Awakening

· The Dominion Series: Book One ·

S.J. WEST

LIST OF BOOKS IN THE WATCHER SERIES

<u>The Watchers Trilogy</u>

Cursed

Blessed

Forgiven

<u>The Watcher Chronicles</u>

Broken

Kindred

Oblivion

Ascension

<u>Caylin's Story</u>

Timeless

Devoted

Aiden's Story

<u>The Alternate Earth Series (A Jess and Mason Bonus Adventure)</u>

Cataclysm

Uprising

Judgment

The Redemption Series

Malcolm

Anna

Lucifer

Redemption

The Dominion Series

Awakening

Reckoning (Spring 2016)

OTHER BOOKS BY S.J. WEST

The Harvest of Light Trilogy

Harvester

Hope

Dawn

The Vankara Saga

Vankara

Dragon Alliance

War of Atonement

Awakening

Preface

Thank you all so much for returning to read the next adventure involving Anna and Malcolm. I know it's been a while since most of you read The Redemption Series, and I thought I would quickly bring you up to speed on where we last left off in *Redemption*.

At the end of *Redemption*, Lucifer finally asked God for his forgiveness and was allowed entry back into Heaven. Helena stole five of the seals from Anna but was unable to retrieve the other two because they had transformed into the souls of Anna's unborn twins. With the added energy of the seals, Helena was able to form a corporeal body and transverse the veil between Hell and Earth.

To escape Anna and the other Watchers, Helena brought up a legion of hellspawn to keep them occupied. During the attack, God sent down two thousand War Angels to help. Not only did God send these angels to help Anna with her Helena problem, but he also sent them to propagate the next step in the evolution of both angel and humankind.

At the very end of *Redemption*, we saw Anna crown Malcolm Emperor of Cirrus and finally declare him as her legal husband.

Awakening takes place a few months after his coronation.

If you feel like you need a more in-depth review of The Redemption Series, you are welcomed to read the chapter-by-chapter summaries I made during my Redemption Read −A − Long on Facebook:

https://www.facebook.com/groups/RedemptionReadALong

All you have to do is ask to join the group. Then, click on the 'Files' tab to access the complete summary. If you don't like Facebook, you are welcome to email me for a copy of the summaries at sandrawest481@gmail.com.

I hope you all enjoy reading this first installment of the Dominion Series!

CHAPTER ONE

Our lives are made up of a multitude of memories. Some memories we cherish more than others, even if they're of bittersweet moments in the timeline of our lives, and some memories take a special place in our hearts because they bring us joy, even during the darkest of days. As I stand on the veranda of the highest tower of the palace, I'm able to survey the cloud city of Cirrus, my home. The responsibility of governing the people who live within my city sits as heavy on my heart as the crown on my head does, but I do not intend to shirk that weight. I've been given the opportunity to make a real difference in the world, and that's exactly what I plan to do.

A pair of warm, familiar hands slide their way around my protruding belly. The sweet sensation of my husband's lips against the side of my neck makes me melt inside, coaxing me to lean my body back against his hard frame for support.

"What are you thinking about?" Malcolm asks me, continuing his loving assault across my bare shoulder.

"How lucky I am," I tell him, closing my eyes as I allow myself a moment to forget about my obligations to the rest of the world, and bask in the love my husband has never been shy about lavishing on me.

"Of course you're lucky," Malcolm says as he rubs his hands against my rather large baby bump, the temporary home of our twins. "You have me in your bed every night to take care of your insatiable appetite for my attentions. What woman could ask for more than that?"

I let out a small laugh as I open my eyes again, and turn around in my husband's arms to look up at him.

It's taken a few months, but Malcolm's hair has finally grown out from the 'haircut' Levi gave him. I let my hands rest against the taunt muscles of his bare chest. The amusement of his own question dances in the depths of his deep blue eyes as he gazes at me.

"I could never ask for more without sounding overly greedy," I tell him openly.

"Well, I can honestly say I've never been stingy when it comes to satisfying your wants," he murmurs, lowering his head and lightly brushing his lips against mine.

"Do you call that a proper kiss?" I ask him, doing my best to sound offended by such a small peck on the mouth. "I know for a fact you can do better than that, Emperor Malcolm Devereaux."

Malcolm lets out a groan of frustration. "You know I hate that title."

"But you love the power it gives you," I tease him.

"Only because it allows me to help you do your job more efficiently and keep the gossip mongers at bay."

"Oh, they still gossip about us," I assure him, not so naïve that I believe those types of people will ever stop talking behind my back, "but now their gossip isn't justified. I finally made an honest man out of you."

"Only for you would I walk the straight and narrow road and conform to what polite society dictates," Malcolm grumbles.

"I know," I say understandingly. "And you know how grateful I am to you for remaining on your best behavior. I've seen you bite your tongue on more than one occasion during our weekly meeting with the royals here. The people of Cirrus can act like spoiled children, but that's only because they've been allowed to behave that way. We both know changing how they think will take some time and patience on our part."

"I need a job that requires me to do more than just play politics, my love," Malcolm sighs deeply. "I almost wish Helena was causing havoc somewhere."

I quickly clamp my right hand over Malcolm's mouth.

"Don't say her name out loud," I admonish him. "You might actually make her appear."

When I take my hand away, Malcolm asks excitedly, "Do you think that would work? I watched a movie once where you could conjure the antagonist if you said his name three times in a row. I wonder if that would happen with her…"

"Please, let's not test that theory out. I've enjoyed having some peace and quiet during the past few months. If I never see her again, it will be too soon for me."

"You do realize that's just wishful thinking on your part, right? She's bound to show herself soon. I would much rather know what her plans are than sit here and speculate about all of the problems she's liable to cause us."

"Yes," I reluctantly admit, "I know that, but let me live the dream of peace while I can, Malcolm. She'll force us to deal with her soon enough. I don't want to jinx things unnecessarily. Everything has been so perfect lately. I don't want anything to change."

"Neither do I," Malcolm says, agreeing with me, even though his expression tells me our idyllic existence won't last forever, no matter how much I want it to remain the same.

We both know Helena is alive and well somewhere. If her corporeal form had been killed, I feel sure I would have felt something through our connection to one another. My War Angel guard, led by Ethan Knight, has been scouring the known universe for any sign of her presence. We had been led on one wild goose chase after another by false reports of Helena-sightings, but any lead to her whereabouts was one that had to be thoroughly investigated.

We now have War Angel battalions on every off-world colony, and stationed in various parts of the Cirrus controlled down-world. Olivia Ravensdale, Empress of Nacreous, and Bianca Rossi, Empress of Alto, were the only cloud city leaders who took us up on our offer for added protection by having War Angels posted in their own cities and down-worlds. I can't say I was too surprised by that, since the other cloud cities were now being governed by either a prince or high-ranking general of Hell.

The coward Abaddon still inhabits the body of Lorcan Halloran, Emperor of Stratus. Thankfully, Lorcan had the good sense to leave his sister, Kyna, and Brutus alone after their marriage. We gave Brutus Malcolm's old position as overlord of commerce in our down-world. Kyna is pregnant, and our children are due to be born only a few weeks apart from each other.

Emperor Edgar Ellis of Virga is ill, from what we've been told, and his son, Callum, is now actively ruling that cloud city. Though, the real

Callum Ellis is dead. He died the moment Mammon forced his soul out of his body in order to wear Callum's skin like a suit.

Nimbo, the cloud city over Africa, is still being run by the demon Agaliarept in the guise of Zuri Solarin. Zuri was made emperor of Nimbo at the tender age of ten. His mother was made regent to rule in his place until his eighteenth birthday. He was now thirty, and being pressured into taking a wife to produce a male heir, but he was still young, continuing to sow his wild oats, from what I was told.

After I killed both the Empress and Emperor of Cirro (the cloud city that controls all of Asia), a battle for the throne ensued among the elite of their royal hierarchy. My brutal torture and subsequent murder of Belphagor while inside the body of Empress Zhin still haunts my dreams sometimes. I have no guilt over the death of Emperor Rui, since he had been taken over by a general of Hell named Botis. Botis signed his own death warrant when he chose to inhabit the body of Horatio Ravensdale, Olivia's husband. After vacating Horatio's body, Botis took over Emperor Rui's body. From the reports we have received, a man by the name of Ryo Mori was successful in securing the most support within the Cirro aristocracy to assume the throne. However, his political victory was a short-lived personal one.

Not long after Ryo Mori was crowned Emperor of Cirro, Baal, one of the last remaining princes of Hell, stole Ryo's body for his own use. Baal once inhabited the body of Raphael Rossi, the now-dead Emperor of Alto. While Baal was Raphael, we were told that he did his best to romance Bianca into his bed. It was well known that the real Raphael was a cad, and would often bring his lovers to the palace in spite of his wife's presence. I wasn't sure if Baal truly cared for Bianca in some way, or if he had had some other ulterior motives we weren't aware of.

I haven't met Baal in his Ryo Mori skin-suit yet, but that would be rectified in the morning.

It took three months to organize, but I was finally able to shame the leaders of the other cloud cities into coming together for a summit on revolutionizing the living conditions for all of our down-worlders. Each leader was feeling the pressure for change from their own constituents, after the citizens of the cloud cities had been forced to watch Gladson Gray's propaganda promos. The summit is scheduled to be held on neutral territory, Mars, and attended by a delegation of one hundred of the most influential royals from each of the cloud cities.

Ethan was currently on Mars with over five hundred of my War Angels to make sure none of the other leaders had nasty surprises waiting for us there. It was strange to know that I currently possessed the power to force the changes that I wanted in the other cloud cities. All I had to do was leave my conscience at the door of the meeting. I had two thousand War Angels under my command who could easily take control over every cloud city in the world if I wished it, but I knew that wasn't God's plan for me or the War Angels He sent to Earth. We were meant to live by a higher standard and prove that war wasn't the only way to foster change.

"Mommy! Dad! Where are you?"

Malcolm takes my hand as we walk from the veranda and back through our bedroom, to the sitting room within our chambers.

Lucas stands in the center of the room, dressed in his favorite blue flannel pajamas, with Luna sitting by his side. My little hellhound puppy isn't little anymore. She is a full-grown hellhound now, and stands almost four feet tall. Her pristine white fur conjures the illusion of being on fire, but her coat is cool to the touch and as soft as velvet. Her eyes have remained blue, showing us that her heart is still as pure as it was when Lucifer first gave her to me. Luna and Lucas have remained inseparable since her introduction into our lives. I was glad Lucas had her, because I knew we couldn't be with him every hour of every day. Not only did our son have a hellhound as his constant companion, but he also had his own personal War Angel guardian, Cade.

Lucas runs towards us. Malcolm lets go of my hand to bend at the waist and pick our son up.

"Where's Cade?" I ask Lucas.

"He forgot to bring up your milk," Lucas tells me. "He should be back in just a minute."

The reason for Cade's absence makes me smile, reminding me of his never-ending thoughtfulness where I'm concerned. It took me a while to get used to his doting, but after Malcolm explained Cade's true identity, I fully understood the reasoning behind his need to take such good care of me.

Apparently, Cade's angelic name in Heaven was Dumah, and he was Seraphina's personal War Angel guard. Even though I am human, or at least partially human, Cade is as devoted to me now as he was in Heaven when I was Seraphina. I'm still amazed by the fact that my soul was the second one ever created, and that Lucifer was not only my father on Earth but also in Heaven. I may have been Seraphina at one time, but I have no lasting memories of her life. I wish I did. I wish I could remember the good times with Lucifer before war was waged in Heaven, but I'm afraid those moments from my previous life are gone forever.

Cade phases into the room, holding a cut, crystal goblet with my nightly warm milk inside. Apparently, he spent some time with Millie to learn more about me before he was dispatched to Earth with the other War Angels. He seemed to remember everything she told him, even the fact that warm milk always helps me go to sleep. With the babies being so active, especially at night, Cade thought the warm milk would help ease my slumber.

As with the Watchers, all of my War Angels were given the choice of picking out their own bodies in which to come to Earth. None of them chose poorly, much to the delight of the women in Cirrus and every other place they are stationed.

Cade stands tall, at six feet and five inches. His hair is short, and light brown, worn parted to the left. His blue-gray eyes hold a kindness in them that is unusual for a War Angel. Or, perhaps it was the only expression I ever saw because of his gentle nature when he was around me and/or Lucas. Whatever the reason, I never doubted his devotion to protect my family.

"I almost forgot it," Cade tells me with a sheepish grin, holding the goblet in his right hand a little higher.

"I'm sure I would have reminded you if you had," I tease.

Cade walks over to us and hands me the goblet of milk.

Malcolm says, "I hope you don't find your soul-mate any time soon, Cade, considering how you've set a precedent for spoiling my wife. Otherwise, I'll end up having to bring her warm milk every night for the rest of her life."

Cade smiles good-naturedly at Malcolm. "I have a feeling you wouldn't complain too much about having to do it. I don't believe I'm the only one who spoils Anna around here."

"Now, gentlemen," I say in exasperation, "I assure you both that I am far from spoiled. There is always room for improvement in the area where serving my needs is concerned."

Malcolm chuckles at my jest. "See, she's spoiled so rotten she doesn't even realize it."

"Mommy's not spoiled," Lucas says, coming to my defense. "She's perfect."

It's my turn to laugh as I rub the top of Lucas' head with my free hand.

"No one, especially me, is perfect," I tell our son. "Though, I love that you think I am."

"You'll always be perfect to me," Lucas declares sincerely.

Secretly, I hope Lucas always sees me that way, but I know, as he grows older, he will come to understand my many flaws, forever breaking the illusion of my perfection in his eyes.

"Open," I hear Vala say from the other side of our chamber door.

As soon as we made the palace our home, I asked Travis Stokes, our technical genius and Vala's savior after Levi destroyed her first body, to install voice recognition devices on all the doors. It made traveling from room to room in the palace a lot easier for her.

After we took up residence in the palace, Vala appointed herself as my personal secretary, dealing with the tedious work of organizing my daily schedules. If you wanted to see me, you had to go through her first. Some of the royals in Cirrus didn't appreciate having to go through a robotic dog to request an audience with me, but I didn't really give them a choice. Vala was part of my inner circle, and there was no one I trusted more to sift through the bureaucracy of helping me run a cloud city than her.

Vala walks in first, but is closely followed by Zane, the shyest angel I've ever met. Zane stands at six feet tall, with short blond hair and emerald green eyes. His full lips give him a permanent pout that most of the women in Cirrus find mesmerizing. Even though quite a few of the ladies have shown interest in Zane, he has abstained from engaging in a relationship with any of them. His behavior contrasts starkly to his brother, Xander.

All angels tend to call each other brother, but in Zane and Xander's case, it is as close to being true as you can get. The Guardian of the Guf, who made Zane and Xander, split the energy of the soul he used to make them. I'm not sure if it was just an experiment on this particular guardian's part, or what his true intentions were at the time, but the result was clear. Zane received the pureness of their shared soul, and Xander the most rebellious parts. As soon as I saw Zane walk into the room, I knew his presence was due to something Xander did. Zane isn't one to bother us about his own personal problems, but he would always come to us if his brother was in need of our help, or if we had to clean up a mess Xander left behind.

"What's wrong, Zane?" I immediately ask, after seeing the distressed look on his face. "Is Xander in trouble?"

Zane sighs heavily before answering. I know he's come to us as a last resort to help him deal with whatever is going on.

"I can't get Xander to come home," he confesses. "He's been inside the Ladies in Waiting for over two days now. He knows we're supposed to be a part of your contingent to Mars in the morning, but he's so drunk he doesn't seem to care. Atticus and Gideon are there now, trying to persuade him to come home so we can sober him up, but I think they're just causing more harm than doing any actual good."

"He's probably run up a hefty bar tab, too, if he's remained drunk for two days," Malcolm mutters with controlled anger.

Since an angel's metabolic rate is so high, alcohol doesn't affect them much unless they drink a lot of it consistently, and for a lengthy amount of time. If Xander was drunk, it meant he had been imbibing quite a large quantity at the expense of the royal family coffers.

"Cade," I say, "would you please tuck Lucas into bed for us while we handle this situation?"

"Are you sure you don't want me to come with you?" Cade offers.

"No," I assure him, "I can handle Xander."

"I don't want you to go inside that place," Malcolm tells me. "Let me deal with Xander."

"You can't handle him without fighting, Malcolm."

Malcolm shrugs. "What's wrong with that? It might actually teach him a lesson in manners."

I shake my head. "It hasn't taught him anything the last five times you've had to drag him out of that brothel. I think it's time I take charge of this situation. Maybe I can shame him into acting like the man he's supposed to be. It might even prevent him from doing it again."

"Good luck with that," Malcolm mumbles irritably. "I'm still going with you, though, to make sure he doesn't do or say something stupid."

"You have my permission to teach him a lesson if he does, but I hope to embarrass him into compliance."

"Depends on whether he's able to actually feel that emotion."

I lean up and kiss Lucas on his cheek.

"You be good for Cade and go right to sleep," I tell my son. "No trying to stay up late to read. Have I made myself clear?"

"Yes, Mommy," Lucas promises as Malcolm sets him back on his feet. "I promise I won't, but can Cade read to me until I fall asleep?"

I look over at Cade and see him smiling down at Lucas.

"I think Cade might be willing to do that for you," I say, giving Lucas an approving wink.

Lucas walks over to Cade and takes hold of one of his hands.

"I'll make sure he gets plenty of sleep," Cade promises us. "You have enough to worry about. The least I can do is make sure Lucas isn't one of them."

"Thank you, Cade," I say, feeling truly thankful that I can place my full trust in him to do exactly what he says.

Unfortunately, if Xander had made such a promise, I would be plagued by doubt that he would keep to his word. I hate that. I hated not being able to trust one of my War Angels. I feel like God sent them to me for a purpose other than countering whatever Helena has planned. Yes, I know they are here to help me take care of her, but I also know He wants them to discover what it means to have a life in which fighting isn't the primary focus. They are the gateways to a brand new chapter in Earth's history. Their children will be allowed to inherit some of their angelic traits, just like I was. I feel sure that will come with its own difficulties, but I also know joining the human and angelic races together will fill the universe with a whole host of grand and probably unexpected possibilities.

"Can I come, too?" Vala asks Lucas excitedly. "I would really like to know how the story ends."

"Of course you can come, Vala," Lucas says, hugging her around the neck.

After Lucas places a hand on Vala's head, I watch as Cade takes hold of Lucas' free hand while touching Luna's back with his other one, and phasing all four of them to Lucas' bedroom.

I return my attention to Zane.

"Let's go get your brother," I tell him.

Zane bows his head and phases to the interior of the Ladies in Waiting brothel, where there will be no actual women of that rank present. I don't like having a whorehouse in Cirrus, but Malcolm convinced me that it was a necessary evil if I wanted to keep the peace in my own cloud city. He argued that some men, and even women, needed such an outlet to relieve their everyday stress and boredom. It wasn't exactly hurting anything to allow it to remain open. The proprietor, a woman by the name of Jade Sands, made sure her establishment was kept clean and, for the most part, orderly. I couldn't really complain about the way she ran her brothel, but that didn't mean I liked having it in my city.

"If he becomes belligerent with you," Malcolm says, a dark undertone to his voice, "I'm phasing you back here and taking care of him myself. I just want you to know that."

I wrap my arms around one of Malcolm's rather large ones and feel how tense his muscles are underneath his shirt.

"That's fine," I tell him, not putting up a fight against his need to protect me. It's one of the traits I love most about my husband. I know he will always stand by my side and watch over me if need be, even though we both know I'm more powerful.

"And if there's anything there that your innocent eyes shouldn't see, I'm bringing you home then, too."

I have to laugh. "Considering what you and I do in the privacy of our own bedroom, I doubt I'll be subjected to anything I haven't seen or done before."

"And that right there shows how innocent of the world you truly are, my love." Malcolm bends down and kisses me lovingly on the lips. "I would rather you kept your idyllic views than see the depravity some people crave."

"I'm not that naïve, Malcolm. I am aware of certain fetishes people have when it comes to sex."

"Knowing about them, and actually seeing them being practiced, are two totally different things. Please, I know you better than almost anyone does. Trust my judgment when I tell you there are certain things you will not want to personally witness."

Slowly, I nod, wondering what it is Malcolm has seen during his long sojourn on this planet that would shock me. "I trust you."

"Good," Malcolm says with a small smile. "Now let's go get our wayward War Angel."

As Malcolm phases us, I begin to wonder if I should have just let him go alone to bring Xander home. With his words of caution, my husband has suddenly made me worry that my decision to go in person was the wrong one.

CHAPTER TWO

I'm not sure why Malcolm is so worried about my 'innocence' being in jeopardy. It isn't like I've never stepped foot inside a brothel before. In fact, he alone holds the dubious distinction of taking me to my very first one. Sure, it was in the down-world, and we were only at Celeste DuBois' place to pick up Lucas, but weren't they all basically the same? Sex, in all its myriad forms, was, after all, just sex. Right?

As soon as we phase into Jade Sands' establishment, I quickly learn just how wrong and naïve my assumption was.

Dark and oppressive are the first words that come to mind as I survey my first cloud city bordello. It takes my eyes a moment to adjust to the dim lighting in the room, but I almost wish they hadn't when I see the people surrounding me. Most of them are dressed in strips of leather strategically positioned across their bodies. I'm not even sure why some of them bothered, considering how much of their flesh is still left on display. Some are wearing outfits made from black lacey material that camouflages very little. Chains and whips seem to be favorite accessories among many in the crowd, and the room's peculiar aroma is saturated with a mixture of sweat and a sickly sweet floral scent, making me wish I could phase back home just to take in a breath of clean air.

Everyone is gathered in a circle, watching three of my War Angels fight in the center of the room. The scantily-clad onlookers are all cheering them on, urging my angels to keep fighting one another. Their thirst for bloodshed sickens me, but it flips a precarious switch inside my soul that is always on the verge of being set off. I assume it's my connection to Helena, more than anything else, that ignites my temper quickly these days.

"Get out of my way," I order the people around me. My threatening tone ensures that I don't have to repeat myself.

When the people standing closest to me recognize who I am, they immediately fall to their knees to show their respect. Eventually, the den of iniquity falls quiet as every human in the room goes down on one knee before me. Silence ensues, except for the sounds coming from the fight itself. My three War Angels are too preoccupied with fighting one another to notice that I'm watching them. They're moving so fast in their brawl that I'm surprised they can even see each other, much less me.

"Enough!" I yell as I stare directly at them, my voice echoing in the near silence of the room.

Gideon and Atticus immediately stop fighting and kneel down on one knee, their heads bowed in deference to my command. Xander, on the other hand, remains standing. Although, standing is a relative term, I suppose. He staggers to the right and catches himself, preventing a fall that would have plastered his face to the floor. I'm surprised he was able to put up such a good fight against Gideon and Atticus, considering how inebriated he appears to be.

When I introduced my War Angels to the world, I didn't try to hide what they truly were or what they were capable of doing. I saw no need to keep their abilities a secret. If God sincerely wanted angel and humankind to come together, the worst thing I could have done was lie about who they actually are. Since teleportation is common in our society, their phasing ability wasn't considered odd. However, their physical strength and their adeptness to phase while fighting was enough to impress most of the general population. The last time I saw God, I thanked Him for sending the War Angels down to me. In a time when half of the cloud cities are being controlled by those who would just as soon see the Earth burn as prosper, I need the added threat of the War Angels as a last resort. I know Lorcan, Callum, and Ryo will stay in line as long as I have the War Angels protecting my interests.

Most of my War Angels are prone to fighting because that was what they were built to do. Their sole purpose for being created was to win the war against Lucifer and his followers. After accomplishing that feat, they didn't have much to occupy their time in Heaven. After living on Earth for the last few months, most of them discovered a newfound sense of purpose as they all followed clues to unearth Helena's hiding place. Some of them are becoming frustrated because she is nowhere to be found, and I'm certain that's part of Xander's problem. He is bored, and one of the ways he has decided to cure that boredom is by drinking and whoring. He knows I don't approve of his behavior, yet he continues to do it anyway. For one so ancient, he acts more childish than Lucas does.

I quickly look down at Atticus and Gideon to check their physical state. Except for a few bruises and cuts, they look fine.

Gideon chose a well-muscled, tall form to come to Earth in, with dark brown hair and chocolate brown eyes that are always filled with a joy for life. He thrives on adventure, and dives head-first into any new undertaking he can find. His heart is that of a child, but his mind is thoughtful and cautious when it comes to protecting me.

Atticus chose a form that is well-toned but not as muscular as some of the other War Angels. I worry over Atticus a lot. He never quite got over the war in Heaven, not that any of the angels I knew had, but Atticus seems to hold on to his anger about it instead of letting it go. I know he is working on his issues through meditation. I'm just not sure it's helping him very much.

"We were just having some fun, Anna. You know what that is, don't you?" Xander says as he wobbles on his feet, barely able to keep his eyes open long enough to look at me.

"Show some respect, Xander," Gideon chastises harshly, keeping his head bowed and only tilting it slightly to speak to his fellow angel.

"Why should I?" Xander asks obnoxiously.

I see Atticus use a fist to whack Xander's left kneecap hard, forcing the other angel to the floor onto both his knees.

"Because she is our commander," Atticus reminds Xander, with barely controlled rage. "And you *will* obey her."

"You're such a follower, Atticus," Xander criticizes before hiccupping. "Why don't you think for yourself for once in your miserable life?"

I see both of Atticus' hands ball into tight fists, and I know he's having a hard time reining in his anger.

"You need to watch your tone, boy," Malcolm says, striding over to stand in front of Xander.

Xander looks up at Malcolm and begins to chuckle. "Just because you've been on Earth longer doesn't make you any wiser than us, Malcolm."

"I'm smart enough to know that you're making a complete ass of yourself by disrespecting my wife in public," Malcolm tells him.

I notice Malcolm also clench his hands into fists by his sides, like he's about to beat Xander into a bloody pulp. From the murderous look in his eyes, I recognize the fact that I only have a few seconds left to handle the situation.

"Xander," I say, knowing I need to step in now before things get out of hand. Both Malcolm and Atticus are on the verge of losing their patience with my wayward War Angel. "Phase home and get some sleep. I need you sober for the summit tomorrow."

Xander looks past Malcolm to me and smiles. "As you wish, Your Majesty."

Xander phases home, defusing the situation for now.

"Atticus and Gideon, please stand," I bid them.

After they're back on their feet, I say, "Thank you for trying to deal with Xander on your own, but next time, please come and get me. I will handle him."

"We didn't want you to have to come to a place like this," Gideon says, looking at the menagerie of scantily-clad people standing around us. "It's not exactly somewhere a woman in your condition or position should be visiting."

"Xander is my responsibility," I tell them, "as you all are. I will do what needs to be done if his behavior doesn't improve. Do you doubt my ability to handle him? Is that why you tried to take care of the situation on your own?"

Both men shake their heads.

"We have no doubt about your capabilities, Anna," Atticus assures me.

"Good," I say. "Now go back to your homes. I'll need you both rested for tomorrow's summit."

Gideon and Atticus bow at the waist before phasing out of the room.

"Thank you," Zane says as he turns to face me. "Xander might not act like it, but he respects you as much as the rest of us do."

"We can discuss his disgruntled behavior later," I tell Zane, not wanting to stay any longer than I already have in the brothel. "Why don't you go to him and make sure he's all right?"

Zane bows at the waist right before he phases to the home he shares with his brother.

Just as I'm about to phase back to the palace, I hear a woman ask, "Won't you stay for a little while, Empress? Since you're already here and all…"

I turn to see Jade Sands leaning up against the doorway at the back of the room. She's a petite woman, standing only about five-feet- five inches tall, even with high heels on. She's waif- thin, with blue eyes and brown hair cut in layers to frame her pretty oval face. The dress she's wearing looks rather conservative for a Madame of such an establishment. It's a long black dress made from a silky material that reaches from the base of her throat to her toes. As she walks over to us, I notice that the dress isn't as conservative as I first thought. The material is solid on the front and back, but the sides are only being held together by links of pewter chains.

"I'm afraid I need to go back home," I tell Jade, desiring to leave her place of business as quickly as possible.

When Jade reaches us, she looks meaningfully into my eyes and says, "I believe I might have something that will interest you, Empress."

"I seriously doubt that," Malcolm scoffs rudely.

As I look into the depths of Jade's eyes, I can tell whatever it is she wants to discuss with me is important to her and shouldn't be ignored. She may run a whorehouse, but that doesn't mean she's unintelligent. In fact, to keep so many customers happy takes talent and an ability to read people. In a way, it's similar to being a leader.

"Actually," I say, "I would like to know what it is you have to show me."

"Anna…" Malcolm says incredulously.

A small smile stretches Jade's lips as she continues to study me. I think she assumed I would dismiss her offer because of who she is and how she makes a living. Not only did I want to know what she had to show or tell me, but I also wanted to prove a point to the others in the room: any citizen of Cirrus, no matter how low on the totem pole of polite society they may be, could come to me if they needed to talk.

"Please," she says, turning slightly and extending her left arm out towards the back of the room, "follow me to my office where we can have a little more privacy."

As Jade begins to walk, I follow. Malcolm quickly grabs hold of my arm.

"Anna," he says urgently, in a low voice, "we should leave this place."

"Trust me," I whisper.

Malcolm sighs and slides his hand down my arm to take hold of my hand.

"Fine, but if something happens and I think we should leave, I'm phasing you back home. I won't be asking for your permission to do it either."

"I won't argue," I tell him.

Malcolm and I follow Jade through the double black doors that lead out of the room we are in, and into a grand foyer. As I look around at all the white marble with gold embellishment, I have to wonder how much money Jade makes with her business. From the looks of it, she's doing quite well; even better than some royals I know.

Jade walks straight across the foyer to another room with a red door. She opens the door and stands beside it, waiting for us to follow her inside.

The room turns out to be her office. The style is rather minimalistic and reminds me of Virga furnishings, with its black and white theme and steel and glass furniture.

"Can I offer the two of you any refreshments?" Jade asks, closing the door behind us.

"No," Malcolm is quick to reply, indicating that he doesn't particularly want me to touch anything in the office, much less accept a drink from someone like Jade Sands.

"Thank you for your kind offer," I tell Jade, being kinder with my refusal than my husband. "But I get the feeling you asked us in here to tell us something you think we need to know."

Jade walks over to her desk and leans back against it.

"I heard that you are as smart as you are beautiful. I'm glad to see the rumor was true. In fact, I was counting on it. It was one reason I let Xander have the run of the place for the last few days. I hoped you might come to fetch him yourself."

"If you have something to say, just say it," Malcolm says, sounding frustrated. "I would like to get my pregnant wife out of this place as quickly as possible."

Jade raises a delicate eyebrow in Malcolm's direction. "Are you always this impertinent?"

"When I feel Anna's safety is in jeopardy, yes," Malcolm answers.

"She's safe here or I would escort her out myself," Jade assures Malcolm. "What happens out there stays out there. This is my private sanctuary. No one is allowed in here except me and those few I invite inside."

"And will you tell us why you've invited us in here?" I ask.

Jade directs her attention back to me. "As you know, a large percentage of our clientele is part of the upper crust of Cirrun society. I always tell my girls and boys to keep their ears and eyes open because people will say things to their lovers that they won't say to anyone else. Lately, I've been getting reports that some of the royals plan to stage a coup and take your throne away from you, Empress."

"On what grounds?" I ask, troubled by this news.

"They're going to argue that your marriage to Emperor Augustus was never consummated, since you ran off with Malcolm on your wedding night. Under Cirrun law, your marriage holds no legal merit because of that fact."

"Do they have any proof that the marriage wasn't consummated?" I ask, not admitting to anything. I don't know Jade well enough to divulge personal information to her. As far as I know, she could be seeking confirmation from me, planning to sell the information to the highest bidder.

"No concrete proof," she admits. "But you need to watch your back, or, in this case, your crown. There are some very powerful people here in Cirrus who want your throne, and they'll sell their souls to get it. I'm one of the people who believe in what you're trying to do for the down-worlders, but I'm afraid I'm in the minority. So, please, be careful."

"Thank you for warning me," I tell her, sensing no deception in Jade. "If you happen to receive any more information that you think I should know, please don't hesitate to contact me."

"Do you really believe you can help the down-worlders?" Jade asks me with a note of cautious hope in her voice.

"Yes, I do," I answer without hesitation. "Do you mind me asking why you care what happens to them?"

"I have family down there," she reveals. "My mother was brought up here by a royal who fancied her when she was younger. He set her up as his mistress and left her a small fortune when he died, but no one in polite Cirrun society would accept her after he passed away. She ended up using his money to start this place. She was able to earn enough to bring a few members of her family here to live. I still have more family in the down-world, but they refuse to leave because they say it's their home. I'm about to admit something to you that I probably shouldn't, but I've been smuggling food and clothes down there for a long time now. Anything you could do to make their lives easier would be very much appreciated by me."

"You have my word that I will try to change things for all the down-worlders," I promise. "But you know as well as anyone that making people want change is hard to do. From what you've just told me about the royals here, they're looking for any excuse to dethrone me and keep things the way they've always been. I won't let that happen. Change is coming, whether they want it to or not."

Jade smiles. "Good. I want you to know that I am a loyal subject. I only have your best interests at heart. You have my word."

When I hold my hand out to Jade for her to shake, I sense Malcolm tense at the offer of physical contact.

Without hesitation, Jade shakes my hand.

"Can we leave now?" Malcolm asks impatiently.

"Yes," I tell him, slipping my hand out of Jade's.

Before I can say or do anything else, Malcolm phases us back home, straight into our bathroom.

"Why did you phase us in here?" I ask, slightly confused by his choice of rooms.

"You need a shower after being in that place, my love," Malcolm says, walking around to the back of me to undo the magnetic closures there. He runs his hands across my shoulders until my dress is pooled around my feet. "And I'm burning this dress."

"Malcolm," I say, having a hard time holding back a laugh at his over-cautiousness, "it's not like we went to a leper colony. It was just a brothel. As I recall, you spent quite a lot of time in places like that before you met me."

"And I know what kind of diseases the people in those places can have," he tells me. "Just do as I ask, please. It will make me feel better."

I turn around to face Malcolm in all my naked glory. "I'll only take a shower if you join me."

"Oh, I already fully intended to do that," Malcolm says, shedding his own clothes in record time. "We're burning my clothes, too."

I laugh. "You are too much sometimes, husband. I swear you seem to think I'm made out of glass or something."

"No," Malcolm says raising a hand to brush his fingers tenderly across my left cheek. "I don't think you're that fragile, but if anything happened to you on my watch, I would never forgive myself. You're too precious for me to lose, Anna. You, the babies, and Lucas are my life, and I'll do whatever it takes to protect you from the things you don't even know about yet. You've led a sheltered life. There are dangers everywhere, my love, and it's my job to make sure you avoid as many as possible. You're still partially human, Anna. That part of you leaves you vulnerable to a lot of things."

"It also makes me strong," I remind him.

"Yes, but not against germs." Malcolm takes one of my hands with his and leads me over to the large shower we have, which is practically a room unto itself. "Besides, you know you like it when I bathe you with my hands, and I promise to make sure every inch of you is thoroughly cleaned."

"Well, since we'll both be clean, does that mean we get to play with one another in bed afterwards?"

Malcolm chuckles. "I swear pregnancy seems to have made you even more demanding in bed than you were before."

"It's perfectly normal," I say, sounding wise beyond my years about such things.

"And how would you know that?" Malcolm asks amused.

"Kyna said she was experiencing the same thing. Poor Brutus barely gets any sleep."

Malcolm chuckles. "I seriously doubt he minds that one bit. I know I don't."

"That's good," I tell him, tightening my grip on his hand as we step into the shower together, "because I predict you won't be getting much sleep tonight."

Much to Malcolm's delight, my prediction proved to be true.

CHAPTER THREE

In the early morning hours, I'm awakened by one of the babies kicking me. The baby kicks so hard, I end up waking up fully and can't go back to sleep. I turn over onto my side away from Malcolm and begin to rub my belly, hoping the soothing action will calm down whichever baby is having an early morning tantrum. I feel another kick that's even harder than the first one and makes me sit straight up in bed.

"Anna?" Malcolm asks drowsily as he sits up, too, and rubs the sleep from his eyes. "What's wrong?"

"One of them has decided I don't need any more sleep." I grimace as I experience another mighty jolt by a tiny foot.

Malcolm gets out of bed and walks over to my side.

"Let's see if I can calm him or her down," he suggests, standing beside me.

I toss the covers off and swing my legs over the edge of the bed. Malcolm kneels down in front of me and squeezes in between my legs. I drop my hand away from my belly, and Malcolm places both of his hands on it, gently stroking up and down. He begins to sing a lullaby to the babies, in hopes of calming them for me. It's a trick we've used before, and I pray it works this time, too.

As I sit and listen to Malcolm's deep baritone voice, I close my eyes and find peace in his song, even if the babies don't.

"Ouch," Malcolm says, quickly taking one of his hands away as I experience another kick. "How are they not tearing you up inside?"

I don't say anything. I have no idea what these kicks are doing to me, but I know I don't want Malcolm to worry.

"I'll be fine," I say instead, hoping I didn't just lie to my husband.

"I'm going to get Desmond." Malcolm stands. "Maybe he'll know what to do."

"Don't bother him, Malcolm," I almost beg. "He's probably sleeping."

"Then I'll wake him up," Malcolm replies, the inflection in his voice indicating that what's happening to me is more important than Desmond getting a full night's rest. "Angels don't need sleep to survive, remember? It's more of a luxury than anything else. I'll be right back."

Malcolm leans down and kisses me on the lips right before he phases away.

I gasp in pain as I experience what feels like both babies kicking me at once. It's something I've never experienced before. I squeeze my eyes shut and begin to pant through the lingering pain.

"Anna?" I hear a familiar, yet unexpected, voice say.

When I open my eyes, I discover that I'm no longer in my bedroom.

I'm in Heaven and sitting in the swing on Lilly's front porch. Lilly is staring at me in shock, which is probably a mirror of my own expression.

"How did I get here?" I ask her.

"You didn't phase yourself here?" she asks, looking startled.

I shake my head. "No; at least, not on purpose."

"I don't know, sweetie," Lilly says as she starts to walk over to me, "maybe you were dreaming and…"

I don't get to hear the end of Lilly's sentence because, after another dual kick by the babies, I phase again. At least this time I have my eyes open so I can see where I phased.

I find myself sitting in the rocking chair in the nursery room of the beach house Malcolm built for me. I turn my head to look at the window with the tree my mother painted depicting my family lineage. Just as I reach out a hand to touch it and activate the holographic butterflies, the babies kick again, and I find myself somewhere I hoped never to return to: Hell.

Instead of waiting for the babies to kick again, I try to phase myself out as quickly as possible. I end up not going anywhere. I attempt to escape a few more times, but each try fails. I can't phase myself. I'm trapped.

"Well, well, well, look who decided to pay me a little visit…"

I turn around and see Helena standing only a couple of feet behind me. The one thing I can't deny about Helena is the fact that she is absolutely gorgeous. With her long blonde hair pulled over to the side, she looks glamorous in an old-fashioned sort of way. She's wearing a sleeveless red dress, but it's made out of crushed silk instead of sequined material this time. Her pale skin glows softly, causing it to give off a warm glow even in the pitch-black darkness of Hell.

"Is this where you've been hiding all this time?" I ask her.

"Hiding?" Helena says, with a tilt of her head as she considers my question. "I wouldn't call it hiding, exactly. It's more like self-preservation."

"I didn't realize you were such a coward," I taunt. "I thought the whole purpose of you taking the seals was to escape this place."

"Oh, I haven't stayed down here," Helena assures me. "Far from it. But, when I sensed your presence here, I had to find out why you would come back."

I don't say anything. I don't want her to know that I'm not in control of my own body. I'm not sure what's going on with the babies, but I do know that the less information I give Helena, the better.

"So, how do you like having a body?" I ask her, trying to find a way to get off the subject of my unexpected arrival in Hell. "Is it everything you hoped it would be?"

"Yes and no," Helena admits. "I mean, I do like the freedom of being able to come and go from here whenever I want, but I can't say I enjoy the bodily functions very much. It's very odd. The first time I had to go to the bathroom was quite an experience."

"One I would rather not hear a recount of, thank you very much," I tell her, grimacing slightly.

"Oh, Sister," Helena says with a small laugh, "you are just too precious sometimes. And look at that belly of yours! You look like you're about to explode at any moment!"

I feared Helena's words might be prophetic, considering how hard the babies' kicks were becoming. Each one seemed harder than the last.

"Tell me, when exactly are you due, dear Sister?"

The question itself was something other people have asked me countless times, but coming from Helena, it takes on a sinister note.

"Why do you want to know?" I reply.

Helena shrugs her slim shoulders. "Can't I ask a simple question without you thinking I have some dastardly ulterior motive?"

"No," I answer succinctly, "you can't. You always have a reason for wanting to know things. Why are you so interested in my babies?"

A slow, malicious smile spreads Helena's ruby red lips.

"I just want to know when I'll become an auntie, Anna. It's as simple as that."

"You're lying."

"Am I? I thought you lost the ability to tell a truth from a lie."

Unfortunately, Helena is right. After I absorbed the second seal from Asmodeus, I lost the capability to tell when someone was lying to me or not. Since the babies each absorbed a seal and held onto that energy as the foundation for their souls, I assumed I would regain the ability as soon as they were born. It is pure supposition on my part, but I'm certain it's a well-educated guess.

"I don't need it where you're concerned," I tell her, unable to keep my disgust for her out of my voice. "I just always assume you're lying."

Helena lets out a throaty laugh. "Oh, my, when did you become so distrustful?"

"The moment I met you."

"Well, I guess that means I won't be able to visit with my niece and nephew anytime I want. How sad for them, really. They'll miss out on Auntie Helena's wicked sense of humor."

"They don't need a crazy aunt like you in their lives, so make sure you stay away from them."

"My, my, that almost sounded like a threat."

"There's no almost about it, Helena.

Stay…away…from…my…children. I don't think I can make it any clearer than that, do you?"

Helena sighs in disappointment. "No, I suppose you can't. But…what about when they get older, Anna? What if they seek me out on their own?"

"Why would they do that?"

"I know their souls are the seals I couldn't retrieve from you," Helena informs me. "I figured that bit out not long after I left you in the desert with my hellspawn. It's the only explanation that makes any sense."

I neither confirm nor deny Helena's deduction. As long as I keep quiet, she won't know for sure that she's right.

"They won't seek you out," I assure her. "I won't raise them to be that stupid."

Helena's smile remains on her face, like it's glued there. She studies me for a moment, as if I'm a puzzle she's trying to figure out. Then, quite unexpectedly, she begins to laugh.

"They brought you here, didn't they?" she asks before clapping her hands together in pure delight. "Now *that* I didn't expect! Although, I can't say I'm all that surprised, now that I think about it."

I bite my tongue, but I have to ask, "Why aren't you surprised?"

Helena shrugs, crossing her willowy arms over her chest. "I have my reasons."

From the guarded look in her eyes and her posture, I know she doesn't intend to tell me more.

The babies kick me again, and I let out an involuntary gasp of pain. The last thing I hear Helena say before I phase is, "Until next time, Sister."

I phase back to my bedroom, where a worried Malcolm is frantically pacing back and forth.

"Thank God," he breathes out as he walks over to me and takes me into his arms. "I saw your phase trail lead to Heaven. Why did you go there without telling me first? I thought you might have gone to get help from my father."

I shake my head. "No. The babies phased me there."

"The babies did *what*?" I hear Desmond ask as he, Jered, and my papa walk into the room from the veranda.

"Oh, cherub," my papa says as Malcolm steps away from me so my father can give me a hug. "We were worried sick about you."

"I'm fine," I say, but hear the doubt in my own words. "I think the babies are just getting stronger, is all."

"Have you been in Heaven all this time?" Jered asks.

"No. After Heaven, they phased me to the nursery of the beach house you all built for me," I answer.

"Why do I get the feeling those aren't the only two places you went?" my husband says perceptively. He's been around me long enough to know when I'm withholding information.

"They took me to…Hell, as well."

I wait for the eruption of heated voices protesting such a thing, but my statement is met with complete and utter silence instead. The four men standing in front of me are staring at me as if I just spoke to them in a language they didn't understand.

"Did she say what I think she said?" Jered finally asks, breaking the silence.

"I think she said the babies took her to Hell," Desmond replies, looking confused.

"Yes," I say slowly, wondering why they're all looking at me so strangely. "That's what I said."

"Why would they do that?" Malcolm asks aloud, but I think he simply voiced the question, not truly expecting an answer to explain it.

"I don't know," I tell them. "I was shocked, too, but…" I falter because I don't want to say what I know I need to next. It will just cause all of them more worry, and that's the last thing I want to do.

"But what?" Jered asks, urging me to finish what I was about to say.

"Helena didn't seem surprised that they phased me down there."

"You saw Helena?" Malcolm yells, making me jump involuntarily.

"Yes. She was in Hell."

"Has she been there this whole time?" my papa asks calmly.

"I thought Slade went down there through one of the fissures that are still open, to search for her," Desmond says, looking confused by the situation.

"Hell is remarkably huge," Jered explains. "He could spend a lifetime there and never find her if she doesn't want to be found."

"She told me she hasn't been in Hell all this time, just part of it."

"You said she wasn't shocked that the babies phased you there," Malcolm says, trying to get the conversation back on track. "Why is that?"

"She wouldn't tell me," I answer, feeling butterflies of worry flutter inside my chest. "I tried to get it out of her, but she kept the information to herself."

"Well," Desmond says, "why don't we worry about that later? Right now, I would like to take a look at the babies, if that's all right with you, Anna."

"Yes, of course."

"Why don't we all go out to the sitting room?" Desmond suggests. "I left my equipment there anyway."

"Are you going to perform a holographic ultrasound?" my papa asks excitedly. "I haven't seen one of those in a while."

"Yes, that's the plan," Desmond tells him. "Come on, grandpa. Let's go see how your granddaughter and grandson are doing this evening."

"I'm hoping they're asleep," I mutter to myself, rubbing my belly because it feels slightly battered and bruised. Considering how hard they were kicking me, I don't doubt that it is.

Desmond asks me to sit down on the couch in the room. Malcolm sits on one side of me, while Jered and my papa stand to watch. Desmond searches inside his tattered, black leather doctor bag sitting on the glass coffee table, and pulls out a slim silver disk. He turns to me and places the disk on top of my belly. He waves his hand over the imaging device and a holographic representation of Liam and Liana appears directly over where the disk is situated.

Desmond studies the hologram for a moment before using his hands to manipulate the image by turning it around in slow increments, to examine the babies from every possible angle. As far as I can tell, they look perfectly healthy. Liam has his hand in front of his face and is wiggling his fingers before his eyes, as if he's trying to make sense of his little appendages.

Liana is sleeping soundly with the thumb of her right hand stuck firmly inside her mouth.

"Oh, dear," my papa says, sounding troubled, "she's a thumb sucker just like you were, Anna. It took me two solid years to finally break you of that habit."

"Then you'll have to share your secret with me," I tell him, feeling an overwhelming sense of pride and joy as I look at my children.

As soon as I speak, I see Liana open her eyes and crane her neck, like she's trying to find me. Liam lowers his hand and does the same thing.

"Can you hear me, babies?" I ask, not really expecting an answer, but receiving something of one as they continue to move their little heads in what appears to be an effort to seek me out. "Go to sleep, Liana and Liam. We have a very big day ahead of us, and I need both of you to be on your best behavior for Mommy."

As if understanding my words, Liana places her thumb back in her mouth and closes her eyes to go back to sleep. Liam also closes his eyes to enter his own world of dreams.

No one says a word as Desmond turns off the holographic ultrasound.

I look over at Malcolm and see a surprised expression on his face.

"Was that normal?" I whisper, not wanting to speak too loudly. I definitely don't want to wake the babies.

"I can't say I've ever seen that happen before," Malcolm admits, also in a low voice.

"Neither have I," Desmond whispers.

I look at my papa and Jered, and see them both shake their heads, indicating that they have never seen babies still inside their mother's womb listen to and obey her instructions.

I'm not sure if I should be worried about this new development or not. All I do know is that I feel a sense of great relief that they are both finally asleep.

"I couldn't phase out of Hell on my own," I tell everyone, because I need to share my worry with them. "I had to wait for the babies to do it for me."

No one says a word. I know we're entering unknown territory where my children are concerned, and that fact worries me tremendously.

Just how powerful are they becoming? Will I be able to control them after they're born?

From what I experienced that night, I would have to say the answer to that last question is a resounding 'no'.

CHAPTER FOUR

I end up not being able to go back to sleep. Malcolm stays awake to keep me company, and we speak in whispers as we lie in bed, wrapped in each other's arms. We stay that way until it's time for us to get ready for the summit.

When I take my nightgown off, I notice tiny foot-shaped bruises on my belly.

"Oh, Anna," Malcolm says, bending down in front of me and kissing each bruise, as if such an action will erase them from existence. "What are they doing to you?"

"It's ok," I tell him, shrugging off the minor discomfort. "They're just bruises. They'll fade in time."

Malcolm stands. "We can take care of them now. I'll get the healing wand."

"Wait," I say reaching out and grabbing his arm to stop him. "I don't want to use it until we know it won't hurt the babies."

Malcolm removes my hand from his arm. "I'll be right back then."

He phases, but returns only a few seconds later.

"Desmond doesn't see any reason why we can't use it. He doesn't think it will harm the twins, and I refuse to have you suffer any more than you have to."

Malcolm quickly strides into our bathroom and retrieves the small healing wand that we keep in there. When he returns to me, he waves it over my belly, almost instantly healing the battered tissue.

"There," Malcolm says after he's finished. "Now I won't worry as much."

Malcom retrieves the dress I had designed to wear to the summit. It's a modest off-white-colored dress with a flowy long skirt and lacey top with gold, pearl, and crystal embellishments across the waist and neckline. It is simple in design, but elegant enough to wear to a meeting with the cloud city aristocracy.

"I have to admit," I say to Malcolm as he helps me into my dress, "I'm a little nervous about speaking in front of everyone."

"Why is that, my love? We've been working towards this day for a long time now."

"What if they don't want to change the way we treat the down-worlders? What if I can't convince them that this is the best thing for all of us?"

"Well, we know Olivia and Bianca are on our side. The others won't be because of what they are, but that's why we put in the stipulation that one hundred royals from each city were required to attend the summit. They are the ones you need to speak to today. Don't worry about the demons who stole the bodies they inhabit. They'll never be on your side. You know that. But if you can convince the people who live in their cities that we need to think about what's best for all of our futures, we might be able to start changing things for the better."

"And what if the information Jade Sands gave us yesterday turns out to be true? If I can't persuade the people who live in my own cloud city that we need to change our ways, why in the world would the people in any of the others side with me?"

"Like you told Jade, no one can prove that you didn't consummate your marriage to the emperor. It's not like there was any video surveillance inside that room to prove otherwise."

"Are you sure about that?" I ask. I know that Empress Catherine, Auggie's mother, was completely paranoid during her reign. I wouldn't put it past her to have had a live video feed inside Auggie's bedchambers that night just to make sure the marriage was consummated. When Catherine ruled Cirrus, she did so with an iron fist. Nothing happened, or didn't happen, for that matter, without her prior approval. Her paranoia about me conceiving a child that wasn't Auggie's led her to make me take her 'treatments' every week. It turned out that she was actually injecting nanites into my system that would activate and poison any man who tried to kiss me on the lips, who wasn't Auggie or my papa.

"I'm positive there wasn't," Malcolm assures me. "We swept the apartment before you even entered the room. Catherine did have something set into place to keep an eye on you and Auggie, but we disabled it so she couldn't see us in the chambers while we searched it."

I feel a little better knowing this tidbit of information that Malcolm never shared before now, but I still feel uneasy about the whole situation. Jade seemed sincere in her desire to warn me about what some of the royals in Cirrus were planning to do. I had no reason to doubt her, but I also had no reason to trust her.

After I'm dressed, I walk over to my vanity and brush out my hair.

"You should wear your crown today," Malcolm suggests as he dons a black, collarless formal jacket over the thin undershirt he's wearing. After its magnetic closure is secure, his jacket looks seamless in the front.

"Must I?" I ask, not really wanting to add more weight to what I was already carrying around with the babies. "It's so heavy."

"You need it to remind people that you're the Empress of Cirrus, and no amount of wishful thinking on their part will ever change that fact. It also shows people that you not only accepted the crown, but the responsibility that goes along with it. It's a symbol of your fidelity to Cirrus, both the people here in the city and the down-worlders."

"That's quite a lot for one crown to symbolize," I tell him, "but I know you're right. Can you get it for me?"

Malcolm phases out of the room, but phases back only a minute later with my gold and blue diamond crown in his hands. Malcolm made me change out the original jewels not long after we took up residence in the palace. He said the color of the rare diamonds accentuated the blue in my eyes. I wasn't entirely convinced I wanted my new eye color enhanced by the jewels, but my husband was adamant that I accept the physical changes that being connected to Helena brought. He urged me not to be ashamed of my new appearance, and I try my best not to be. But, the fact of the matter is, every time I look at myself in the mirror, I am reminded of Helena. She was in my thoughts every day, and I didn't know how to get her out.

Malcolm walks over to me and says, "Turn around."

I swivel on the small bench I'm sitting on to face him. Very carefully, he sets the crown of Cirrus on my head. "That's better. Now you look like someone to be reckoned with."

I turn back around to look at my reflection. I couldn't argue with Malcolm's estimation. I did look more grown-up with the crown on than I did without it. The girl I once was isn't in the face of the woman staring back at me now. A lot has happened since I first met Malcolm, for better and for worse. I am counting on things to get better from here on out, though.

I stand up from the bench with Malcolm's help.

"Is Ethan here yet?" I ask.

"He'll be here in exactly five minutes."

"Do the War Angels have the same compulsion to be on time everywhere they go, like the Watchers?"

"I think it's a curse my father put on all of his angels," Malcolm replies with a small chuckle. "One of these days, I would like to be late for something."

"I feel very confident that I can find a way to make you late for an appointment," I tell him with a small, suggestive smile. "I can think of a few pleasurable ways I can make that wish come true for you."

"I'm sure you can," Malcolm replies before leaning down to give me a kiss on the lips. "Unfortunately, now isn't the time to be late for a meeting. If anything, we should probably be early."

We hear a knock on the door to our chambers.

"It appears Ethan may agree with you," I say, already knowing who is at the door as we walk into the sitting room.

Malcolm walks over to the double doors of the room and opens one of them. Standing on the other side, dressed in their black formal leather uniforms, are two of my War Angels. The gold embroidered 'WA' symbol over their hearts marks them as being part of my War Angel army. Malcolm was the one who came up with the idea for the emblem. He said it was a figure once used for the Watcher Agency back in Jess' day. He saw no reason to let such an iconic signature go to waste.

Ethan Knight, the War Angels' commander in Heaven and my second in command here on Earth, stands tall at just over six feet. He has short brown hair and piercing brown eyes. He keeps a well-trimmed, thin beard and mustache that makes him look rather dashing, if I'm being honest.

Atticus is standing to Ethan's right, and looks completely healed from the wounds he sustained in his fight with Xander the night before. As always, he's wearing a serious expression on his face, and I make a promise to myself to find time to make him smile one day, possibly even relax enough to laugh.

"Is everything ready?" Malcolm asks Ethan as he moves away from the door to let my escorts to the meeting inside.

"Yes," Ethan replies. "We've done a systematic sweep of Mars and haven't found anything there that might harm Anna during the summit."

"You searched the whole planet?" I ask, slightly amused by this idea. Ethan smiles. "Malcolm insisted."

I feel a little exasperated by Malcolm making them search everything so thoroughly, but I also know the task makes him feel more at ease about my safety, so I let it slide this time.

"I thought you might want to get there a little earlier than the other leaders," Ethan tells me. "It might give you a slight advantage to watch them arrive with their delegations."

"Have the royals from Cirrus arrived there yet?"

"No. You will be the first."

"Then let's go and get settled," I tell them. "If I'm the first one there, it might also remind them that I'm the one who asked for this meeting."

Malcolm holds out an arm for me to take. I slip my hand over his arm, and he phases us to the designated location of the conference.

Olivia Ravensdale took charge of designing a building for us to all meet in on Mars. She used the polymeric material all of the structures in Nacreous were made from, which could take on any form and mimic any material you wanted. This is the first time I've seen the building. The circular shape and stadium-style seating arrangement reminds me of a miniature version of an Ancient Roman coliseum, except this structure has a glass ceiling and cushioned seats.

There are seven defined sections, one for each cloud city. At the front of each section is a dais with either one or two golden thrones. Each chair has a winged-back design, which seems to be a subtle reminder to the other leaders of the world that I have an angelic army at my disposal. I have to smile at Olivia's subtle adeptness at psychological warfare. Below each dais is a gold placard inscribed with the name of that section's cloud city.

Already stationed in the room are more of my War Angels. Xander and Zane are situated at the door up the stairs and directly behind where I will be sitting. Gideon and Ethan's second in command, Roan, are standing on either side of my dais to protect my flanks. Ethan and Atticus take their places in front of the dais on the ground floor. Malcolm helps me up the stairs to our chairs. After we sit down, I look around the room, wondering what will happen that day.

Olivia Ravensdale, Empress of Nacreous, and one of the few cloud city leaders I consider an ally, teleports into the center of the room alone. When our eyes meet, she smiles.

"Anna, my dear, I should have known you would be the first one to arrive. Hello, Malcolm, I hope you're in a patient mood today."

"So far, but we'll see how long that lasts," Malcolm replies. "I doubt I'll stay in a decent mood, considering the people we'll have to deal with here."

"True," Olivia sighs, being the only other cloud city royal who knows the real identities of the other leaders. "But let's hope we can work over the obstacle they present. I'm just relieved everyone agreed that I should be the one to preside over today's proceedings."

"No one has a beef with you," Malcolm says. "Thankfully, none of the others are aware that you know who they really are."

"And let's keep it that way," I suggest, not wanting to place Olivia in the cross hairs of anyone who might want to take her place as Empress of Nacreous.

I assume the only reason no demon has taken over Olivia's body is that they don't want to rule over the poorest of the cloud cities. Being situated over Antarctica limits the wealth it can obtain from natural resources. I am thankful for that fact. I don't want to lose one of the few friends I have in the world the same way I did Auggie.

Lucifer released Levi's soul from Auggie's rotting corpse, and, as far as we knew, he hadn't taken on a new identity yet. It would be just like Levi to kill Olivia and assume her form just to spite me. It was one reason I limited my contact with Olivia. I didn't want to place a target on her back because of our friendship.

A few minutes later, other royals and cloud city leaders begin to arrive. I am grateful Ethan came for me early so I can observe the way people are acting as they enter the room. It also gives me a chance to listen in on some of their conversations. However, most of the whispers I hear come from my own citizens. The few conversations I can make out seem to confirm what Jade Sands said. I end up hearing plenty of disparaging remarks about my character, and how I don't deserve to wear the crown of Cirrus.

From one lord seated directly behind me, I hear the word 'whore' associated with my name, and have to clamp my hand down firmly on Malcolm's arm to prevent him from rising out of his seat and attacking the man.

"Don't," I beg my husband, and, with that one word, Malcolm remains seated, even if the muscles in his jaw are as tense as piano wire. "We don't need to give these people an excuse to leave these proceedings so they don't have to listen to what I need to say. You're Emperor of Cirrus, Malcolm, and that title requires you to contain your temper, especially when you don't want to."

"Doing nothing goes against my nature, Anna," Malcolm growls between clenched teeth.

"I know," I say sympathetically, "but for my sake, contain your natural impulses during this meeting. I'm sure that won't be the only disparaging remark you hear today concerning my character. Just remember that they're only words used by ignorant people, Malcolm. You, our family, and friends know the real me. That's all that matters."

"I don't suppose you would give me the privilege of teaching that man some manners," Gideon says to me from his post beside my chair. "I'm sure a man who is so cowardly he has to talk behind his empress's back instead of to her face," Gideon says loud enough to ensure the man who spoke can hear his words, "would be easy to break in half."

"Stand down," I order. "We have too much to lose here."

Gideon shakes himself somewhat and spreads his legs farther apart in a more defensive stance, as if changing his body position slightly will help lessen the aggravation he feels.

"If you change your mind about that," Gideon tells me ominously, "let me know."

I feel fortunate that Atticus isn't standing beside me. Considering his issues with anger, I'm not entirely sure he would have listened to my order like Gideon just did. All of my War Angels are protective of me, and fighting to preserve my honor is probably their natural inclination. But here, in this place, politics are more important than brute strength. I know I have an army that could force the changes I desire, but that isn't the way I want to win. If politics doesn't work, I'm not sure what my next step will be. Thankfully, we aren't at that point yet, and I have to keep my faith that everything will turn out for the better in the end.

The first of the world's leaders to enter the arena is Lorcan Halloran. The real Lorcan had been a sadist of the worst kind during his short life. It's odd to think that the demon who took possession of his body, Abaddon, is actually better for the cloud city of Stratus than Lorcan ever was. Abaddon has feared me since the moment I defeated him during our duel over Kyna's honor. He knows I can kill him with just one touch, and that knowledge helps me keep him in line. As Lorcan walks up the Stratus dais towards his throne, I see him shake his head slightly at the chair's angel-wing design, but he makes no comment as he sits down in it.

Next to enter are Callum and Edgar Ellis. I am surprised to see Edgar in attendance, since we all thought he was on his deathbed. He doesn't look well, but his age-lined face is filled with a grim determination to have his voice heard at this meeting. I know his presence means he intends to fight the changes I want to implement to improve the lives of the down-worlders. Edgar is part of the old guard, and will struggle until his dying breath to keep things the way they always have been. I pity Edgar. It's sad knowing that Mammon is now inhabiting Callum's body without Edgar being any the wiser about the situation. If Edgar were told, he would probably have a heart attack on the spot, leaving Mammon free to reign over Virga unchecked.

Emperor Ryo Mori teleports in next. This is the first time I've seen him in person. I'm saddened by the fact that I will never get to meet the real Ryo Mori. Baal now inhabits his body. As far as I'm aware, he is keeping his head down and performing his duties as Emperor of Cirro efficiently. I'm not sure if he just hasn't had a chance to reveal his real agenda, or if he truly just wants to keep his position and live out Ryo's natural lifespan in peace. I hope he chooses the latter option, because I have enough on my plate as it is. The body of Ryo is quite handsome, with classic Asian features and a commanding presence. As he takes his seat on the Cirro dais, Ryo looks over to me and bows his head slightly, showing a reverence I didn't expect to see from a prince of Hell.

One of the few royals I consider a friend, Bianca Rossi, teleports into the room. Bianca is a rare beauty, who caught the eye of the royal family in Alto at an early age. When she married Rafael Rossi, it appeared to be a fairytale match made in Heaven, but the marriage proved to be a nightmare for Bianca. Rafael was a philanderer, and he didn't care who knew it, not even his own wife. Rafael's body was inhabited by Baal at one time, but after Alto fell out of the sky, he vacated that body, leaving the cloud city with only Bianca as its ruler. Honestly, the people of Alto couldn't have asked for a better person to lead them during these trying times.

I happen to notice Ryo stand from his seat when Bianca enters the room. After she sits on her throne, she glances in his direction and smiles politely at his gracious show of respect for her. Ryo bows at the waist and retakes his seat, but his eyes remain on Bianca.

"What's that all about?" I ask Malcolm, knowing he saw what I did.

"I have no idea," Malcolm muses. "Maybe Baal is actually in love with her."

It wasn't beyond the realm of possibility. While Baal was inside Rafael, we heard reports that he tried to woo Bianca. Perhaps he truly does care about her in his way, and wants to start fresh in his new form. Whatever his purpose, I know I will need to keep my eyes on him where Bianca is concerned.

We all wait for the last cloud city emperor to make his appearance, Zuri Solarin from Nimbo. Zuri is known to be brash and not very reliable, so none of us are particularly surprised that he is late for the meeting. As I survey the delegation from his cloud city, I notice quite of lot of them whispering to one another and laughing as if they are in on a joke that the rest of us aren't privy to. Something is going on. I just don't know what.

After fifteen minutes of waiting on Zuri, I can tell Olivia is becoming agitated by his blatant disregard for those of us who showed up on time. She stands from her throne and addresses the crowd.

"I see no reason why we should delay starting this meeting any longer," she says to us. "Emperor Solarin can join in on the discussion when, or if, he ever decides to show up."

We all see a man from the Nimbo delegation stand to his feet, with his hand raised.

"Empress Ravensdale," the man calls out, "may I be allowed to speak?"

"Do you have an explanation for your emperor's absence from these proceedings?" Olivia asks agitatedly.

"Only partially, Your Majesty," the stranger answers. "Emperor Solarin swore us all to secrecy because he wanted to bring his surprise in person."

"Surprise?" Olivia questions, looking slightly troubled and confused by the man's statement.

"Yes, Your Majesty."

"And is it this *surprise* that is causing his delay?"

I notice quite a few in the Nimbo delegation smile or snicker at Olivia's question.

"Most assuredly, Your Majesty. Perhaps you could give him a few more minutes to…"

"I'm here! Sorry for the delay! I hope you can all forgive me for being so tardy today."

Zuri Solarin is now standing in the center of the room, though I didn't see the flash of light that usually accompanies teleporting into a space. He's a handsome black man with an easy smile and a twinkle in his eyes, but I instantly know the man standing before us is no longer the real Zuri Solarin.

He isn't even the demon we all thought still inhabited Zuri's body, Agaliarept. I would recognize that leer even if it were displayed on the face of a dog.

The man standing in front of us is Levi.

I sense Malcolm's body tense at the sight of Levi, and slowly place one of my hands on his arms to keep him seated before he can pounce on the Emperor of Nimbo and cause an international incident.

"Let's see what he's up to," I whisper to Malcolm. If I know Levi at all, I'm certain his late arrival was calculated to make sure all eyes were focused on him.

"In the future, Emperor Solarin," Olivia says, not having a clue who she's really speaking to, "perhaps you should manage your time more wisely so you don't waste any of ours."

"I couldn't agree with you more, Empress Ravensdale," Levi says, using Zuri's mouth to make his apology.

Levi turns to look directly at me. "I meant no disrespect, Empress…uh…" Levi scratches the side of his stolen Zuri head as if he's confused about something. "What exactly are we supposed to call you now? Amador or Devereaux?"

"Devereaux," I answer, wondering why Levi has chosen this moment in time to reappear in my life. Why is he here? What is he up to? The only thing I'm certain of is that his presence does not bode well for the success of this meeting.

"I meant no disrespect, Empress Devereaux," Zuri says, bowing at the waist, even though it's obvious to everyone present that his words and action are disingenuous. "I do hope the reason for my delay will be enough to get me out of the dog house with you."

"And what is your excuse?" Olivia questions tersely. "We were told you had a surprise to share with us."

Levi's smile widens. I catch him looking in my direction out of the corner of his eyes before addressing Olivia's question. It's almost like he wants to make sure I'm watching him.

"Indeed, I do have a surprise, Empress Ravensdale," Zuri says, sounding extremely excited, almost giddy with anticipation, in fact. "Indeed... I... do. As you know, my people have been begging me to ensure the lineage of my family's name. So, I decided to remedy that oversight on my part." Zuri looks around at everyone present in the room as if he's about to reveal something extraordinary to us. "Ladies and gentleman, please allow me the pleasure of introducing you to my wife, the new Empress Solarin of Nimbo."

As if on cue, Zuri's new wife teleports into the room, to stand by her husband's side.

I stare at Zuri's wife, feeling as if I've suddenly become trapped inside my own worst nightmare.

Helena simply stares back at me and smiles.

CHAPTER FIVE

I'm instantly surrounded by all six of my War Angels. I have to lean to the far left to look past Ethan in order to keep my eyes on Helena and Levi, who are standing in the center of the room.

"Let me kill her for you," Atticus whispers to me a little too eagerly. "We can end this here and now."

I sit up straight and look at Atticus, who is standing to the right of Ethan.

"No," I tell him in a low, urgent voice. "Don't attack her unless she becomes a threat to the people here. We will not start a war with the people of Nimbo because of her."

Atticus' brow lowers ominously, showing me how displeased he is with my order, but he turns back around to keep an eye on the two in the center of the room.

Malcolm leans over and whispers in my ear, "You should go home. Let me handle things here."

I shake my head. "No. I will not cower in her presence. That would give her too much power over me."

"We don't know what she's capable of, Anna," Malcolm stresses worriedly. "We don't even know what kind of powers she might have."

"I am not leaving," I say resolute in my position, "so stop asking."

Malcolm huffs in frustration, but he doesn't say anything else. He returns his watchful, and decidedly hateful, gaze to Levi and Helena.

Helena smiles sweetly at my War Angels before turning her gaze to the others present in the room.

"And does your wife have a name, Zuri?" Olivia asks hesitantly, understanding that something is definitely wrong with the situation after witnessing my War Angels surround me like a protective barrier.

"Please, forgive my manners," Zuri replies respectfully. "Olivia Ravensdale, it gives me a tremendous amount of pleasure to introduce you to Helena Solarin."

I see Olivia's body stiffen slightly. She knows who Helena is and why she's so dangerous, but I don't want Helena to understand the depth of Olivia's knowledge concerning our world of angels and demons.

"It's very nice to meet you, Helena," Olivia says, quickly recovering from her initial reaction. "Congratulations on capturing the heart of one of the world's most eligible bachelors. Tell me, how did the two of you meet?"

"We met through my father," Helena tells Olivia. "Honestly, I've had my eye on Zuri for quite a while now. My father recently passed away, and Zuri has spent a great deal of his time helping me cope with the loss. I'm not sure I would have made it through my grief without him by my side the last few months."

Well, that certainly explained where Levi had been hiding out all this time. I knew he was up to no good. I just didn't know what.

I sit back straight in my chair because leaning to one side in my condition isn't prudent. I find myself staring directly at Ethan's backside. It's a nice one but not exactly something I want to be staring at for the rest of my time at the summit.

"Ethan," I whisper to gain his attention.

Ethan turns his head to look back at me and raises his eyebrows, silently asking me what it is I want.

"I need you to move so I can see," I tell him.

Ethan's eyebrows lower and I know he doesn't like my request. He wants to remain exactly where he is in case Helena tries to throw a fireball or lightning bolt at my head. I understand his need for caution, but I also know that he's a War Angel with quick reflexes. Even if Helena tries to kill me, I feel safe in the knowledge that at least one of my angels would be able to stop her.

Reluctantly, Ethan takes a step to the left, giving me at least a small gap between him and Atticus to watch Helena and Levi continue their charade as husband and wife. The sight of them together sickens me. I want to tear Levi's new face off, and trap Helena back in Hell where she belongs. However, neither is a viable option at the moment. I will simply have to bide my time until we can come up with a plan to handle them both.

"That was quite nice of Zuri," Olivia comments to Helena. "I think I speak for everyone here when I say we wish you the best of luck in your marriage to one another."

Helena briefly glances in my direction. "You probably don't speak for everyone present," Helena turns her head to look back at Olivia, "but thank you for your well wishes."

"If the two of you would please take your seats, we will begin discussions on the matter that we're all here to deliberate on."

Levi holds out an arm to Helena to escort her to the Nimbo dais. Once they're seated there, all eyes return to Olivia, except mine and those of my contingent of War Angels. We're keeping a close eye on the two most dangerous creatures in the room. They're not dangerous because of the magical powers each of them wields. They're dangerous because we don't know why Levi and Helena have decided to team up. Whatever their agenda, I doubt it's just coincidence that they've chosen to present themselves at the summit together. I fear my vision of uniting the up-worlders and down-worlders is about to blow up in my face somehow.

"As you all know," Olivia begins, "we are gathered here to discuss the motion presented by Empress Anna Devereaux of Cirrus. I would like to give her a chance to explain her vision for her own cloud city and for the down-worlders who live within her territories. Empress Anna, you have the floor."

Ethan moves a little further to the left of me and turns to lend me a hand as I stand from my chair.

"Thank you," I tell him, smoothing out my dress as I prepare to address the assembly.

There aren't many friendly faces in the crowd staring back at me, but I keep in mind what Malcolm told me earlier. I need to convince the royals at the meeting that raising the standard of living for those in the down-world is in the best interests of all of us.

"Thank you all for giving me this moment to speak with you today," I say. "I am truly humbled that you have given me this opportunity to ask for your help in a matter that is dear to my heart. I know that many of you have seen the videos concerning the conditions the down-worlders have to survive in."

"Are you responsible for those blasted things?" I hear Edgar Ellis ask accusingly.

I turn my attention to him and answer, "Yes, it was my idea to produce them."

A low murmur moves through the crowd like wildfire, but I can't tell if people disapprove of my involvement in the making of the videos or not.

"Do you realize the trouble those things have caused, girlie?" Edgar asks.

"Edgar," Olivia says in an admonishing tone. "You will address Empress Deveraux with the respect she deserves."

"I thought I just did," Edgar snickers, before he starts to cough uncontrollably.

Callum rubs Edgar's back, trying to ease his father's discomfort.

Edgar's snide remark does not sit well with Olivia.

"The delegation from Virga has lost its privileges in this meeting. Edgar, you and your son are to remain silent so that people who are serious about learning more on this matter can discuss it freely." Olivia turns her attention back to me. "I apologize on Edgar's behalf for his outburst, Empress Anna. Someone as old has he should have better manners."

I try to remember what it was I wanted to say to the people in the room.

"As I was saying," I begin again, "I know that many of you have seen the videos. I also know that many of you weren't aware of the conditions the down-worlders have to live in. The time has come for those of us who have so much to give back to those who have very little. Some of the down-worlders don't even have enough food to eat to survive. I've witnessed things during my time in the down-world that would make most of you weep. I stood and watched a mother lose her child because it was born too soon. I've seen people sleeping in the streets because they can't afford a home of their own. There are people starving to death because they're not allowed to eat the food they grow and harvest for us. Now is the time to stand up and fight for those who can't fight for themselves. Even if they could, they would probably be too malnourished or ill to ask for your help. All of us have lived in luxury for far too long. We need to take responsibility for the people in our down-worlds. They break their backs to provide us with the comforts we enjoy each and every day. If we don't take care of their needs now, we won't have anyone left to make the things we all need to survive. It doesn't take much to ease their lives enough to make them happy. The down-worlders are human, too. I think that's a fact that many of you have forgotten over the years because you never have to see them. We have to stop being so complacent about this issue, and strive to be the leaders we were meant to be. I ask that you consider following Cirrus' lead in sharing cloud city technology with your own down-worlders."

"Heresy!" Edgar bellows, gaining the support of most of the Virgan delegation behind him.

"It is not heresy," I calmly tell Edgar. "It's called doing the right thing and showing respect to your fellow humans."

"Empress Anna is right," Bianca speaks out, standing from her throne. "We should all be ashamed of the way we've been treating our down-worlders. To be honest, it wasn't until those propaganda videos began playing that I realized how appalling conditions are on the surface. We cannot keep hiding in our cities in the sky, pretending that they don't exist. Those people do exist and they need our help!"

"I completely agree with Empress Bianca," Ryo Mori says, standing from his seat as well. "In fact, I've decided to start a program similar to

Empress Anna's that will hopefully elevate the living standards of my own down-worlders."

"As have I," Olivia states, showing her support for my idea. "Empress Anna is correct. We cannot turn a blind eye anymore. We have to take responsibility for the people we lead, whether they live in our cloud cities or in our down-world territories."

"Excuse me…"

All eyes turn to Helena as we wait for her to continue to speak. She has her right hand raised in the air, as if asking for permission to say more.

"Speak freely, Empress Helena," Olivia says, with a note of hesitation. Olivia may have never met Helena before today, but she understands the threat she poses to all of us well enough.

Helena stands and smooths out the silky red dress she is wearing.

"I can't say I'm opposed to Empress Anna's… *suggestion*, but I wonder if she's thought it through completely."

"What part in particular?" I ask Helena.

"Well…and perhaps it's just my untrusting nature shining through here…but what happens if the down-worlders decide to take the technology we give them and use it against us? I mean, if conditions are as deplorable as you say, I would assume there is a great deal of animosity among the down-worlders in all of our territories. What happens if they decide to band together to destroy us?"

An excited murmur comes from the royals in attendance.

"I have to admit," Levi says from his chair, "my wife does make an excellent point."

"The down-worlders only want what the rest of us want," I tell them. "They want enough food to feed their children and a decent home to raise them in."

"Well, that's all well and good," Helena concedes, "but it doesn't answer the question I just asked."

"I don't believe they have any desire to war with us," I reply. "They simply wish to live freely."

"And just how much freedom do you intend to give them?" Levi asks. "I don't think any of us will argue against sending them more food to eat or even helping them build better homes to live in, but giving them our technology is just unrealistic, in my opinion. They're like children down there, and should be treated as such. Would you give the babies growing inside your womb the means to destroy you after they're born? That's basically what you're asking us to do."

"The down-worlders aren't children," I argue. "You're purposely trying to sow fear and suspicion where none is warranted. Giving them part of our technology will only help us all in the future."

"Yet, you just said that they want to 'live freely'," Helena says. "Your words, not mine. If they're allowed to live free, who will grow our food or make our clothes? Just how much freedom do you intend to give the down-worlders?"

"Enough freedom to make them feel like they're human beings again," I argue. "We pay them very little for the work they do for us."

"Oh, so now we're supposed to increase their wages as well?" Helena asks, as if I'm asking for the moon. "What next? Are we supposed to invite them to live in the cloud cities with us too?"

"I doubt many of them would want to do that," I tell her.

"Because they hate us?" Helena asks cunningly.

"Some do," I admit.

"And you still don't think they will use our own technology against us one day? Didn't we learn anything from the Great War? Aren't we supposed to gain knowledge from our past mistakes?"

"I hope we have," I reply. "I hope we learned that running away from a problem simply creates more complex ones. We abandoned those who weren't rich enough to buy a place in the cloud cities. The down-worlders were left to fend for themselves, and almost destroyed the world."

"Exactly!" Helena says triumphantly, like I just made her point for her. "And now you want to give these same people the means with which to destroy everything we've built? Like my husband said, I don't think any of us will argue too strenuously about giving the down-worlders more supplies, but I suggest we keep cloud city technology right where it is: in the hands of level-headed people."

I see many of the royals in the crowd begin to nod their heads in agreement with Helena's proposal.

"Sending them extra supplies is a start," I concede, "but I hope those of us who have already decided to share our technology with our down-worlders can prove to the rest of you that it's the only way to ensure our future. Our technology can make their work go faster and produce more products for all of us to consume. Simply sending them more supplies is a shortsighted plan. We all need to look towards the future, and the best way to assure mutual prosperity is to make things more efficient."

Fortunately, I see people in the crowd nodding in agreement with what I just said. I let out a small sigh of relief, feeling like I won a minor victory.

"Perhaps it's the down-worlder in you that makes you sympathize with them so readily," Helena says disparagingly. "Tell me, Empress Anna, what does it feel like to be the only ruler here who bought her crown?"

Involuntarily, I bristle at Helena's words, but quickly pull myself together because I don't want to give her the upper hand.

"My husband died, and the people of Cirrus asked me to remain on the throne to lead them," I inform her.

"We've all heard the rumors, you know," Helena says to me.

Out of the corner of my eye, I see Edgar Ellis lean forward in his chair to listen closely to Helena's next words. Unfortunately, he's not the only one in attendance who seems interested in Helena's salacious gossip.

"Tell us, Anna," Helena continues, "what exactly happened to poor Auggie?"

"He became ill and died from the sickness," I tell her. It was the only story we could come up with that explained Auggie's odd behavior and change in physical appearance. "It affected his mental faculties and caused his body to decay."

"And what exactly happened to his body?" Helena questions. "As far as I know, no one ever saw it. You didn't even have a funeral for the Emperor of Cirrus. Instead, you had a wedding to marry your lover so you could crown him emperor."

I hear a few snickers in the crowd, but they don't affect me. I'm used to their judgmental attitude by now.

"I married the man who saved me and showed me what true love is," I tell Helena. "Auggie turned into a monster. Just ask the people of Cirrus how much he changed."

"Yes," Helena says musingly, "he did seem to change for the worse. Yet, was it just coincidence or by design that he made this odd transformation right after your wedding to him?"

I can see where this line of questioning is leading.

"Are you accusing me of something?" I ask, already knowing the answer to my question.

Helena shakes her head. "Not I, but someone who was very close to Auggie is extremely eager to ask you a question."

The door above the Nimbo section opens up to allow my accuser entry into the proceedings.

Catherine Amador walks into the room, causing almost everyone present to gasp in surprise.

I haven't seen Catherine since the night I rescued her from Levi's torture, and arranged for her to be taken to Mars on a freighter ship. I look at her hands, and notice she's still missing her right one. I thought she would have had a prosthetic one attached by now. When I look into Catherine's eyes, I don't see the pathetic creature who was staring aimlessly and trembling like a wounded animal on my bed that night. I see a proud woman standing before me now, with a grim look of determination on her face.

"The former Empress of Cirrus," Helena says, "seems to think you poisoned her son on your wedding night, and that's why you ran off to the down-world with your lover. She came to Zuri and me with her suspicions, and I thought it was only right that you allow her to speak with you."

Watching Catherine enter the room has thrown me for a loop. I didn't expect her presence at this meeting, but now I know how naïve I was to think I would never have to set eyes on her again.

"You are no Empress of Cirrus," Catherine tells me scathingly. "You are a traitor and a harlot, and I call for your immediate removal from the throne!"

Everyone erupts into excited chatter over this new and scandalous development.

"Please, everyone," Olivia says, trying to calm the people in attendance, "let's remember who we are and why we are here. Catherine," Olivia looks up at her, "this is not the time or the place to make unfounded accusations against the reigning empress of your cloud city."

"Unfounded?" Catherine asks incredulously. "How else do you explain the changes in my Augustus? Everyone here knows what a sweet-tempered young man he was. In fact, I believe the poisoning started even before the wedding night. I noticed small changes in his behavior, but didn't put the pieces together until it was too late. Anna and my son couldn't have possibly had time to consummate their marriage vows before she ran off with her lover."

More excited chatter erupts, and again Olivia asks everyone present to calm down.

"I didn't kill Auggie," I tell Catherine. "You know how much I loved him."

"But you loved Malcolm Devereaux more!" Catherine points an accusing finger at me. "I know you went to Overlord Deveraux's bedroom the night before the wedding, Anna. Do you dare deny that fact?"

I think about lying, but telling one lie always leads to having to tell another one.

"No," I admit. "I don't deny that."

"Excuse me…" Helena says. "I have a question. How do you know Anna's marriage to your son wasn't consummated? Besides the time constraint, of course."

"He told me," Catherine says, but I see her tremble slightly at the memory. I can only assume it's something Levi told her while he was pretending to be Auggie.

"But you can't prove it one way or the other," Malcolm says, rising from his seat to stand by my side. "It simply becomes your word against Anna's. We all know what you're trying to do here, Catherine. You want the throne back for yourself, and you're desperate enough to do and say anything, even a blatant lie, to become Empress of Cirrus again."

"I think the people of Cirrus deserve someone better than that whore to lead them!" Catherine says vehemently.

The crowd erupts. Some of them take my side and some of them take Catherine's side.

When I look over at Helena and Levi, both of them are smiling at me in triumph. This was their plan all along. They didn't care about the issue of whether or not down-worlders should be given cloud city technology. They wanted to see me dethroned in shame.

"Please, everyone!" Olivia says loudly. "Calm down and remember why we're all here."

"Might I make a suggestion?" Levi says, standing from his seat to draw the attention of those present. "It seems like Anna's claim to the throne was supported by the people in her city after Auggie's death. Perhaps the people of Cirrus deserve the chance to voice their opinion on the matter. At the time, they thought Anna was their only choice, but now that Catherine has recovered from her injuries, they may want to go back to an Amador ruling them again."

"What are you suggesting?" Edgar Ellis asks.

"I think both Anna and Catherine have a rightful claim to the throne. I don't think it really matters whether or not Anna and Auggie consummated their marriage. The fact is that the people of Cirrus asked her to lead them. If I were a citizen of Cirrus, I would be open to having a vote on the matter. Let them decide which empress they want leading them into the future. It seems like the only fair thing to do."

"This is not a decision for those of us in this room to make," Olivia says. "Only the people of Cirrus can call for such an election."

"Well," Helena says, crossing her arms and tilting her blonde head slightly as she considers the delegation from Cirruns who are sitting behind me, "why don't we ask the ones present what they think should be done to settle this matter?"

I hear someone behind me stand and say, "I think we should have a vote."

Another person from my delegation stands and says, "I think we should have a vote, too. Some of us want Anna to remain in power, but she won't be as effective with the specter of Catherine haunting her reign. We should get past this gossip-mongering first so she can continue the good work she's trying to do."

Silently, I thank the man who just spoke. I pray there are many others who view me the same way.

"I have no problem with having a public vote," I declare to the assemblage.

"Well, I guess it's settled then," Olivia says, looking over at me. "May the rightful ruler come out victorious."

CHAPTER SIX

To say that I am having a very bad day is an understatement. Not only has Helena made herself known to the world, but Catherine is trying to reclaim her control over Cirrus. I couldn't care less about the prestige of holding the title of empress. The only reason I fought so hard to retain it was to help my people, both those who reside in the cloud city and the down-world. Now, everything I want is in jeopardy. My dream of forging a peaceful coexistence between both worlds is slowly disintegrating before my eyes. All I know is that I need to win the support of the people of Cirrus and retain my claim to the throne.

Olivia calls an end to the meeting, for which I am eternally grateful. Before I can stop him, Malcolm takes hold of my hand and phases us directly to the couch in the family room of the palace. When we first accepted the castle as our home, we fashioned the room in the same style as Malcolm's office in New Orleans.

The room is twice as big as his old office, and the walls are lined with shelves of real leather-bound books. I find that actually holding a book in my hands and being surrounded by the aroma of ink on paper makes the stories I read feel more real for some reason. Sometimes, I almost feel as though I'm reading someone's diary, depending on the author's style of writing. I suppose, in a way, I am. Each author, especially the good ones, places bits and pieces of themselves within the words of their novels. The tactile sensation of physically flipping a page to find out what happens next in the story brings a new sense of excitement to reading for me. I love the experience. One of the missions I have set for myself is bringing back factories that publish real books for people to have in their own homes. I consider it a lost art form that needs to be revived.

"Are you all right?" Malcolm asks me, his voice filled with concern.

"I would be lying if I said I was," I tell him, standing from the couch to pace in the open area between it and the fireplace. Unlike the down-world, the inner workings of fireplaces in Cirrus are holographic. They emit real heat, but the flames and the wood aren't real. When we visit our beach house in the down-world, I always ask Malcolm to make me a fire. The scent of burning wood and the ability to roast marshmallows over open flames are two things I love to share with my family.

"How are we going to get rid of Helena now?" I ask, feeling frustrated by the whole situation. "She did the one thing I never thought she would: present herself to the public. Every person in every cloud city will know who she is by the end of the day."

"All they'll really know is that she's the new Empress of Nimbo. They won't know she's literally Hell on Earth, and we'll have to keep it that way for as long as we can. Otherwise, there will be chaos in the streets. We don't need for people to feel frightened in their own homes because they don't know what she's capable of doing."

"And Levi," I say in disgust, feeling as though I might throw up from letting his name pass over my lips. "I can't believe he's helping her! I can't fathom how two people so narcissistic can stand to be around one another, much less pretend that they're married. At least, I hope they're pretending." I shudder in revulsion at the thought of the two of them being together in the biblical sense.

"What I can't believe," Malcolm says, shaking his head in dismay, "is Catherine's betrayal of you after everything you did for her."

"She can't possibly believe that I would actually poison Auggie, can she?" I know I shouldn't, but I feel my heart ache over her false accusation. I may have never liked Catherine, but I didn't want her thinking that I could be capable of such an atrocity.

"I think she's been brainwashed by Levi and Helena," Malcolm says with certainty. "They've devised a plausible scenario that provides Catherine with a way to make sense of everything Levi did to her as Auggie. She was a total mess when you rescued her. I'm sure she doesn't even remember half of that experience. The human brain has a way of protecting itself by repressing memories that are just too traumatic to rationalize."

"But while she healed on Mars, she was told that we helped her escape on Captain Vitor's ship, and that we were paying her bills."

"I guess we should have visited her there to keep track of who she was speaking with. If we had, we would have known Helena and Levi were poisoning her mind against you."

"Against us," I correct. "If I lose my crown, so do you."

"I couldn't care less about a stupid crown," Malcolm declares, standing from his seat and walking over to me. "My only concern right now is you. You are too good a person to have to go through what you did at the summit. It couldn't have been easy to hear all those terrible things being said about you, to your face *and* behind your back. I want you to know it took every ounce of will power that I possess not to go bash Edgar Ellis' face in with my fists."

"He's always disapproved of our relationship. You know that."

"Yes, I'm fully aware of his disdain for us, but it doesn't change the fact that I wanted to do bodily harm to the man today. Trying to defame you in public is disgraceful, even for a senile old coot like him."

"Well, don't feel guilty for your natural urges to quiet Edgar. I assure you, you weren't the only one in that room who wanted to slap him silly."

Malcolm reaches for both of my hands and holds them up to his chest.

"I promise that you will retain your crown. No one is better for Cirrus than you are, Anna. I'm sure the people here can see that."

"Not if what I heard being said behind my back at the summit is what they actually think of me. Who wants to publicly support a harlot?"

"You are the furthest thing from what that word means," Malcolm says vehemently. "And I don't ever want to hear you say something like that about yourself again. Don't let people wear you down with their words. You let them win that way. You know who you are, and you have a clear vision for this city and the down-worlders. We know what Catherine will do. She'll keep things the way they are, and that's not good for anyone. Change is hard for some people to accept. You have to show them that the old way to do things won't work forever. We have to prepare for the future for our children's sake. You and I know what's coming. If my father's plan for the War Angels to start the next step in human and angel evolution takes place, we need to prepare everyone for the adjustment. It's quite possible that some of your War Angels will find wives in the down-world. Those people can be even more backwards in their thinking, just because they haven't been exposed to as much."

"I almost feel sorry for Liam and Liana," I tell Malcolm, voicing a thought I've been keeping to myself. "They won't have a lot of choices in their lives. Once they're born, we'll have to start grooming them to not only lead humankind into the next era, but angelkind as well. That's a lot of responsibility to be born into."

"They'll be fine," Malcolm tells me, drawing me into his arms. "Don't worry about them. They're our children. I feel sure they'll be so stubborn that ruling people will come naturally to them."

"I hope we can teach them that leading is a privilege, not a right. We both know what can happen to people who think a little too much of themselves. A good ruler shouldn't expect people to follow them because of who they are. They should expect people to follow them because of what they do."

"Then we'll teach them that," Malcolm assures me. "I, for one, won't allow them to act like over-privileged brats, and I know you wouldn't have any patience to put up with them acting that way either. If anything, we might end up being more strict with them than with Lucas."

"I hope we treat all of our children equally, but I have a feeling you're right."

"You and Auggie were raised knowing you would rule Cirrus together one day, and the two of you turned out to be excellent leaders."

"That's true," I say, feeling better about the situation. "If we teach them right from wrong, and always let them know that we love them, they'll be fine."

Malcolm leans down and kisses me on my cheek. "Good. Now, we need to figure out how we're going to win this election."

"I'm not even sure when it's supposed to take place."

"Stay here," Malcolm says. "I'll go ask Olivia if she has any ideas."

Malcolm lets go of me and phases back to the summit room on Mars.

Almost like they were waiting on their father to leave the room, the babies kick me in unison, and phase us to the one place I don't want to go.

Helena is standing in front of a large glass window, looking out at the cloud city of Nimbo, her new domain. Since Nimbo is situated above Cairo, Egypt, the architecture of the city resembles the ancient ruins from that territory's past. Most of the structures are made from real limestone.

The room I'm standing in is most likely inside the large gold pyramid the Solarin family has resided in since they took control of Nimbo. Hieroglyphs decorate the walls of the sitting room, depicting significant moments from the Solarin family history. Within the center of the room is a seating area defined by four tall columns with ornate tops painted with shades of aquamarine and red-orange.

Helena turns to face me with an almost serene smile on her face.

"I didn't expect you to seek me out again so soon, Sister," Helena says, almost sounding genuinely pleased that I'm with her again.

"It wasn't my decision to come here," I inform her, not wanting Helena to think I would ever seek her out on purpose. I try to phase out of the room, but it appears that particular ability is not under my discretion anymore.

Helena already figured out that the babies were the ones who phased me to her in Hell, and I certainly don't want her to think that I deliberately came to her for a friendly chitchat.

"I think your children can sense what's best for you better than you can, Anna."

"And why is coming to see you best for me, pray tell?"

Helena's face loses its smile, and her expression turns serious.

"You need to lose the election. Don't fight Catherine for the crown. Trust me; losing is better than winning in this case."

"If you think I'm going to intentionally lose to her, you don't know me at all, Helena."

"If you care about living," she yells, "you will do what I say!"

"Are you threatening to kill me?" I ask, feeling my own temper rise.

Helena shakes her head resolutely. "No. That is not what I'm saying at all. I have no desire to kill you, but can you honestly say the same thing about your intentions for me?"

I decide not to reply. My answer definitely isn't one she will want to hear. To be honest, I'm not even sure I'm strong enough to kill her. My gut tells me that she and I are on fairly even ground where our powers are concerned. In fact, I fear Helena is more powerful than I am. She was able to steal five of the seals, only leaving me with two. Even though the energy of those two seals was transformed into the souls of my children, I am still able to draw on some of their power. However, I wasn't sure what would happen once Liam and Liana were born. I assumed my power would diminish, leaving me more vulnerable to Helena.

Yet she just said that she had no plans to kill me. Then why did she want me to relinquish my claim to the throne? How did that further her agenda? Maybe if I actually knew what her scheme entailed, I could make an educated guess as to her real purpose for asking me to throw the election, one she helped orchestrate into being.

"Even if you have a good reason for wanting me to give up my crown, I wouldn't do it because that isn't in the best interests of my people."

"If you care about your citizens so much, then do what I say! I can promise that if you win, all hell will break loose in Cirrus, and you'll wish you had listened to me."

"Stop the theatrics, Helena. You won't be able to intimidate me into doing what you want."

"Why do you have to make everything so difficult, Anna?" Helena asks wearily. "Besides, wouldn't you much rather live in the quaint home Malcolm built for you on the beach and raise your children without having to worry about their safety all the time? Why do you want to live a life of strife when you could live one of peace?"

"Peace is what I'm struggling to build," I try to explain, even though I know trying to reason with Helena is a lost cause. She is the personification of Hell, after all. How do you explain to someone who thrives on hate and pain that peace has to be fought for on Earth?

The creation of the cloud cities did accomplish one thing: They brought about the end to all war. We hadn't had one since the Great War, but that peace had come at a tremendous price. It was a price paid by the downworlders, and it was time to find a new way to handle things.

"Anna…"

I turn around to find Cade and Ethan standing behind me.

"How did you know I was here?" I ask them in surprise.

"We just followed your phase trail," Ethan replies, keeping a wary eye on Helena.

Cade is staring at her, too, but his eyes aren't filled with hatred like Ethan's are. He looks a little shell-shocked, like he's looking at a ghost. The

War Angels have been searching for Helena for so long I can only imagine what's going through his mind as he sets eyes on her for the first time.

"We should get you home," Ethan tells me.

When I look back at Helena, I notice she's keeping her eyes locked on me and ignoring the two War Angels who have come to my aid.

"Heed my warning, Sister," Helena tells me ominously. "I would hate for you to have to live with regret."

I feel Ethan gently grab hold of my arm. I make no protest as he phases me back home.

When we arrive in the family room in the palace, I turn to Ethan to thank him, but end up saying something completely different.

"Where's Cade?" I ask in alarm, hoping Helena hasn't done something to him.

"Stay here," Ethan tells me urgently. "I'll go back to check on him."

I do as I'm told and remain exactly where I am. I doubt I could have phased back to Nimbo on my own anyway. My capability to do something that should be second- nature to me has been temporarily suspended by the little scoundrels growing inside my womb.

A few seconds later, Cade and Ethan phase back into the room.

"Why didn't you phase home with us?" I ask Cade. "Did she keep you there somehow?"

Cade doesn't move or say anything. He just stands there and stares at me with a blank expression on his face. I'm not even sure he heard my question.

"Cade," I say, taking a step closer to him, "what's wrong?"

Cade begins to shake his head. I see him swallow hard, but he remains silent.

"Anna asked you a direct question, soldier," Ethan says, taking on a forceful tone. "Answer her."

Cade swallows hard again before he says, "I think I just met my soul-mate."

CHAPTER SEVEN

Since the moment the War Angels entered my life, I've tried my best to get to know as many of them as possible. Since there are two thousand of them, that task is an almost impossible one. The angels who have been included into my personal guard are the ones I've formed the closest bond with.

We appointed Cade to be Lucas' guardian angel because his soul struck me as being the purest out of all the War Angels under my command. Plus, he was great with Lucas. The two of them had become practically inseparable, and I knew Lucas loved having someone to spend time with who liked the same things he did. Cade had even taken on the responsibility of teaching Lucas how to fight properly with a sword and in hand-to-hand combat. Since our royal duties took up most of our days, Malcolm and I were extremely grateful that Cade had been sent to us when we needed someone like him the most.

As I continue to stare at Cade in complete shock, I can't fathom how such a pure soul could have Helena as a soul-mate. How was that even possible?

"What did you feel when you saw her?" I ask Cade in a whisper, fearing his answer will be a confirmation of his earlier statement.

"I felt like the universe opened up to reveal a piece of myself that has been missing from my life, and I didn't even know it until that moment."

I sigh in defeat because Cade just described how I felt when I first met Malcolm.

"This is insane!" Ethan roars, looking at Cade like he's completely lost his mind. "There's no way you can be that creature's soul-mate!"

"Ethan," I say in a calm voice, "no one is able to choose who their soul-mate ends up being. You can't blame Cade for this."

If anyone should be blamed, it should be me.

When God revealed that I had once been a Guardian of the Guf named Seraphina, he also told me that I was the one responsible for the creation of soul-mates. After Lucifer was banished from Heaven, Seraphina had been so heartbroken over his exile that she devised a scheme to bring him back one day. She asked the Guardians of the Guf to break her angelic soul apart and reform it into a human one so that she could one day find a way to reveal humanity's beauty to Lucifer. The process not only broke Seraphina's soul, but also every soul that had ever been created or ever would be created. Those who were fortunate enough to meet their soul-mate were never the same again. Usually, it was a time of celebration. This time, however, I couldn't be happy for Cade because I knew his soul-mate would only lead him down a dark and twisted path.

Could this be part of God's plan? Does He hope Cade can teach Helena how to love, like my mother showed Lucifer? In my heart, I have a very bad feeling about this new development. I'm not even sure Helena understands how to love someone besides herself. She's a creature unlike any other in existence, and none of us knows exactly what she is capable of doing.

"You are forbidden to ever go to that woman again," Ethan orders heatedly. "Do you understand me, Cade?"

"I'm going to have to countermand that order," I tell Ethan, being the only person besides God who he will obey. "You don't understand the pull of a soul-mate, Ethan. It's not something you can turn on and off at will."

"Do you actually *want* him going back to her?" Ethan asks skeptically.

"Of course not, but I won't set him up for failure either. There may come a time when he won't be able to stop himself from seeking her out. I can't fault him for doing something that he can't avoid."

"I won't purposely go to her without your knowledge," Cade says like a promise to me. "She's the enemy, and I will never choose her over you, no matter what."

I reach out and touch Cade's arm. "I know that, Cade, but I also want you to know that I won't think any less of you if you do feel an overwhelming need to go to her. Follow your heart in this matter. I trust your judgment."

"This is ridiculous," Ethan says in frustration. "I say we figure out a way to kill her before she has a chance to wheedle her way into Cade's heart any further."

"I can't risk doing anything directly to her while I'm pregnant. Not unless I absolutely have to," I tell them. "I won't endanger the lives of my babies for something I don't even think will work."

"Then what are we supposed to do about her?"

"I assume this conversation concerns Helena?" Malcolm says, phasing back into the room with Olivia by his side.

"We should continue talking about this later," I tell Cade and Ethan, not wanting to speak about the latest development in front of Olivia. She has enough on her mind at the moment.

Cade and Ethan bow to me and hastily phase out of the room.

Malcolm looks at me with an unspoken, but silently asked, question on his face. I discreetly shake my head, indicating that now is not the time to discuss the latest problem to affect our lives.

"I hope my presence hasn't interrupted something important," Olivia says, being as astute as ever about the things happening around her.

"Your presence is always a welcome distraction here," I assure Olivia as I walk over and kiss her on the cheek.

"I'm so sorry about what happened at the summit," Olivia tells me, looking distressed over the whole situation. "I had no idea any of that would happen."

"You've visited with Catherine since her recovery, haven't you?" I ask.

Olivia nods her head. "Yes, I have. And before you ask your next question, no, I had absolutely no idea she was going to ambush you with such a ludicrous accusation. If I had, I would have stopped her."

"Which is probably why she didn't mention it to you," Malcolm says.

"I would presume so," Olivia agrees.

"Has she ever said anything to you about her suspicions concerning my involvement in Auggie's death? Did she tell you Zuri and Helena were visiting her on Mars?"

"She doesn't like to talk about Auggie because it upsets her so much. As for you, she detests the fact that you're wearing her crown, but she's never even hinted that she would try to orchestrate a coup. As for Zuri and Helena, I knew Zuri visited her recently, but I didn't realize he was filling her head with poison about you. If I had, I would have put a stop to it at once, since it seems he and Helena are the ringleaders of this whole fiasco."

"Since you're a friend to both Catherine and me," I say, "I think you should be the arbiter of the election. I trust you to make sure it's kept above-board."

"It would be my honor," Olivia says, nodding her head as she accepts the responsibility. "Now, although I love Catherine as a person, I never respected the way she ruled Cirrus. I will make sure the election stays fair, but, secretly, I hope you win, Anna. You are the leader of the future, not only of Cirrus but also of the world. Catherine has no idea what she's up against, considering the creatures who are ruling some of the other cloud cities. We need someone in charge who they fear, and you are the only one that they do."

"Not necessarily," I hate to admit. "Helena is also a force to be reckoned with. She might even be more powerful than I am. We have no way of knowing without testing her abilities, and I would rather not do that if I don't have to. She is definitely an unknown variable that we need to be cautious of."

"Tell me," Olivia says, looking hesitant to voice her next words. "I know you were searching for Helena's location before she revealed herself. How exactly did you plan to deal with her once you found her?"

"Our primary motivation for finding Helena was to keep an eye on what she was doing and to resolve any problems she might cause. Honestly, I'm not even sure we can kill her, if it ever comes to that."

"But her body is corporeal, correct?" Olivia asks. "Can't you simply slice her throat or stab her in the heart?"

"It's certainly something we will try if she proves to be a threat we can't handle any other way," I say, "but I don't think it will be that simple. She has five of the seals within her. For all we know, they've made her invincible. Without attacking her outright, we have no way of knowing how strong she is, and now is not the time to try to assassinate the Empress of Nimbo. If people found out that I ordered an attempt on her life, it wouldn't matter who supported me during the election. I would be cast out of Cirrus just to keep the peace with Nimbo. For now, we will have to play the game Helena has set into motion. All we can do is see where it all leads us."

"Hopefully, not down a dark path," Olivia says, but I can see the doubt in her eyes. She knows just as well as I do that we've already been set on a gloomy course.

"Well," Olivia says, "I will speak with Catherine to make sure she agrees to have me as the arbiter for this election. It's never been done before in any cloud city. I may need a few days to gather what I need and get things set up, but I don't see why we can't have the election a week from today. Do you agree?"

"The sooner the better," I say.

"Well," Malcolm hedges, "not *too* soon. We still have some campaigning to do. The more people we can persuade to support you between now and then, the better."

"Very true," Olivia agrees, nodding her head. "Let me see what Catherine would like to do, and I will contact you after things have been decided."

"Thank you, Olivia. I don't know what we would do without your help."

Olivia grins and winks at me. "You don't have to worry. I will be around for quite some time."

Olivia holds out her palm to bring up her holographic controls before teleporting herself back to Mars to speak with Catherine.

"Ok," Malcolm says, "so what was that all about with Ethan and Cade?"

I tell Malcolm about everything that happened after he left.

He looks down at my belly and scowls, like our children betrayed me by phasing to Helena.

"Liam and Liana," he says in a stern voice, "I am very disappointed in you. *Very* disappointed. Stop taking your mother to that devil woman!"

"They can't possibly understand how dangerous she is," I tell Malcolm, rubbing one hand against my belly to take the sting out of Malcolm's words. "I wish I could figure out a way to break this connection I have with Helena. Maybe then they wouldn't feel drawn to her."

"Do you think that's the reason they keep going to her?"

I shrug my shoulders. "I have no way of knowing. It's either that or they're drawn to her because she has the other seals. Those are the only two possibilities I can think of."

"Agreed. They do seem to be the only links between her and them."

"I hope we can break that bond one day," I say worriedly. "It's going to be difficult to keep them safe if they keep phasing to her after they're born."

"We'll figure something out." Malcolm takes me into his arms to comfort me. "We always do."

I remain silent as I stand within the circle of my husband's embrace, drawing on his strength. We stay that way until my feet begin to hurt.

"I need to sit down," I tell him.

After we sit on the couch in front of the fireplace, Malcolm says, "So, Cade thinks he's soul-mates with Helena. How is something like that even possible?"

"That's exactly what I asked," I reply, leaning my back against the couch to relieve some of the pressure the babies are placing on my lower back. "I don't know, but I'm worried about him, Malcolm. Have you ever known anyone able to resist the urge to be with their soul-mate?"

Malcolm shakes his head, much to my dismay. "Never. He's doomed."

The situation isn't funny, but his words and look of disillusionment make me let out a small laugh over Cade's dilemma.

"He promised me he wouldn't go to her without telling me first, but I wonder if that's the right thing for him to do."

"I know what you're thinking, and I would caution you to not assume Helena is anything like Lucifer. Lucifer started out good, but then he let his vanity and greed get the better of him. Helena has never been good. She was born from Lucifer's hate and anger. I don't believe she's redeemable, Anna. I know that might be hard for you to hear because you like to see the best in people most of the time, but trust me when I tell you not to get your hopes up that the same scenario that helped Lucifer find redemption will work with

Helena. I don't think it will. I think that only pain and suffering will come from this."

"Is it wrong for me to hold out hope for her?"

"No, it's not wrong. It's just who you are, my love, and I wouldn't want you any other way. I simply don't want you to get your hopes up only to have them dashed."

"Let's talk about something else," I say, feeling a desperate need to change the subject. "How am I going to convince the people of Cirrus that I'm the candidate they should support?"

"I think we need to do a discreet poll of our own to see how many allies you have at the moment."

"And how should we go about doing something like that?"

"I think we should host a ball here at the palace to see who your true friends are in Cirrus."

"How exactly is a ball going to tell us that?"

"Well, anyone who refuses to come can automatically go into the 'need to be persuaded' pile. Out of the people who do attend, we can either assume they are on your side, or they're simply curious to see what will happen at the ball. We can have people mingle and listen to what's being said. It won't be an exact count, but we should be able to get a good idea of how much work will need to be done to ensure your win."

"Malcolm," I say, hoping he doesn't get too upset with what I'm about to say, "I don't want you to spend any of your money on this election. If I can't retain the crown because of who I am, I shouldn't win."

Malcolm squints at me. "I can appreciate you wanting to win that way, but you know as well as I do that Catherine will be using everything at her disposal to persuade people to vote for her."

"But she doesn't have any money."

"She doesn't need it, Anna. She can promise favors to those who will hold their vote hostage. Unfortunately, you know the royals here expect something for their support. I had to spend a great deal of money to make sure people didn't oppose you retaining your position as empress, and even more to ensure my own coronation. It's just the way things are done, my love."

"It doesn't feel right," I say stubbornly, "and I don't want us to do it."

Malcolm sighs heavily. "Is that your only request? Are you going to tie my hands in any other way?"

"No."

"Good."

"Wait," I say, worried I may have just consented to something even more corrupt than bribing. "What else do you have planned? I don't want to win by promising special favors either, Malcolm."

"I understand."

I wait for him to say more, but he doesn't.

"You're not going to do anything illegal, are you?" I ask, worried now that I should have put more restrictions on what I would allow him to do during his campaigning for my sovereignty.

"Truly, my love, your lack of faith in my natural ability to persuade people is troubling. I can be rather charming when I want to be, you know."

I can't prevent a smile as I look at my husband.

"I know exactly how charming you can be," I tell him, reaching out to touch the side of his face. "I have the proof of your charm growing inside my womb."

Malcolm grins proudly. "They are proof of my virility," he says brashly. "My charm is what persuaded you to marry me in the first place."

"I was doomed the moment I laid eyes on you," I tease, reminding him of his words about Cade's fate.

"Admit it," Malcolm says, sliding over to sit closer to me, "even if we hadn't been soul-mates, you still wouldn't have been able to keep your hands off me."

I let my gaze travel leisurely from Malcolm's long dark locks of hair down to his legs.

"I wouldn't have been able to resist you," I murmur. "I'm not that stupid."

Malcolm chuckles. "That is a word I would never associate with you, Anna. Ever."

Malcolm leans in and begins to kiss me tenderly on the lips, but I've had a rough day and need more than his gentleness. I coax his lips and tongue into a familiar dance, telling him with actions instead of words about what I need.

Malcolm pulls back for a moment to look into my eyes before asking, "Are you sure?"

"I need you to remind me how beautiful the world can be, and that's never more pronounced for me than when we make love. Today's been horrible. I need for you to make it better."

Malcolm stands to his feet and picks me up easily in his arms.

"It's a great sacrifice on my part," he tells me through a smile, "but I'm willing to do whatever is required to make you happy."

I laugh just as Malcolm phases us to our bedroom.

My heart sinks slightly when I realize our play will have to be delayed. Through the open door of the room, I can hear Lucas and Vala out in the sitting room, talking.

Malcolm sets me on my feet, having heard them, too.

"I guess we'll need to wait a little while," I tell him only slightly disappointed. How could I be upset that our plans will have to be delayed when our son is in the next room, waiting to see us?

Malcolm reaches up and plucks the Crown of Cirrus from my head. I'd become so used to its weight, I had forgotten it was even there. He sets it down on the table beside our bed before taking one of my hands with his. When we walk into the sitting room, we find Lucas, Vala, and Luna in the middle of the floor where Lucas has his Tinker Toys spread out across the area rug in the room. Cade is standing by the entryway to the veranda, looking lost in thought as he watches Lucas play.

As soon as our son sees us, he jumps up and runs over to me.

"Cade said you had a bad day," Lucas tells me. "We made you something to help put you in a better mood."

"Oh, a surprise!" I say excitedly for my son's benefit. "What is it?"

"I'll go get it, Lucas," Cade says.

Cade phases, but returns only a few seconds later. In his hands, he's holding a small white bowl filled with one of my pregnancy indulgences.

For whatever reason, I have been craving strawberry ice cream topped with crushed potato chips and shaved milk chocolate. It was something I had never eaten before in my life, but about two months into my pregnancy the thought of the combination practically had me drooling. The first time Malcolm and Lucas made it for me, I sat and ate almost a whole pint of it at one time.

"You boys spoil me," I tell Lucas and Cade as he walks over to hand me the bowl of ice cream.

"That's what we're here for!" Lucas proudly proclaims.

I take a spoonful of the ice cream into my mouth and swear I hear the angels in Heaven begin to sing.

"Thank you so much," I tell them both. "I really needed this right now."

"Don't worry, Mommy," Lucas tells me, hugging me from the side since my belly doesn't exactly make it practical for him to hug me from the front. "Cade told me about the election. I know you'll win."

"Did you have a vision of me winning?" I ask Lucas, hoping for some good news about our future.

"Not exactly," Lucas admits, dropping his arms so he can take a step back to look up at me. "But I never see us not living in the palace. I'm pretty sure that means you'll win."

"Well, I'll take that as meaning that I win, too," I tell him.

"What are you trying to build?" Malcolm says, examining Lucas' contraption.

"A spaceship," Lucas tells his father proudly.

"Want some help?"

Lucas walks over to Malcolm, and takes his hand to lead him to his play area as a reply.

As I take another spoonful of my ice cream treat into my mouth, I notice Cade still has a distant look in his eyes as he watches Lucas and Malcolm play together. There's an aura of sadness surrounding him now that was never there before.

"Cade," I say, drawing his attention. "I think I need some fresh air. Would you like to join me on the veranda?"

It may have sounded like a request, but it was really more of an order so we can speak in private.

I start walking towards the veranda without waiting for his answer.

Cade follows me out, remaining silent.

Once we're outside I take in a deep, cleansing breath of air and set my bowl of ice cream down on top of the stone railing.

"You don't look very good," I inform Cade, granting him my full attention.

"I feel even worse," he admits with a melancholy smile.

Cade closes his eyes and rubs his forehead with the fingers of one hand, looking slightly frustrated.

"You know," he begins, "when I learned that we were going to be allowed to come to Earth, I did hope that I would meet my soul-mate. I wasn't counting on it, but I think we all want to experience that once-in-a-lifetime connection to someone else."

"Just because she's your soul-mate doesn't mean you have to be in love with her, or that she's the only one you can feel love for. People who aren't soul-mates fall in love every day, Cade. I don't want you to feel like your chance to find someone good to build a life with here is gone. It's not.

You can choose to love someone more worthy of you. Helena doesn't deserve your notice, much less your love."

"For some reason, I feel like my life ended today."

I walk up to Cade and grab both of his arms to make sure he is looking at me before I speak.

"Your life on this Earth has just begun," I declare. "Don't let Helena take away the joy you've found here with my family and the people on this planet. There is so much in your life to look forward to, Cade. I know it will be hard, probably impossible, for you to put her behind you, but I think that's exactly what you have to do for the sake of your own sanity."

Honestly, I had harbored a small hope that Cade might be able to soften Helena's heart one day, but Malcolm's earlier warning to me that such a thing would probably never happen seems true in this case. If I could break Cade's connection to Helena, I would. As things are, I'm incapable of breaking my own link to her.

"I'll try," Cade promises. "Don't worry about me, Anna. You have enough to think about without my problem being added to the list."

I lean up and give Cade a kiss on the cheek.

"You're my friend," I tell him. "I always worry about my friends, even if they don't want me to."

As I take a step back, I ask, "Would you mind telling me why you stayed behind in Nimbo when Ethan phased me back home?"

"I wanted to force her to look at me," Cade says. "I knew she had to feel what I did when I first phased into the room, but she refused to look at me. After you left, she didn't have much choice."

"Did she say anything to you?"

Cade nods. "Yes. She told me to stay away from her because she had too much work to do, and I would only get in the way."

It seemed like an odd thing for Helena to tell him. It was almost kind coming from her.

"I think she's determined to ruin my life any way she can," I proclaim. "I'll be honest with you, Cade. I'm not even sure love is an emotion Helena is capable of feeling, and even if she is, I'm not sure she would acknowledge it."

"When I saw Malcolm sit down to play with Lucas a moment ago, I realized that's something I want to do with a son of my own one day. I can never have that with her, can I? She doesn't exactly strike me as the mothering type."

"No, she doesn't strike me as that either. My best advice to you is to keep your eyes open for a woman who can genuinely be the partner you deserve in life. She's out there. I just know it."

Cade's shoulders straighten a little as he stands a bit taller.

"I'll try to do that," he proclaims. "I know I can."

It sounds more like he's trying to convince himself of the fact, but I perceive it as him taking charge of his own life.

I just hope he truly can.

CHAPTER EIGHT

(From Helena's Point of View)

Love. What an absurd human concept. Practically since the beginning of time, people have used that emotion as a crutch to help explain away their weaknesses. Instead of owning up to their own failures as sentient beings, they use 'love' to explain away the reasons they do certain imbecilic things in their lives. Pathetic.

I would have more respect for them if they just admitted their mistakes. Then again, I suppose I wouldn't have had so many lovely, tainted souls as my playthings during the long years Lucifer and I reigned together. I hate to acknowledge it, but I miss the old bastard. Even though he eventually became as weak as the humans he always loathed, I do miss having someone around who understands the real me.

As I stare at the War Angel standing in front of me, I have to wonder what's going through his mind. Does he imagine that I'll submit to the unwelcome feeling I have for him that's irritating the pit of my stomach? I feel an inexplicable urge to kiss him and slap him all at the same time.

Anna and her other War Angel phased away, but this one stayed behind. Presumably, to declare his undying love for me, even though he doesn't know me at all. How preposterous is that? How can you fall madly in love with someone you just met?

"What's your name?" I demand to know.

"Cade," he says, staring at me like a lovesick puppy.

I don't like puppies. Never have, never will. The hellhounds were the only things close to such an animal that I could stand, and even then I hated the pesky little mongrels until I could train them to accept their fate as my loyal minions. Once their eyes went from bright blue to pitch-black, I knew all of the goodness they'd possessed had been drained out of them. It was only then that I knew they were ready to do whatever I commanded.

I study Cade and wonder if he's trainable, too. Maybe I can transform him into something I can tolerate to have around, but do I really want to invest the time in such an endeavor?

"Do me a favor, Cade: Stay away from me. I have a lot of work to do, and you'll only become an obstacle that I'll have to get rid of eventually. If you treasure your life, keep your distance from me, and I will keep mine from you."

The other War Angel phases back, looking between Cade and me as if he doesn't understand what's going on. I'll admit he's not the only one in the room who is confused by the unexpected turn of events.

"We need to get back to Anna," the other one tells Cade. He doesn't even wait for Cade to respond before phasing them both back to the palace in Cirrus.

Right after they leave, the gold double doors to my personal chambers open, and Levi steps in.

"I received word that Anna phased in here," Levi says as he walks over to me in his stolen body of Zuri Solarin. "Where is she?"

"Why? Are you ready to trade me in for your old flame already, Levi?"

Levi rolls his brown eyes at me. "Please, give me more credit than that, Helena. I just wanted to find out why she was here. I thought she would still be licking her wounds from today's events, not seeking out more humiliation. Though my little dove got what she deserved, if you ask me."

"No," I say, smiling tightlipped at Levi, desperately trying to keep myself from ripping out his heart and shoving it down his throat on the spot, "in point of fact, I didn't ask you; just like I didn't ask you to come into my chambers uninvited. I thought I made it perfectly clear that you are to stay away from me."

"I don't see how I can do that and still make the people of this cloud city believe that we love one another."

"Love, love, love!" I say irately, unable to hide my irritation at the word. "Why do humans treasure it so much?"

"I have no idea," Levi admits, looking baffled. "It's always mystified me as well, but they seem to like falling into it with each other all the time. More often than not, it leads to their downfall in some way. I really don't know why they even bother."

"Anna seems to believe her love for Malcolm actually gives her strength."

"Then she's deluding herself," Levi scoffs. "He's one of her many weaknesses, and makes her exploitable. She'll never find her true self until everything she loves is ripped away from her."

"You are a cruel, heartless bastard," I say, at least admiring that much about Levi.

"What can I say?" he replies with a cocky grin. "It comes naturally to me."

"Too bad I won't let you harm anyone she cares about."

"Yes," Levi says, narrowing his eyes on me. "Why is that exactly? You still haven't given me a good reason."

"I don't have to give you a reason. Just do as I say, and I'll make sure you live through this."

"What's to keep Anna from killing me, now that she knows who I am? We didn't exactly leave one another on the best of terms."

"Anna won't do anything to either one of us."

"How can you be so confident about that?" Levi asks skeptically.

"The reasons are more political than anything. Can you imagine the reaction if the Empress of Cirrus killed both of the leaders of Nimbo? It would be quite the scandal. Anna isn't desperate enough to publically do something that bold, at least not yet."

"Can she kill you?"

I shrug my shoulders. "I have no idea. I don't think so, but I'm not going to purposely test my theory either. I've worked too hard to get to where I am."

"Do you think you're immortal?"

"You just asked me that, you imbecile. Changing the words doesn't make it a different question."

"I'm just trying to make friendly conversation with you, Helena."

"No, you're not. You want to know if you'll ever be able to get rid of me. It's what I would want to know if our positions were reversed. Frankly, I don't know the answer, Levi, but I wouldn't count on finding a way to dispose of me any time soon. You and the others will have to bide your time to see how things play out between Anna and me."

"For what it's worth, I hope you accomplish whatever it is you're trying to by dethroning her."

"Don't worry about my motives," I warn Levi, not wanting him to dig too deep for the answer. "My true agenda is none of your concern. Just enjoy the ride, Levi. All you need to do is take care of Nimbo so I can deal with my own affairs, and don't come back into my rooms unless I call you. Is that understood? I might not be as nice next time."

Levi inclines his head in my direction, showing his acquiescence to my request before he phases away.

"I hate being surrounded by idiots," I mumble to myself, turning back to face the window and continue my observation about my cloud city.

It is rather beautiful, in a gaudy sort of way. Apparently, gold is a plentiful commodity in Nimbo's down-world. Almost every building has something gold attached to it. If not a gold statue then a roof made out of it. Humans and their desperate need for expensive items to show off their wealth. Superficial halfwits.

I decide to go back home, back to Hell, and see how my preparations are coming along. If I've learned anything during my long existence, it's that being prepared for every eventuality is always the best course of action. I can't count on people to act the way I want them to. It's not like my home, where anything I want is simply a thought away. I have to admit it's rather irritating living in the Earthly veil, but, at the same time, a bit exhilarating.

Who knows? Maybe things will work out the way I want.

So far...so good...

CHAPTER NINE

(Back to Anna's Point of View)

Cade and I go back into the sitting room, where Malcolm and Lucas are having a lively discussion about the design of our son's imaginary spaceship. Malcolm is arguing that they should build it one way, and Lucas has dug in his heels, informing his father that he thinks they should do it another way. I've always found these moments rather amusing between the two of them. It's our own version of David and Goliath, and, as in the Bible, David always wins.

After I finish eating my ice cream, I ask Cade, "Do you know where Atticus is right now?"

"When we returned to the palace, he and the others decided to blow off some steam in the training room."

"Would you mind taking me down there?" I ask.

"Of course I will."

Malcolm looks up at me from his spot on the floor by Lucas.

"Do you want me to go with you?" he asks, standing to his feet.

I shake my head. "No. You stay here and play with Lucas. I won't be gone long."

Malcolm looks at Cade. "Make sure my wife doesn't tire herself out, and, for goodness' sake, don't let her pick up a sword. I swear I think she forgets she's pregnant sometimes."

Cade smiles. It's nice to see a genuine look of amusement on his face.

"You have my word that she won't be sparring with the others."

"I'm not a child, you know," I say to them both. "I think I can decide what I can and cannot handle."

Malcolm walks over to me and loosely wraps his arms around me.

"You think you're indestructible," he tells me. "The fact is, you're not, so humor me and don't get into a brawl down there."

"I'm only going down to talk to them," I promise. "Besides, they all know I could beat them in battle. It's not even a fair fight, if you think about it."

Malcolm laughs heartily. "That is very true. They would have to be fools to accept a challenge from you."

"I'll be back in a bit," I say, rising up to kiss Malcolm chastely on the lips. "Don't worry."

"I'll always worry," Malcolm tells me in all seriousness. "It doesn't matter where you go or what you're doing. Your safety will always take top priority with me."

"Well, this is something you don't have to worry about," I declare.

Malcolm drops his arms from around me as I place a hand on Cade's arm. He phases us down to the training room on the first floor of the castle. The room is similar to the one my papa and I had in our home here in Cirrus. Everything from weapons to sparring partners is holographic, but the holograms are able to mimic the real feel of a weapon and opponent.

However, the War Angels never use the room's holographic capabilities. They always prefer to use the weapons they brought down with them from Heaven, and to fight against one another. I can understand their need to make the combat as real as possible. It's always more fun that way.

We find Atticus and Xander in the center ring, which is just a large, white, padded square in the middle of the room, sparring against one another. They've chosen hand-to-hand combat this time, which always seems to make a fight more personal for some reason. I suppose it's the direct physical contact between opponents. Fighting with a weapon places a certain impersonal distance between combatants. A one-on-one fight can be more exhilarating and gratifying, especially if you have a lot of pent-up rage that needs to be expelled. With the ferocity of the fight between the two men in the ring now, it's obvious they both have some anger issues to work through.

I asked Malcolm once why it seemed like some of the War Angels acted like the war in Heaven happened only yesterday. He reminded me that time moves differently in Heaven, and for them it was almost as if the war ended only a short while ago. Many of them are still trying to cope with the aftermath of killing so many of their brethren. Malcolm likened it to humans who used to suffer from something called post-traumatic stress disorder. I didn't know what he was talking about at first because war had not been a factor within my lifetime. I did understand the concept, though. It seemed like some of them were able to compartmentalize what happened during the war and put it behind them. Others, like Atticus and Xander, weren't as lucky and seemed to have to deal with the aftermath every day of their lives. I hoped, in time, all of the War Angels would be able to find a way to put the war behind them. Unfortunately, all I could seem to offer them was another conflict to fight in.

Also standing in the room are Ethan, Zane, Gideon, and Roan. Roan is Ethan's second in command, and has spent a great deal of his time on Earth searching for Helena's whereabouts. He is quiet, for the most part, but ever-vigilant in his duties.

"Come on, you wuss," Xander taunts Atticus as the two of them circle one another like wild animals. "You can do better than that. Just pretend I'm Helena."

Xander changes the gait of his walk and begins to shake his hips, placing one hand on his waist and the other one near his neck like he's bouncing a head full of curls.

"Come on, you stupid War Angel," Xander says in a high-pitched feminine voice, which forces me to suppress a giggle as I watch his antics. "Show me you have more in between those huge elephant ears besides air, you big, burly half-wit."

With a growl, Atticus charges Xander, grabbing the other War Angel around the waist and slamming him onto the floor. Xander quickly phases out of Atticus' hold to straddle his back. Xander grabs a fistful of Atticus' curly brown hair and yanks so hard I fear he might break the other man's neck.

"Stop letting your anger dictate your actions, Atticus. That's always been the problem with you during a fight. When you see red, it's like your brain shuts down and you can't think straight."

Atticus phases out from underneath Xander, appearing behind him and swiftly kicking Xander in the center of his back, causing him to sprawl onto the mat.

"And you've always been horrible about watching your back," Atticus growls.

"Gentlemen," Ethan says loudly, drawing the attention of the two on the mat, "we have a guest."

Ethan looks pointedly at me.

"Don't let me interrupt you," I tell them. "I only came down here to make sure everyone was all right after what happened at the summit."

"Isn't that a question we should be asking you?" Gideon says, looking worried over my welfare.

"I'm fine," I reassure them, belatedly realizing that they can all tell the truth from a lie. "Well, maybe fine isn't the right word, but I'll make it through this. None of you should worry about me."

"We all know you're strong," Zane tells me, "but no one should have to go through being accused of murder when the fact is that you saved this world from complete annihilation. I just wish we could say that in public."

"The fewer people who know, the better," I reply. "I'm just relieved they accepted you all so easily."

I notice Roan avert his gaze from me with a troubled look on his face. It's then that I know I may have been given the sugarcoated version of my angels' acceptance into polite society.

"Have things not been going as smoothly as I was told?" I ask, in a tone that warns lying is not permitted. I immediately pounce on the person who appears to be the weakest link concerning this issue. "Roan?"

Roan looks back at me with a surprised expression on his face for being called out to answer my question.

Gideon reaches over and slaps Roan hard on the backside of the head, causing his fellow angel to stumble forward slightly.

"Now you've gone and done it," Gideon complains. "Why is it so hard for you to pretend?"

Roan stands back up straight, rubbing away the ache on the back of his head.

"I'm not a good liar," Roan answers. "I never have been."

"Why would you all feel the need to lie to me in the first place?" I ask, confused by this turn of the conversation.

"I wouldn't exactly say that we lied," Ethan replies, even though I can hear his guilt clear enough. "It's more like we let you think everything was going smoothly. We didn't want you to get upset over something that you can't control."

"So tell me the truth," I demand. "What have you been hiding from me?"

"A lot of the humans are wary of us," Zane starts to explain. "It's a perfectly natural reaction. None of us blames them for it. I think they just need to get to know us better, and it's going to take some time for our presence to seem natural to them. I don't think any of us can make that happen any faster than it is. Change is always difficult. Their acceptance of us isn't going to happen overnight."

"I wish you had told me this sooner," I tell them, before realization sets in. "Has Malcolm known about this all along?"

Everyone seems to find a place to divert their eyes so they don't have to meet my gaze.

I sigh heavily, but say nothing. Their lack of an answer tells me everything I need to know.

"What can I do to help?" I ask them.

Ethan shrugs, finally meeting my eyes again. "I'm not sure there's anything you can do, to be honest. Like Zane said, it's just going to take some time for the humans to accept us."

I stand there silently for a moment, trying to think of some way to aid my angels in their quest to assimilate into human culture.

"We're having a ball tomorrow night," I inform them. "I want all of you to attend it."

"We're your personal guard," Ethan says, looking confused. "Of course we'll be there."

"No," I say with a shake of my head. "I don't want you there as my guard. I want you there as my guests."

It's Ethan's turn to shake his head. "Your safety is our top priority, Anna. It always will be, especially now with Helena as an open threat."

"Malcolm and the other Watchers can take care of my safety for one night, Ethan. This is the perfect opportunity for you to show the people in Cirrus who you truly are. All they've seen of you so far is your aggression."

"Well, it's not like we're beating people in the streets," Roan says, sounding slightly offended by my statement.

"It's not your actions, exactly," I correct. "But you all tend to wear a certain look on your faces while you're protecting me."

"Look?" Gideon questions. "What kind of look?"

I'm at a loss as to how to explain what I mean, so I try to show them. I scrunch up my forehead, narrow my eyes, and purse my lips. For added effect, I place my fists on my hips and strike a fierce pose for the boys.

I bear witness to something the universe at large has never seen before, and marvel at the wonder of its sound.

Atticus begins to laugh.

He's soon joined by his brothers, and the room is filled with the heavenly sounds of my angels' amusement.

I can't hold my posture for very long because their laughter is infectious, and I'm not above laughing at myself.

Once we're all able to catch our breaths, I tell them, "That's the side of you people need to see. They need to know that you're not that different from them. Show the humans who you really are. I know they'll love you as much as I do."

I watch as my words have the desired effect. Everyone nods in agreement.

"What are we going to wear?" Gideon asks.

I have to smile because his expression is so serious. Besides, it's a completely natural worry when you attend your first social event.

"Let me worry about arranging your clothing," I tell them to take that worry off their shoulders. "I'll have Malcolm's tailor in town make sure you all have something special to wear."

"You said this was a ball?" Xander asks worriedly "So there will be dancing, right?"

"Of course," I answer.

The boys all look at each other like I just announced they would be expected to jump through a series of flaming hoops. Then the reason for their discomfort dawns on me.

"Have none of you ever danced before?" I ask.

"Not a step," Ethan confirms, "at least not in these bodies or to human music."

"Dancing is easy," I assure them. "I can teach you how to do it."

They all instantly say no, and shake their heads as they back away from me as if I suddenly contracted the plague.

"I promise I won't hurt you," I tell them, finding this the only explanation for their sudden wariness of me.

"It's not that we think you would hurt us," Roan says. "I think we're all pretty certain that we would end up hurting you. I would rather not be responsible for breaking your feet, Anna."

"Oh," I say, waving a hand at them like they're crazy for even thinking such a thing, "I can assure you that won't happen."

"How can you say that with so much confidence?" Zane asks dubiously.

I use one of the gifts handed down to me by my ancestor Jess, and float a couple of inches off the floor.

"If my feet are nowhere near yours," I say, "there's no way you can hurt me."

Thankfully, none of the boys can find an objection to this arrangement, and we begin the very first dance class for War Angels.

Most of them pick dancing up quickly. Xander is the only one who seems to have difficulty learning the movements.

"I can't do this," Xander says in frustration, stepping away from me during his turn. "My body just doesn't move this way."

"Would it help if you thought of dancing like it was a fight?" I ask him.

Xander's brow furrows. "How am I supposed to do that?"

I turn and hold out my hand to Roan, who accepts it readily.

"Watch me teach Roan a minuet. It's a dance with steps specifically timed to the music. It might be easier for you to learn because you'll be able to memorize the movements beforehand."

It takes me two tries to teach Roan the steps to the minuet, but on the third run through, he has it down pat.

I turn to Xander and hold out my hand. "Are you ready to give it a try?"

Xander nods and accepts my hand. On his first attempt, Xander dances the minuet perfectly.

I give him a big hug afterwards and say, "See! I knew you could do it."

Xander looks at me a little sheepishly before saying, "I'm sorry about last night. I was rude to you, and you didn't deserve having me talk to you like that. All you've ever been is good to us since we came here. I know I've been a handful, but please don't give up on me just yet. I can do better. I can be better."

"Thank you for saying that," I tell him, knowing he had to swallow a lot of pride to admit his faults to me.

Men in general don't like to show weakness, and my War Angels are no exception to that rule. In a way, I almost feel like a mother figure to all of them. They look to me for guidance through the ins and outs of living amongst humans. I knew there would be an adjustment period when they were first sent to me, but I guess I didn't realize just how hard it would be for some of them to adapt.

"Does anyone else have any concerns about the dance?" I ask them.

"I think we're prepared," Ethan answers, but doesn't sound completely confident about his statement.

"What else is troubling you?" I ask him.

Ethan rubs the back of his neck while looking hesitant to say what's on his mind.

"It's just," he begins, but stops to collect his thoughts. "Well, humans seem to like small talk. I'm not sure I know enough to keep a conversation going."

"Are you kidding me?" I ask, flabbergasted. "All of you will be highly sought- after companions, because you know the one thing almost every human is curious about."

"What's that?" Zane asks.

"What Heaven is like," I answer. "I can assure you that at least one person will ask each of you that question. I suggest you prepare your answers beforehand."

Vala walks into the room, catching my attention.

"Is anything wrong?" I ask her.

"No, Anna," she answers, coming to sit in front of me. "Malcolm asked me to come down here to make sure you were all right. It's been over an hour since you left us."

"Has it been that long?" I ask, not realizing so much time had passed.

"You should probably get back to your family, Anna," Gideon suggests. "I think you've prepared us well enough for tomorrow night."

"All of you are a part of my family," I tell them. "Don't ever forget that, ok? If you need me, just come to me, and I will move Heaven and Earth to help you."

"Of that, I have no doubt," Ethan says to me with a confident grin. "We're fine, for now. You've had a rotten day. I think spending time with Malcolm and Lucas would do your heart some good."

"Malcolm said he needs your help with the invitations to the ball," Vala informs Ethan. "He wants you and your men to hand-deliver them to certain invited guests."

"Why would he want that?" I ask Vala.

"I believe his plan is to make those people feel important. Having an invitation hand- delivered to you by an angel of God will more than likely do the trick."

I couldn't argue with my husband's logic. If anyone knew how to play on peoples' vanity, it was Malcolm. He had lived on Earth longer than almost anyone else alive, except for the few remaining Watchers. He was an expert in making people do what he wanted without them even knowing why they were doing it.

I feel lucky to have him on my side to guide me through the politics of it all. I just hope it's enough.

CHAPTER TEN

I take Ethan's advice and spend the rest of the day with Malcolm, Lucas, Vala, and Luna in our private chambers. We're pressed for time in dealing with the preparations for the ball, but, luckily, we have an excellent staff in the castle who knows exactly what to do. They require very little supervision, and only come to us when they need our opinion on matters. I do, however, stress the fact that the event shouldn't be overly-extravagant and wasteful of precious resources.

The living conditions in the down-world are always at the forefront of my mind. I can still remember the homeless people I saw in the streets of New Orleans, and the ramshackle town where I witnessed a mother's rage over losing her newborn daughter in Stratus. Those memories propel me forward to find ways to make the world a better place for everyone living in it. Is it a fool's dream to hope for so much change? Perhaps. Yet, it's one well worth pursuing, and I will strive to achieve my life's ambition until the day I die, if it takes that long. I aspire to achieve my goals within my lifetime, but I'm not a fool. I know it might take longer, and I plan to instill in my children the importance of helping those who don't have the power to help themselves.

Once we put Lucas and the pups to bed, Malcolm takes special care of me. During my pregnancy, he has been an attentive lover, like always, but even more gentle and unselfish about satisfying his own physical needs. His touches have been light and only meant to satisfy, demanding nothing in return. His kisses pluck the strings of my heart like a tender caress, declaring his love without needing to say the words. Though, he professes his love to me all the time, seeming unable to stop himself from doing so. I'm not even sure he realizes how often he says 'I love you' to me, but I have zero complaints about that fact. He makes me feel loved and cherished in every possible way. What more could a woman ask for?

While Malcolm and I make our final walkthrough of the grand ballroom in the palace to approve of what's been done, Lucas asks us a simple question.

"Can I invite Bai to come?" he says innocently.

Even though Linn did consent to move her family to Cirrus after Daniel's death, she and her children have kept their distance from all of us. Within the past few months, we have sent countless invitations for Bai to come to the palace to play with Lucas, but each time our invitation was politely declined. We eventually stopped telling Lucas about the invitations we would send out, because each rejection seemed to dampen the joy in his eyes.

It's obvious that Linn still despises me for killing Daniel, even though she knows it was an accident. After Levi sent me Millie's severed head in a box, I completely lost the ability to reason and think straight. When my friends tried to stop me from killing him, Daniel received the brunt of my anger and frustration. When Daniel placed his arm around my waist to prevent me from killing Levi, my anger and hatred of Levi was so great in that moment that, when I went to push his arm off me, I lost control of my powers for one split second, killing Daniel in the process. I can still remember staring at the black ash from his passing, on the palms of my hands. How could I expect Linn to forgive me for taking away the father of her children, when I couldn't even forgive myself for what I did?

"We'll see," Malcolm answers, trying his best not to get Lucas' hopes up over the prospect, but from the smile that appears on our son's face, I can tell it's already too late.

"We're going to invite her, Luna!" Lucas announces to his faithful companion as he runs down the grand staircase.

"No running!" I admonish.

"Woohoo!" Lucas yells, leaping off the last step and paying absolutely no attention to me.

"What are we going to do now?" I whisper to Malcolm. "He obviously thinks Linn will let Bai come this time."

"I know," Malcolm says. "I've been thinking about how to get the two of them together."

"I don't think Linn will ever let that happen," I reply, feeling despondent about the situation. "If Bai was to ever marry Lucas, Linn would be permanently connected to our family. I seriously doubt she wants to be around me that much."

"Do you remember what Lucas told you at our wedding reception?" Malcolm reminds me. "He saw his marriage to Bai in the future. We have to make sure that happens, Anna."

I look over at Malcolm as we come to the bottom of the stairs to stand on the open floor of the ballroom.

"Why is this so important to you?" I ask. "Other than the fact that you want to make our son happy."

Malcolm looks over to make sure Lucas is well out of earshot before saying, "I have a theory."

"What kind of theory?"

"Do you remember what I told you about Gabe and how he sacrificed himself to save us on alternate Earth?"

"Yes," I say, feeling a coldness seep underneath my skin at the reminder of Malcolm's adventure in that other reality. "I remember what you told me. I'm so happy Gabe has a second chance at life on Earth in Lucas."

"I don't believe he's the only vessel who was sent back," Malcolm reveals to me for the first time.

"What?" I ask in surprise. "Why haven't you mentioned this to me before now?"

"I guess I was afraid to hope that I was right." Malcolm shrugs. "But, the more I think about it, the more it just makes sense."

"What makes sense, and more importantly, who do you think was sent back?"

"I think Bai is JoJo reincarnated," Malcolm whispers.

"Gabe's wife?"

"Well, they never had the chance to actually marry in their first lives, but they were as devoted to one another as any married couple."

"What is it that makes you think Bai is JoJo, besides the fact that Lucas saw them getting married?"

"When we returned home from alternate Earth, God visited us inside the vessels' inner realm right before we returned to our Earth. He whispered something to JoJo and said it would bring her peace to help adjust to the loss of Gabe from her life. He didn't allow her to keep the memory of what He told her, but He did allow her to keep the calm it brought her. I've been thinking about it a lot, and it just seems like the most logical conclusion. It would make sense that God told her they would be together in the future and have a second chance to live out their lives together on Earth. If you add in the fact that Lucas has already seen himself marrying Bai, I don't think there can be any other explanation."

"Do you remember the dinner party we had when we invited Lucifer over?" I ask.

"Yes, of course."

"He didn't tell us at the time, but he told us later that he recognized Lucas as having Gabriel's soul. Since Gabe and Gabriel's souls are forever linked, you were able to figure out that Lucas is Gabe. I've always meant to ask, why didn't you know who Lucas actually was before that moment?"

"The souls of the vessels were hard to identify. None of us knew who they were when we first met them, not even Lucifer. I've always just assumed that archangels have a different type of sixth sense when it comes to souls and, that after meeting the vessels and knowing which archangel they carried, they were able to distinguish between them more easily."

"If that's true, then Lucifer had to know Bai was JoJo. She was at that dinner party, too."

"He probably did."

"I wonder why he didn't tell us."

"Lucifer only told us about Lucas to explain how Mammon was able to hide him in the Garden of Eden. Everything happened so fast after that, there really wasn't a good time to tell us about Bai. I don't think he was hiding the information. I think he just either didn't see the need to tell us, or simply ran out of time."

"Oh, Malcolm," I say, looking over at Lucas as Luna chases him around the room, "if what you believe is true, we have to find a way to get Lucas and Bai together. Do you think we should tell Linn this story? Surely she wouldn't deny Gabe and JoJo a chance at a happily-ever-after in this life."

"Anna," Malcolm says, taking both of my hands with his, "I think you need to go to Linn in person and have a talk with her face to face."

I shake my head. "She doesn't want to talk to me. You know that. I've invited her to the palace almost as much as I have Bai."

"I know, but if you go to her home, I don't think she will turn you away."

"You want me to force her to talk to me after everything I've put her through? Have you lost your mind?"

"Please, my love," Malcolm practically begs, "do this for our son. Gabe and JoJo deserve another chance at happiness. JoJo was never the same after his death. She tried her best to move on for their son's sake, but there was always the shadow of Gabe's loss following her. We all saw it, but were helpless to do anything about it. You and I can help them achieve in this life what they were denied in their first ones."

I sigh because I know what I have to do. I want my son to be happy. I want JoJo and Gabe to finally live out their lives together.

"Ok," I agree. "I'll do it."

Malcolm brings me into his arms and hugs me. At first, I assume the embrace is only meant to thank me, but then I hear him sniffle. I pull back slightly and see that he's holding back an ocean of tears.

"Oh, Malcolm," I say. I don't have to ask him what's wrong. I know how much he loved JoJo and Gabe. He's told me a lot about his time with Jess, Mason, and the vessels. I feel as though I know them all, too, and I understand how much he misses being with them.

"I'll do whatever it takes to persuade Linn to let Bai spend time with Lucas," I promise him. "JoJo and Gabe will get their happy ending."

Malcolm nods, but is too choked up to make a reply. I draw him back into my arms, being forever thankful to have a man like him in my life. Malcolm is one of the strongest men I know, and, when it comes to his loved ones, he'll do whatever it takes to make them happy, even if it means sacrificing part of his own happiness to do so. I not only want to bridge the divide between Linn and me for our families' sake, but I also want to mend what was broken in our relationship because of Daniel's death.

I've given her months to mourn, hoping in time she could at least find a way to tolerate me in her life for the benefit of our children. I didn't relish the idea of forcing my presence on her, but I know the longer I let Linn's hate for me fester, the harder it will become for her to absolve me of my sins. I doubt Linn will ever be able to completely forgive me, but perhaps we can find some common ground to build another type of relationship with one another.

I sympathize with her pain and loss. If the tables were turned, I don't think I would be able to forgive her for taking away the man I loved either. I only need to find a way for her not to punish our children over something I did out of anger and thoughtlessness.

"I should go to her today, before I lose my nerve," I tell Malcolm.

Malcolm pulls away from me. "Do you want me to go with you to try to help explain things? Or, possibly act as a buffer between the two of you?"

"There's no guarantee she'll let you inside her home either. She hasn't let any of us near her in months."

It was true. Brutus, Jered, Desmond, Malcolm, and my papa had all gone to Linn's home to see her after she moved to Cirrus, but none of them were allowed entry inside. As far as I know, Linn hasn't stepped foot outside her home since she moved into it. Becoming a shut-in wasn't healthy for her, and I refused to be the reason she cut herself off from the world.

After Malcolm and I give our final approval on the preparations for the ball, I feel the need to take something to Linn's home. I have one of the kitchen staff prepare a basket of sweets. If Linn doesn't want to eat them, I feel certain her children will, especially Bai. As I recall, she had quite the sweet tooth.

I ask Vala to make sure my War Angels have everything they need to attend the ball while I'm away.

"Socially," I tell her, "they're a little awkward. They don't know what's expected of them. I at least want to make sure they're dressed correctly. I can do that much to help."

"Of course, Anna," Vala says, "I'll take care of them while you're gone. Don't worry."

"I never worry when I ask you to do something for me," I assure her. "I trust you completely."

"So, have you thought about what you will say to Linn when you see her?"

"No," I confess. "I don't know what I'm going to say. I'm not even sure she'll let me inside her home, Vala. What if she turns me away, like she has everyone else? Do I just barge in and demand that she accept my apology?"

"I don't think that will work. Maybe enough time has gone by, and she is finally willing to listen to your heartfelt request for her forgiveness in person."

"I hope so," I reply with a heavy heart.

Malcolm phases into our chambers with the basket of sweets from the kitchen.

"Are you ready to go?" he asks.

"Yes," I reply, self-consciously smoothing out my dress. "Do I look ok?"

"You look beautiful," Malcolm replies, leaning down to give me an encouraging kiss. "You always do, my love."

I take a deep breath, hoping it calms my nerves, but I quickly find out that it doesn't.

"I'm ready."

"Good luck!" Vala says, right before Malcolm phases me to the front door of Linn's residence.

The home we bought for Linn was a five-bedroom, two-story dwelling made of white bricks. When her family left Cirro, Linn gave the orphanage she and Daniel operated to a couple who had worked for them for years. They promised to keep the home for displaced children running, since Linn didn't feel she could do a good enough job while she grieved the loss of her husband.

This was the first time since she moved here with her family that I stood on her stoop.

"Do you want me to stay out here?" Malcolm asks.

"Yes, I might need a ride home. Stay with me until we know whether or not..."

I stop in midsentence because I hear Linn scream from somewhere inside the house. Without even bothering to knock, Malcolm slams the front door open and rushes in.

"Linn!" he yells urgently, hastily setting the basket of sweets on the table in the foyer.

A second scream can be heard, but we also see Bai run into view on the second-floor landing this time. The look of utter horror and worry on her face quickly disappears when she spies us over the railing.

"Anna! Malcolm! Please help!" she begs tearfully.

Malcolm grabs my hand and phases us up to Bai.

"What's wrong?" Malcolm asks. "Where is your mother?"

Without wasting time to reply, Bai begins to run down the hallway. Being more mobile than I am, Malcolm runs with her as I slowly make my way down at my own pace. Bai stops at a set of open double doors, and I assume the entryway leads into one of the bedrooms. I see Bai and Malcolm run into it just as Linn lets out a bloodcurdling scream.

When I finally do reach the entrance to the bedroom, I'm not prepared for what I see.

Linn is lying on the bed with her legs up and bent at the knees. Her brow glistens with a fine sheen of sweat as she pants to catch her breath. I lean my shoulder against the doorway to prevent myself from collapsing to the floor in utter shock. Malcolm sits down on the edge of the bed and takes one of her hands. I feel as though my world has been turned upside down and sideways as I stare at a very pregnant Linn in labor.

"How far apart are the contractions?" Malcolm asks.

"Less than a minute," Linn answers, breathing hard.

"Do you have a doctor on the way?"

Linn shakes her head no.

"Anna!" Malcolm shouts. "Come over here and hold her hand. I need to get Desmond."

I hesitate. Why would Linn want me to hold her hand? I was responsible for killing the father of her soon-to-be-born child. Did she even want me in the room with her?

"Anna!" Malcolm barks.

Whether she wants me or not, I'm all that's available besides a very flustered and frightened Bai. I walk over to the bed and take Malcolm's place beside Linn as he stands and phases.

I try to take hold of Linn's hand as Malcolm requested, but she snatches it away.

"Don't touch me," she growls, just before screaming out in pain again.

I'm at a loss. I have no idea what I should be doing.

I look over at Bai and ask, "Why didn't someone call for a doctor? Where is everyone else?"

"She didn't want anyone here except me," Bai answers, looking distressed. "She said she could do it all on her own, and just needed me here to clean the baby when it comes out."

"I've given birth four times," Linn says in between short breaths. "I didn't think I would have any problems."

"Is something different about this birth?" I ask.

Linn frantically nods her head, finally allowing herself to break down into sobs. "Yes! It's never hurt like this before."

Thankfully, Malcolm phases back into the room with Desmond.

Desmond sets his doctor bag down on the bed.

"I've got you now, Linn," Desmond tells her in his soothing tone. "I'm going to make sure this baby comes out just fine."

"Get her out of here!" Linn shouts to Malcolm before looking at me. "I don't want her anywhere near Daniel's baby. Get her out! Now!"

Malcolm grabs my hand, and we walk out of the room.

I break down into tears because the hate I just saw on Linn's face makes me realize she will never be able to forgive me.

Malcolm takes me into his arms and tries to cradle me with his love and support.

"She's in pain," he says. "She doesn't know what she's saying right now, Anna."

"Yes, she does," I sob, feeling the loss of Daniel rip my soul apart all over again. Perhaps it wasn't only Linn's disgust for me that has kept me from coming to her, but also my own overwhelming guilt.

Even though Daniel forgave me for what I did to him, I haven't forgiven myself. I doubt I ever will. His death will always be a permanent mark on my soul. For a thousand years, he waited for me to be born so I could claim my birthright, and how did I repay him for his loyalty? I murdered him for trying to help me. Linn will never forgive me. She will never be my friend again. She will always see me as the woman who robbed her of years of happiness with Daniel.

"Take me home," I beg Malcolm. "Please, just take me home."

CHAPTER ELEVEN

Malcolm phases me to the sitting room in our chambers. He sits down with me on the couch, and holds me while I attempt to bring my emotions under control.

"I shouldn't have asked you to go over there," he says, sounding like he's admonishing himself for doing something ill-advised.

I pull back from him and look at his guilt-stricken face. "I'm glad we did. She needed our help. I still can't believe she was going to try to have that baby all by herself. What was she thinking?"

"I think she was just being stubborn," Malcolm replies.

"Do me a favor," I say. "Go back there and make sure they're all ok. It would make me feel better."

"Are you sure?"

I nod. "Yes."

Malcolm kisses me on the lips before standing.

"I won't stay long."

As soon as Malcolm phases to Linn's home, God appears, standing in front of me and looking worried.

"Is Linn's baby all right?" I ask, fearing He's come to deliver bad news in person.

"Her baby is fine, Anna. Right now, it's you I'm worried about."

God walks over and sits down on the couch beside me. "I know the last couple of days have been hard on you."

"That sounds like the understatement of the century."

"I'm sorry all of this is happening to you at once, but you're strong, Anna. You'll make it through this like you have the other tribulations you've had to face so far."

"Will it ever get easier?"

"What? Life?" God says with a sympathetic smile.

"Yes."

"Everyone has to face their own personal trials during their lives. Right now, Linn is facing one that involves raising her children without their father by her side. She's also trying to deal with her feelings about you."

"What is there to deal with?" I ask dejectedly. "She hates me. I think that's painfully obvious."

"She doesn't hate you, Anna. She's just conflicted. There is a part of her that still loves you as a friend, and because she knows how special you were to Daniel. If it wasn't for you, she never would have met him."

"What do you mean?"

"The only reason Daniel was still on Earth is because he was waiting to help you succeed in your mission. I know for a fact that Daniel would have asked for a mortal life a long time ago. So, in a way, you were the one who allowed them to find one another."

"I didn't think about it like that," I admit, feeling a smidge better. "But it doesn't change the fact that I'm the one who took him away from her forever."

"Not forever," God reminds me.

Since I have God's undivided attention, I ask, "Is Bai JoJo? Did You send her back so she and Gabe can finally build a life together?"

"Yes."

"That was nice of You. I didn't realize You were such a hopeless romantic."

"I try to reward those who deserve it. Gabe sacrificed his life to save a world of lives and to ensure the safe return of his loved ones back home. His deepest, most heartfelt desire was to be raised by a mother and a father who loved him unconditionally, and to build a life with JoJo and grow old with her. They both had to give up their memories of their previous lives, but he and JoJo decided it was worth the sacrifice."

"Will they ever remember everything?" I ask. "From both of their lives?"

"When they return to Heaven, they will remember their lives before and the ones they are living now."

"So we shouldn't tell them who they really are."

"You can if you want, but it would only serve to confuse them. I believe it's better to let them be who they are now and see where their lives take them. Each life is an unchartered adventure for the one experiencing it. It's hard to tell what course a person's life will take, until they make a decision to step forward and commit to a specific path."

"I don't suppose You would be willing to tell me if I'll ever defeat Helena..."

"I have faith you'll be able to handle her," He tells me with a small, encouraging grin.

"I have to say, that's more than I thought You would tell me. It was almost an answer."

"Almost," God agrees, sounding surprised at Himself for being even marginally helpful.

I'm silent for a moment because I'm not sure if I should ask my next question. God sits and waits patiently, like He knows I need to ask Him something else. And why wouldn't He know? He is God, after all.

"Why do the babies keep phasing me to Helena?" I finally ask.

"I think you already know the answer, or at least suspect what the answer is."

"So it's either my connection to her or the seals that are causing it?"

God remains mute, but that's all the answer I need.

"Will I ever be able to break my connection to her?"

"I'm sorry; I can't answer that, Anna. In time, you'll find the answer out on your own."

God stands, and I know my time with Him is over.

"How are my mother and father?" I ask Him.

"They're happy," God says, smiling. "And so am I. Thank you for bringing my son back to me, Anna. It's been so nice to talk to Lucifer without there being a subtle animosity hanging between us on his part. His return has brought Me a great deal of joy."

"I have one more question before You go," I say, not wanting Him to leave just yet. "Are You sure I'm the right one to lead the War Angels? I don't feel like I've done a very good job with them so far."

"You're doing fine. It will just take some time for them to acclimate to their new existence. They're all grateful to be here and to have a mission to accomplish. I hope being on Earth will allow them to learn that there is more to life than just fighting. I want them to yearn to build lives and families of their own."

"Speaking of building families...I suppose You know Cade is Helena's soul- mate."

"Yes."

"There's no way she'll ever be the person he wants her to be."

God remains silent, not giving me a hint one way or the other if my supposition is correct.

"Cade will find his way," God finally replies, even though the statement tells me nothing.

"Thank you for coming," I tell Him. "It always feels nice when You're near."

"I'm only a prayer away," God reminds me with a small grin.

I smile. "I know, but I don't like to monopolize Your time."

"One of the perks of being omnipotent is that I can be in several places all at once. So never believe you are bothering Me, Anna."

"I'll keep that in mind."

As God phases, Malcolm returns, as if on some preordained cue.

"The baby is fine. It's a girl," Malcolm says, retaking his seat on the couch beside me.

"And Linn?"

"She's doing well. Desmond is going to stay with her through the night, so you'll only have me, Brutus, and Jered watching your back this evening."

"That's plenty. I don't think we'll have any problems with anyone we invited."

Just as the words leave my mouth, I feel like I've jinxed the evening ahead.

"I've …uh…done something I'm not sure you will approve of…" Malcolm says hesitantly.

"Is this going to make me mad?" I ask, bracing myself for what seems like a confession.

"Maybe," Malcolm admits. "I invited Jade Sands to the ball."

I stare at Malcolm for a moment because I'm confident I didn't hear him correctly.

"I thought you didn't like her?" I ask, remembering Malcolm's reaction to being in Jades' establishment, the Ladies in Waiting brothel.

"It's not so much that I don't like her. I just didn't like you being in her place of business. At least she tried to warn us about the views of some of the people here in Cirrus."

"Is she your friend now?" I ask amused by the idea.

"More of an ally, I would say."

It only takes me a second to figure out why Malcolm would want Jade at the ball.

"We're not bribing, and we're not blackmailing people either, Malcolm."

There could only be one reason that Malcolm would want Jade in attendance that evening: to show those present that she's a friend of ours. Considering the fact that so many of the royals use the services she provides at her establishment, I can only imagine the source of material she has to pull from to blackmail people into voting for me.

"I knew you would say that," Malcolm says. "That's why I vetoed her offer to do just that."

"Then why did you invite her to come tonight?"

"On occasion, the threat of something is just as good as actually doing it. If people see that Jade supports you, they may think twice before voting against you. Also, the news of her appearance will spread like wildfire. Even those who don't attend the ball tonight will know that she was here. It might be enough to make them reconsider not voting for you. I'm certain there are a lot of people who don't want to get on Jade's bad side."

"But she won't actually release any of her information, will she?"

"Well, she certainly won't if you win."

"And if I lose?"

"Let's not even consider that a possibility."

My thoughts return to Linn.

"Is there anything else we can do for Linn? Should we hire a nanny for her, to help take care of the baby? Why was she in so much pain during the delivery? She said she felt like something was wrong this time."

"We are doing something for her," Malcolm answers. "She asked me to bring her other children here until she feels better. They're all in Lucas' room, playing."

"Oh, Malcolm," I say excitedly. "What was Lucas' reaction?"

"He was happier than I've seen him in a long time," Malcolm replies with a big smile. "It was like he and Bai hadn't been separated for months. You'll be proud to know that I've already sent over one of our servants to help Linn take care of the baby, and the answer to your last question is she was in so much pain because it was a breech birth. Desmond was able to turn the baby, though. After that, the little girl came right out. And, Anna, she told me to tell you that she was sorry for how she acted. She knows you were only trying to help her."

"Does she want to see me?" I ask hopefully.

"I think we should give her a little more time, and wait to see if she asks you to come to her. You were right. That's probably what we should have done all along, but I'm still grateful we went over there. If we hadn't, it's possible we could have lost both her and the baby. Poor Bai might have been scarred for life, watching her mother and little sister die. I believe we were meant to be there for her today."

"Speaking of destiny, your father came to see me after you left."

"Did He have anything important to say?"

"He confirmed that Bai is JoJo, but other than that, nothing specific. I think He was here to lend me His support more than anything else."

There's a knock on the door, and Malcolm tells the person to come in.

One of the maids walks in, carrying my dress for the ball. It's a royal purple gown that falls slightly off the shoulders, with a beaded neckline and a loosely draped front to comfortably camouflage my belly.

"Excuse me," she says, "I came to help the empress prepare for the festivities this evening."

"Is it that late already?" I ask, not realizing so much time had passed.

"Yes, Your Majesty," the maid says with a curtsy. "Your guests should be arriving in a little more than an hour."

Malcolm stands and holds out a hand to help me stand too.

"While you're getting ready, I'll keep an eye on the kids. I think Brutus said he was going to bring Kyna here a little early so the two of you can have some time together."

"I would love that," I say, missing my friend dearly. "It's been a couple of weeks since I last saw her."

"Well, she should be here in a few. I'll come back in a little while to change clothes." Malcolm kisses me before phasing.

I feel ashamed when I look back at the sweet young maid who has come to help me get ready for the ball. I have no idea what her name is. When we took up residence at the palace, Malcolm went through all the servants and fired the ones who seemed a little too loyal to the old regime. The young lady standing in front of me was a new hire, and we hadn't been properly introduced yet.

"I hate to sound rude," I tell her, "but I'm afraid I don't know your name."

"It's Jenny, Your Majesty," she replies, curtsying again.

"I'm pleased to meet you, Jenny. Do you think you can make me presentable enough to go to the ball? I fear I look like a complete wreck."

"Oh, no, Your Majesty," Jenny says with a shake of her head. "You could never look bad. You're far too beautiful."

"With flattery like that," I say, "I may just have to make you my personal maid, Jenny."

"I would be honored, Your Majesty," Jenny says, with yet another curtsy.

"Jenny, there's something you will have to do for me if you're going to be helping me every day."

"Anything you need, Your Majesty."

"You're going to have to stop curtsying every time you address me. I really don't need for you to do it."

"Of course, Your Majesty." Jenny almost forgets what I just told her, but catches herself and stops the curtsy she was just about to perform.

"Now, how do you think I should wear my hair?" I ask.

For the next half hour, Jenny applies my makeup and styles my hair. Both are kept simple and elegant. We decide to just straighten my hair out and pull the front portion back. Jenny encourages me to wear the Crown of Cirrus, because Empress Catherine always wore her crown to formal functions. I don't argue, but not because it was something Catherine did. I decide to wear it as a subtle reminder to those who will be present that I am still empress, no matter how many of them want to see me dethroned.

Jenny is helping me into my dress in the bedroom when I hear Kyna shout out, "Anna! Are you here?"

"One minute, Kyna! I'm putting my dress on!"

"No rush, sweetie! We're not going anywhere."

After Jenny closes the back of my dress, I rush out of the room and into the awaiting arms of the most beautiful redhead in the world. The hug between Kyna and me is a bit awkward, since we're both pregnant, but we make it work.

"How do you remain so stunningly beautiful even though you're carrying two babies around?" Kyna asks enviously. "I feel like a water balloon, considering all the fluid I'm retaining."

"I think that's just because of the summer heat in the down-world right now," Brutus tells his wife. "And you're just as beautiful as Anna. I tell you how gorgeous you are every day, even though you continue to refuse to believe me."

"Whatever the cause," Kyna says, puffing out her cheeks with air before saying, "I feel horribly bloated. I may just have to come spend the rest of this pregnancy with you here in Cirrus, Anna."

"We could definitely make that happen," I assure her. "It's not like Brutus can't phase back and forth between here and your home in the down-world."

"I've been suggesting it for weeks, so don't think I'm the reason for the delay," Brutus says in his own defense.

"I know," Kyna sighs, "but there's no place like home when you're about to give birth. Have you gone through the nesting phase yet, Anna?"

"Nesting?" I ask, not quite sure what she's talking about. "I guess not. Why? What have you been doing?"

"What hasn't she been doing?" Brutus laughs. "That might be a shorter answer."

Kyna rolls her dazzling emerald eyes at Brutus. "I've just been cleaning up a bit is all, and reorganizing a few things."

I shake my head. "No. I can't say I've done any of that. Have either of you been told about Linn?"

"Linn?" Brutus asks looking worried. "What about her? Is she all right? Has something happened to one of the kids?"

I go on to tell them about Bai being JoJo reincarnated, and the condition we found Linn in when we went over to her house.

Brutus tears up when he learns Bai's true identity.

"I can't believe they both came back," Brutus says, sounding emotional about Gabe and JoJo's new chance at an Earthly life together, "but it makes perfect sense. Bai's always been very artistic. JoJo was a world-famous fashion designer, you know."

I nod. "Yes, I know. She's the one who made my white leather outfit. I miss being able to fit into it."

Brutus' face lights up, as if he's just had a brilliant idea. "She's also the one who made the talismans to protect us lowly Watchers from an archangel's power to kill us."

I see where he's going with this. "Do you think Bai can make the War Angels something to protect them?"

"In theory, yes," Brutus says, looking thoughtful, "but I don't know if her powers have awakened yet."

"Lucas had his first vision of me when he was three-years-old," I say. "It's quite possible that Bai's gift is active, too."

"Maybe she's noticed something out of the ordinary happen with a piece of her artwork," Brutus suggests. "We should probably ask her."

"Let's wait on that for a little while," I recommend. "She and Lucas are playing with each other for the first time in months. I don't want to do anything to disturb that. I think they both deserve some time together, don't you?"

"Absolutely," Brutus agrees.

"So how are things going in the down-world, Overlord?" I ask. "You might as well give me a report while you're here."

Brutus brings me up to date on the marketing side of things in the down-world. While he's giving me his report, Malcolm comes back to change clothes for the ball.

"How are the children getting along?" I ask as he bends down to give me a kiss while I sit on the couch.

"Lucas is happier than I've seen him in months," Malcolm says proudly.

"That's wonderful," I reply, suddenly feeling the urge to be with my son, but not wanting to overstep my bounds with Bai in Linn's absence. I would like to get her permission first before making myself a part of Bai's life again.

"I'll be right back," Malcolm tells us as he walks into our bedroom to get ready for the evening's festivities.

He steps back into the sitting room only a few minutes later, looking dashing in his black collarless suit with his long hair pulled back into a ponytail.

My heart skips a beat as I watch him walk over to me, and I'm as grateful as ever that I'm able to call Malcolm Xavier Devereaux my husband.

"We should probably go downstairs," Malcolm tells me. "Our guests will be arriving soon."

I stand up from the couch with a little help from my husband. I feel an ache in the small of my back and begin to rub it.

"When tonight is over," I whisper to Malcolm, "I think I'll need one of your special massages. My back is killing me."

"Of course, my love; you know I'll do anything you need."

The twinkle of amusement in Malcolm's eyes promises more than just a back massage, and I do nothing to alter his train of thought.

The custom in Cirrus is for the emperor and empress to remain seated on the dais, in their thrones, while guests arrive. I don't care to do that this evening. Malcolm and I decide to greet our guests as they enter the room. It seems like the more polite thing to do, and, since I am campaigning for their votes, I want them to know that I truly do appreciate them attending the ball.

When we reach the ballroom, Jered and my papa are already there, as well as Slade, which surprises me.

"Slade," I say, genuinely happy to see him, "I didn't realize you would be here this evening."

"Me neither," Malcolm grumbles, looking accusingly at Jered.

"I thought we could use all the help we could get tonight," Jered replies, not making any excuses for his unilateral decision. "He's still one of us, even though you try to forget he exists."

Jered. Never one to mince words with my husband, he was one of the few people Malcolm allowed such leeway.

After the coronation ceremony, Malcolm banished Slade to the mining colony on Neptune. It was obvious that my husband still held a grudge against his fellow Watcher for his one-time betrayal. I could understand Malcolm's reluctance to trust Slade again, but I had hoped he would be able to find some leniency in his heart for Slade by now.

"I'm only here to help Anna," Slade tells Malcolm, looking uncomfortable in the face of my husband's scrutiny. "After that, I'll go back to Neptune as ordered."

"Good," is all Malcolm says before averting his eyes from Slade, obviously not being able to stand having the other man so close.

"It's good to see you again, Anna," Slade says to me before kissing me on the cheek. "I've missed you."

"You should come here more often," I tell him. "I would like to see you occasionally, even if some don't."

"I am always at your disposal," Slade says, bowing his head slightly in my direction.

"You look lovely tonight," my papa proclaims proudly was he walks up to us. "You're practically glowing."

"Thank you, Papa. I just pray the evening goes well, and I hope people actually show up to lend me their support."

"Oh, they've already formed a line outside the palace," Jered informs me. "You may have more people coming than you planned for."

As if it was coordinated, my War Angel guard all phase in at once. I smile in delight when I see them. Besides their formal black-and-white-feathered capes and War Angel uniforms, I've never actually seen any of them in casual clothing.

All seven of them are wearing suits similar in style to Malcolm's, and each is a different color.

"You look like a rainbow," Malcolm comments dryly as he scrutinizes their attire.

I have to admit, he's right. All seven colors are represented, but at least the tailor chose to go with dark jewel-tone versions of the colors instead of bright ones.

When I notice my War Angels begin to look self-conscience about their suits, I walk over to them.

"You all look very handsome," I say, knowing they'll be able to tell that I'm speaking the truth. "I love the different colors. They make you each stand out as individuals instead of a unit of guards."

"Thanks, Anna," Ethan says, sounding relieved.

From the looks on their faces, I can tell they all needed to hear me say what I just did. In a way, this is like their coming-out party. They will have an opportunity to mingle with the citizens of Cirrus as 'real' people, and not as part of my own personal army. Their purpose for being sent was clear to everyone who saw them. They were built for winning wars, and nothing would stop them from being victorious in any battle I sent them to fight.

"Empress and Emperor Devereaux," the herald calls down from the top of the stairs, "are you ready to receive your first guests?"

"Yes," I reply, "please let them in."

Malcolm and I stand side by side at the foot of the stairs, while Jered, Brutus, and Slade stand behind us for added protection. Kyna takes charge of my War Angels, and strikes up a friendly conversation with them all.

"Announcing the arrival of Empress Olivia Ravensdale of Nacreous!" the herald says.

I look up the stairs and see Olivia dressed in a long black dress, with gold lace appliques along the bottom and over the sheer material on top. She's wearing a small gold crown on her head, marking her as Empress of Nacreous.

"Announcing the arrival of Empress Bianca Rossi of Alto!"

Bianca is dressed in a pale pink gown made of silk. It's a simple style with its gathered shoulder straps, low-cut front, and free-flowing skirt.

"I didn't know you invited them," I whisper to Malcolm.

"I thought you could use their support."

"You thought right."

When I look back up the stairs to watch my friends descend, I catch myself gasping as I view the next guest who is about to be announced.

"Announcing the arrival of Emperor Lorcan Halloran of Stratus!"

"Now *him* I didn't invite," Malcolm growls irritably. "What the hell does he think he's doing, coming here?"

"I was wondering about that," Olivia says as she steps off the last stair to stand before us. "I assume you probably didn't invite the others either."

"Others?" I ask in confusion just before the herald announces the arrival of someone else I didn't expect to see that evening.

"Announcing the arrival of Emperor and Empress Solarin of Nimbo!"

When I look back up the staircase, my shocked gaze is met by Helena's amused one.

CHAPTER TWELVE

"I sure as hell didn't invite *them*." Malcolm scowls as Levi and Helena begin to descend the staircase.

"Don't make a scene," I discreetly warn Malcolm. "That's probably what they want—to make us look bad in front of everyone. We'll just need to steer clear of them this evening. There's nothing else we can do."

I turn to look at Brutus, who's standing behind me.

"Go to Kyna," I urge him. "Make sure Lorcan keeps his distance from her. If she needs to leave, I won't be upset."

"She's not going to let him run her off." Brutus doesn't look happy about this fact. "You know how stubborn she can be."

As Brutus walks off to be with his wife, I look over to the other end of the room and see Kyna staring at Lorcan with unabashed hatred.

"What a wonderful idea," Lorcan says as he stands in front of us, "to have a party to see how many supporters you actually have in your fair city."

"Considering you know this party is for my supporters," I say, "I'm surprised you decided to grace us with your presence this evening, Lorcan."

"Really?" Lorcan says, seeming to find my statement curious. "You shouldn't be surprised. I want you to win, Anna. I truly do."

I glance over at Ethan who is standing only a few feet away, watching over us. I notice him nod his head, answering the question I was silently asking him. Apparently, Lorcan just spoke the truth. Yet why would he want me to win the election? It didn't make sense. His life would be much easier if I didn't hold a public position of power.

"I feel a bit parched," Lorcan declares, clearing his throat to emphasize the point. "I believe I'll go get some of that delicious champagne your down-worlders make."

Lorcan leaves us, but his spot is quickly taken up by Helena and Levi.

"Home sweet home," Levi says, looking around the ballroom. "I must say, I do sort of miss the old place."

"It does seem to have a bit of a rustic charm to it," Helena agrees as she looks around the room for the first time.

"What are you doing here?" I ask Helena in a low voice. "Even if you weren't who you are, the fact that you publicly supported Catherine yesterday should have been enough to keep you away from here tonight."

"Well, aren't sisters supposed to support one another in times of crisis?" Helena says through a practiced smile. "Besides, I had a feeling the others would show up. I thought you might need a hand with them."

"Announcing Callum Ellis, the Crown Prince of Virga!"

"See," Helena says, as if Callum's presence is proof that I need her help. "Everyone is here, but they don't have your best interests in their hearts like I do, Anna. They actually want you to win this election."

"Why would they want that?" I ask, not understanding the reason the others want me to remain in control of Cirrus, when it would seem like the opposite should be true.

"Come along, my dear," Levi says to Helena before she has a chance to answer me. "We shouldn't monopolize Anna's time. She has a long line of guests to greet."

Levi whisks Helena away before she has a chance to answer my question, not that she would have anyway.

After Callum arrives, the herald announces the arrival of the Emperor of Cirro, Ryo Mori.

"Why are they all here?" I ask Malcolm as Ryo follows Callum down the stairs to us. "It doesn't make any sense."

"I don't know," Malcolm replies, "but I do know I don't like it."

"I came to offer my apologies," Callum says to us as he makes a show of bowing to me. "My father was out of line yesterday. I hope you can forgive the ramblings of an old man who isn't as sharp as he used to be."

"Your father seemed very much in control of his faculties to me," I reply curtly.

"Even if he was, he represents the old regime of Virga, and I am its future. I hope our two cities can build a lasting friendship with one another, Empress Devereaux. I cherish my peaceful existence. I would like to keep living that way."

Callum doesn't wait for either Malcolm or me to make a reply before he bows to us and walks off.

When Ryo Mori stands in front of us, I desperately want to slap him silly because I know Baal is living inside the skin-suit of Cirro's new emperor.

When Baal resided inside the body of Raphael Rossi, Bianca's husband, he, Mammon, Levi, and Helena concocted a plan to kill me by channeling two seals into me at one time. Their plan backfired, of course, but I hadn't forgotten it. I never would. The experience didn't kill me, but it almost drove me over the edge to eternal darkness. It was only the strength of Malcolm's love that brought me back to myself before I was lost forever.

"It's a pleasure to finally meet the both of you," Baal says through Ryo's mouth. "I know I haven't been in power for very long, but I hope Cirrus and Cirro can continue to enjoy a peaceful trading relationship with one another. I, for one, hope you both maintain your positions here in Cirrus."

"Why?" I have to ask, knowing not one of these people cares a whit about me.

Ryo grins, but the look is grim, not joyful.

"Because the alternative is far worse," he answers before bowing to us and heading further into the ballroom.

For almost half an hour, Malcolm and I stand and greet the rest of our guests. By that time, my feet are hurting and I have to sit down. I would have much rather found a quiet spot to sit with some of our friends, but we are expected to sit on our thrones during a ball at the palace. My feet are so sore I really don't care where I sit.

One advantage to sitting on the dais is that it gives us a perfect view of the entire room. Thankfully, Helena and Levi are behaving themselves and each acting seamlessly as newlyweds as they hold hands, dance, and laugh with one another. I can almost imagine Helena being a normal person, but know in my heart that such a fantasy is just that, a fantasy. She isn't normal. In fact, she epitomizes the meaning of 'abomination to God'.

I pay close attention to Cade's movements. I can see him making an effort to involve himself in small talk with some of the people in the room, but his eyes always seem to find their way back to Helena. She, on the other hand, has no problem ignoring his presence. In fact, it's almost as if Cade doesn't exist in her world. It's further proof to me that she is utterly dead inside and exists in an empty shell. How can she ignore her soul-mate? Either she is incapable of love, or she is a very good actress and hiding her true feelings. It's impossible to tell which is the truth.

My other War Angels seem to be having a good time, and mingling with the people of Cirrus rather well. I even saw Xander ask a lady to dance a minuet with him. I couldn't have felt prouder.

However, I do notice one person missing from the ball.

I lean over and say to Malcolm, "I thought Jade Sands was going to be attending."

"She'll be here," he says confidently. "Women such as Jade like to make a statement when they walk into a room. I didn't expect her to arrive with everyone else."

It's almost an hour into the ball when Malcolm's supposition about Jade is proven correct.

"Announcing the arrival of Jade Sands and her escort, Lord Gladson Gray!" the herald announces.

"Well, I have to say I didn't expect that," Malcolm tells me as we watch Jade walk down the stairs on the arm of Gladson, the most debonair rebel against the old regime.

Jade is dressed more demurely than the last time I saw her. The dress she's wearing isn't as conservative as most of the others in the room, but it's also not the least bit objectionable. The nude-colored, sheer tulle material is decorated around the edges and across the bodice with a silvery lace applique. Jade's ample bosom is covered, yet definitely a stand-out feature. Her hair is styled in a loose bun that almost gives her an air of innocence, which is quite a feat considering her profession.

I want to laugh at the expression on Gladson's face. He's blushing like a school boy who just brought a woman of ill repute to meet his parents.

I have to admit I become rather impressed with Jade as she walks down the stairs. Even with the ruckus her presence is causing amongst our guests, she looks at the other partygoers as if she's above their petty whispers about her unexpected arrival. I know from my previous visit with her that she is a strong-willed woman, but it isn't until now that I realize just how resilient her character truly is.

Gladson escorts Jade up to the dais, and the room goes completely silent. There is an air of anticipation from the crowd as they wait for my reaction to Jade's presence.

"Welcome, Lord Gray," I say to Gladson. "I'm glad to see that you were able to make it this evening."

"I wouldn't have missed it for the world," Gladson responds with an easy grin. "Empress and Emperor Devereaux, would you please allow me the pleasure of introducing Ms. Jade Sands."

Jade curtsies to us.

"Welcome to my home, Ms. Sands," I say. "I'm happy to see you were able to accept our invitation as well."

More than a few gasps can be heard at my shocking revelation. If Malcolm's plan is going to work, the people in the room need to know that Jade wasn't just brought here by Gladson as his date. She was invited by us to prove that she is our ally.

"Thank you for extending your kind invitation," Jade replies smoothly. "Business would have been slow tonight because of your party anyway."

I have to prevent myself from giggling at her remark, but Malcolm obviously doesn't feel the need to restrain himself. His laughter echoes against the walls of the room, causing some of our guests to cringe guiltily.

"I can well imagine how few customers you would have available this evening," Malcolm agrees.

"I'm confident we'll more than make up for the loss tomorrow night," Jade assures Malcolm. "We almost always have a house full of patrons."

"I'm sure you do," Malcolm says, still looking amused. "I hope you enjoy yourself this evening, Ms. Sands. If you need anything, please let us know. We do anything we can for our friends."

"As do I," Jade replies loudly enough for everyone in the room to hear. She curtsies to us once again, declaring to all those present that she supports my claim to the throne of Cirrus.

Gladson starts to escort Jade to the refreshment table, but is stopped by an unexpected question.

"Lord Gray," Helena says, taking a few steps forward, away from the gathered crowd, "I was wondering, are you proud of yourself for helping Empress Anna make those propaganda videos to brainwash the populace of the cloud cities?"

Gladson turns to face Helena. "Revealing the truth isn't brainwashing, Empress. I didn't say anything that wasn't true."

"So causing arguments to break out among the royals was all in the name of peace? A bit hypocritical of you, isn't it?"

"We simply started a discussion within the cloud cities that was long overdue," Gladson replies in a calm voice, but I can see a storm brewing in his eyes.

"I think that's quite enough, Helena," Malcolm declares, standing to his feet. "I won't allow you to berate a dear friend while he is in my home. Please remember your manners as our guest, or I will have to ask you to leave."

Helena stares at Malcolm for a moment before bowing her head. "Of course, please accept my apologies. I meant no disrespect."

The word 'liar' comes to mind, but I refrain from saying it aloud.

"I think it's time we took a spin around the dance floor," Malcolm tells me. I assume he wants to take people's minds off the small disturbance with dancing. "Are you up for it?"

"I would love nothing more," I tell him.

Malcolm lends me a hand to make it easier to rise from my throne. The small orchestra, which has been providing the music all evening, strikes up a waltz, and Malcolm expertly leads me around the dance floor. Other couples quickly join us. I happen to notice Ethan ask Lady Sophia if she would like to dance with him. The woman is certainly no fool. She jumps at the chance to dance with the commander of my War Angel guard.

"Should we warn Ethan about Lady Sophia?" I ask Malcolm, remembering quite well how jealous I became of the woman when Malcolm spent most of his time with her on the night of my wedding party. I knew she had a reputation for taking any man she found desirable into her bed, and thought for sure Malcolm would end up succumbing to her charms later that evening. Thankfully, he didn't. Instead, I learned the connection of sensing pain from a soul-mate went both ways. I phased to Malcolm's room in Cirrus that night and learned that a soul-mate can travel to wherever their other half is, even if they have never been to that particular spot before.

"Let him have some fun," Malcolm tells me. "I've heard Lady Sophia can be quite generous with her lovers."

"Oh, really?" I ask, feeling the green-eyed devil of jealousy rear its ugly head inside my heart. "And you just heard this, correct? It's not from any personal experience on the subject?"

Malcolm grins. "Are you jealous?" he asks incredulously. "You have no reason to be. You are the only woman in Cirrus I've ever bedded."

"Bedded," I giggle. "You make it sound so old-fashioned."

"I am old-fashioned," Malcolm professes. "I make no apologies for being that way."

When we pass by the spot where Cade is standing, I inadvertently miss a step in our waltz and my foot lands on top of one of Malcolm's feet.

"I'm sorry," I apologize, but quickly turn my head to find Cade again, which causes me to step on Malcolm's foot a second time.

"Anna," Malcolm groans in pain, "what's wrong? You're usually a better dancer than this."

"Look who Cade is talking to."

Malcolm looks up and sees what I do.

Cade is talking to Helena. I watch as he seems to convince her to walk out onto the balcony with him, where it's more private.

"Should we go out there and drag him back in?" I ask Malcolm, concerned for Cade's safety.

"No," Malcolm says, but doesn't sound convinced about his answer. "Cade's wise enough to make his own decisions. We don't need to stick our noses into his personal affairs."

"But she's pure evil, Malcolm," I say, worried about Cade surviving the night if he spends too much time with Helena. "Cade's heart is too pure to see her for who she truly is."

"Give him a little more credit than that, my love," Malcolm says. "Let him deal with this situation in his own way."

I want to protest against what Malcolm just said, but I also know he's right. Cade is his own man, and he will have to make his own decisions where Helena is concerned, right or wrong. For me, it isn't a matter of *if* she will break his heart, just *when*.

I silently make a promise to Cade that I will be there for him after Helena shows him her true colors. If there is one thing I know about, it's the heartbreak a person can suffer through when they think their soul-mate doesn't care about them. It seems like a sick, twisted joke that the universe would pair two souls that are like night and day to one another. There has to be a reason. Perhaps one day we'll learn what it is.

CHAPTER THIRTEEN

(From Helena's Point of View)

I would almost rather tear my eyes out of their sockets than touch Levi one more time this evening. It's taking a great deal of willpower on my part not to rip his hands from their wrists so he can't run his fingers across my skin again. He seems to be taking a great deal of pleasure from torturing me with his touch. The sad thing is that I only have myself to blame. I'm the one who asked him to play up our newly-wedded bliss while we are at Anna's party.

My purpose is two-fold. Firstly, I want the people attending this little soiree of Anna's to believe Zuri Solarin is madly in love with his newly-wedded wife. As long as Levi does what I tell him to, I might even let him remain in the body he's chosen for a little while. Secondly, I want to torture that doe-eyed War Angel who keeps watching my every move. He's an irritating distraction that I don't need right now. I have too many plans set into motion. I can't have him dividing my attention when I'm so close to having what I want.

As I watch Malcolm effortlessly twirl Anna around the dance floor, I can't help but notice how she looks at him so adoringly. It's like he alone brings light into her life, and nothing will ever diminish the way she sees him. How my sister can let a man control her emotions so completely is beyond my comprehension. I would never let a man have that much power over me. *Never*.

"Do you have a minute?"

I tilt my head to the right and take a deep breath before expelling it in a huff of aggravation. I contemplate what effect ignoring Cade's presence would have, and quickly conclude that he won't budge until I at least acknowledge his existence. Begrudgingly, I look to my left and see him standing there, a pleading look in his eyes.

"What do you want?" I ask irritably, eyeing him up and down. I can't deny that he's attractive. I would have to be blind and stupid not to notice that he's physically perfect, and his blue eyes are so clear I can see straight into the deepest recesses of his soul. Ugh, how can someone be so...good?

"Can we talk," he whispers to me, "in private?"

"What for?" I ask curtly.

"Please, Helena. I just want to talk."

"And if I talk to you, do you promise to leave me alone forever?"

"If that's what you truly want afterwards, I will."

"Fine. Where do you want to have this little heart-to-heart of ours?"

"The terrace is empty."

I make my way through the crowd, with Romeo following close behind me. Once I'm outside, I take a deep breath to clear my head. I have to admit, my sister's city is beautiful, in a human sort of way. I can well imagine her growing up in a place where there was always light of some kind. I, on the other hand, was raised in a place where neither the sun nor the moon was able to reach. The dark is where I'm most comfortable. It's my home, my sanctuary.

I turn to face Cade and ask, "So, what is it you're so desperate to talk to me about?"

"How are you?"

His question confuses me for a moment. I think it must be the sincere tone he used to address me. I quickly think back through my life and try to remember if anyone has ever asked me such a question before. I don't remember it ever being asked, and am at a loss as to how to reply.

"What does it matter to you how I am?" I ask defensively, because it's the only response I can think of.

"It's just a question, Helena," Cade says as a small, confused smile tugs at the corners of his generous lips. "I simply want to know how you are this evening."

"I'm fine," I snap, hoping rudeness will end this line of questioning.

"You seem to be doing everything you can to prove your marriage to Zuri Solarin is real."

I have to let out a derisive laugh. "Well, if you want proof that it is, I have a signed marriage contract."

"I didn't say prove it legally. I said making it appear as if it's a real marriage. You seem to be doing everything you can to show the world that the two of you are in love. Levi is incapable of having such an emotion, so I know it's just an act on his part."

"And do you think I'm acting?"

"I know you are."

"You seem awfully sure of your answer."

"I am."

"Why?"

Cade remains silent, but I know where this is going. I certainly wasn't born yesterday.

"Listen," I tell him, hoping reason will cease his need to get to know me, "you need to stop whatever fantasy you might have playing out in that little brain of yours about where this is going between the two of us. Love is not going to conqueror all here."

"Do you love me? Are you even able to love?"

"What does it matter?" I yell, losing my patience. "You need to move on and forget this…this…*thing* between us. Grow up, Cade. Fairytales don't actually exist. They're just stories to make children feel like they have something to look forward to when they become adults."

"I'm not looking for a fairytale romance, Helena. I'm looking for the real thing, and you could have a happily-ever-after if you just let yourself."

"Wow, you're more insane than I thought if that's what you truly believe."

Cade doesn't say anything. He just looks at me like he's trying to figure out how to respond.

"Lucifer really did a number on you, didn't he?"

"Lucifer," I scoff, with a roll of my eyes. "His ultimate downfall was finding his soul-mate. I refuse to follow his path. He would have been a lot better off without meeting Amalie. All she did was make him weak and vulnerable."

"Vulnerable to you?" Cade asks knowingly. "I heard you fed off his pain to make yourself stronger. Was it worth it?"

"Was what worth it? Torturing him?"

"Yes."

"Of course it was worth it, you ninny! Look where I am today! I finally made it to the world of the living. He may have thought he could keep me trapped down there forever, but he sorely underestimated me. He shouldn't have done that...and neither should you."

"Is that a warning?"

I shrug. "Take it the way you want to. I really don't care."

"Isn't it tiring?"

"Tiring? I have no idea what you're talking about. Use your words more effectively if you actually want an answer from me."

"Isn't it tiring to hate the world so fiercely?"

I grin tight-lipped at Cade. "I don't hate the world. Why do you think I fought so hard to come here?"

"I don't know. Why did you?"

"I want to rule it, once and for all. This is my domain now, and I want to bring pain and suffering into it."

"That's already here."

"Not enough!"

"Why?"

"Why, what?"

"Why would you want to bring more pain and suffering into the world?"

"To finally finish my father's work. He could never completely bring himself to destroy the Origin after his little trip to that alternate reality Jess took him on. I tried to persuade him to find all the princes and finally open the seals, but he refused to spend the time necessary to get the job done. He had all that power at his disposal, and he never did anything with it! How absurd is that? So, no, I feel zero guilt for making him relive his worst memories so I could grow stronger and finally do what he couldn't. He got what he deserved, if you ask me. And you want to know what the worst part is? I think he enjoyed having me torture him. It was the only way he could see his precious Amalie again. He was such a sad sack I started to feel sorry for myself for having to put up with him. To tell you the truth, I'm glad he's gone. He was becoming a complete bore."

"What does it feel like to be filled with so much hate?"

"Good."

"I think you use your hate to hide behind," Cade tells me. "You're scared to let yourself feel love."

"I'm not scared," I say disdainfully. "I'm just too smart to fall into its trap."

"What about friendship? Is that a fairytale, too?"

"Why? Do you want to be my friend, Cade?"

"I would settle for that."

"You're pitiful," I say with a shake of my head. "You act like a starving dog, waiting for me to throw you a scrap from my plate. So, if you can't have my love, you'll take my friendship instead. Is that about right?"

"I think you need a friend, Helena. You've never had one before."

I don't say anything because I know he's right.

"I don't need friends," I say, trying to believe in my own words, but he seems to hear my doubt. His damn eyes light up with hope.

"Everyone needs at least one friend," he tells me. "I can be a friend to you, Helena, if you just give me a chance."

"As my friend, what would you want from me?"

"Nothing you don't want to give. I just want you to know that, if you need someone to talk to, I'm here for you."

"And why would I want to talk to Mr. Perfect about my less-than-perfect problems? So you can go scampering back to Anna and tell her everything I say?"

"I would never betray your trust in me, not unless you told me something that would allow me to save a life. I won't have the blood of an innocent on my hands."

"Well, that will certainly put a limit on our conversations."

"Does that mean you want to be my friend, Helena?" Cade asks, sounding amused by me.

"We'll see," I say, not committing one way or the other. "But you won't be able to change me, Cade. Don't even try."

I stomp off the veranda and back into the ballroom.

"What did that big lug want?" Levi asks me, handing me a glass of champagne from the refreshment table as he watches Cade reenter the room.

"None of your business," I tell him tersely. "And stay away from him or you'll have me to answer to."

"Why would you put a War Angel under your protection?" Levi says, sounding a little too interested in the answer.

"What did I just say? What part of 'it's none of your business' did that teeny-tiny brain of yours not understand? Even someone with your limited intellect should be able to comprehend that."

"I just…"

"Stop talking," I interrupt. "If you say one more word to me tonight, I will send you to the lowest levels of Hell where not even God Himself will be able to find you. Is that understood?"

Levi stares at me with pure hatred before nodding and looking away from me. He hates it that I can put him in his place so easily. I, on the other hand, revel in the fact.

"Let's go," I say, setting my champagne glass back down on the table. "I've seen all I need to see here tonight."

Just before I teleport back to Nimbo, I catch a glimpse of Cade out of the corner of my eye. He's watching me closely, but I make sure I don't look directly at him. I think we've said quite enough to one another for one night. Possibly too much.

CHAPTER FOURTEEN

(Back to Anna's Point of View)

I feel a sense of relief when Helena and Levi decide to leave the ball early. They're one less complication to the evening that I have to worry about.

Halfway through the night, I notice my papa approach Olivia and strike up a friendly conversation with her. Within a few minutes, he's taking her hand and leading her out onto the dance floor for a waltz.

"Well, it's about time," I hear Malcolm mumble beside me as we sit on our thrones to keep watch over the festivities.

I look at him and ask, "What do you mean by 'it's about time'?"

Malcolm nods to my papa dancing with Olivia. "Andre finally plucked up his nerve to show Olivia he's interested in her."

"*What*?" I say a little too loudly, which draws the attention of almost everyone in the room. I quickly smile to reassure them that everything is fine.

"Haven't you noticed how he is around her?" Malcolm asks, looking confused by my surprise. "You're usually more observant about such matters."

"No," I admit, returning my attention to my papa with new eyes as I watch him dance with Olivia. "I haven't noticed."

Malcolm is right, though. Usually I'm more observant about the emotional states of the people around me. I suppose a match between my papa and Olivia isn't that unexpected. They were close in age. Olivia is a few years older, but she doesn't look it. The thought of my papa finding someone to love and build a normal life with never even crossed my mind for some reason.

During my childhood, my father lavished me with all of his love and attention. I suppose I selfishly thought that would continue until the day he died. Now that he's showing a romantic interest in a woman, I realize I was only thinking about him as my papa, not as a man. It shouldn't come as any great surprise that he's attracted to Olivia. She and I had become close friends over the past few months. The Empress of Nacreous was a regular and welcome guest in our home. In fact, now that I think back on her visits, I should have recognized the signs of their mutual attraction a long time ago. I shouldn't have needed Malcolm to tell me something that was so painfully obvious.

"You're okay with them being together, aren't you?" Malcolm asks, sounding concerned over my continued silence on the matter.

"Of course I am," I say without reservation. "I want him to be happy, and I love Olivia to pieces. There's no one else I would rather see him with."

"He wanted to wait until he knew whether or not she has feelings for him, too, before saying anything to you."

"You seem to be quite knowledgeable about this subject. Has he been talking to you about his feelings for her?"

"Of course," Malcolm says. "He's my best friend, Anna. He came to me for some advice. He wasn't sure if it was too soon after Horatio's death to approach her. Andre didn't want to look like a lecher taking advantage of a widow."

"No one could ever see him that way." I feel conflicted about this new development in my life. I want my papa to be happy, but I suppose I'm having a selfish moment and don't want things to change.

If my father and Olivia decide to get married, he'll have to move to Nacreous to be with her. I'm not sure if I'm ready for such a drastic change.

"Anna," Malcolm says, urging me to look at him. "He's dedicated his life to you. You should be happy that he's found someone he can respect and love for the rest of it."

"Is she his soul-mate?" I ask quietly.

Malcolm shakes his head. "No, she isn't, but you know not everyone can be as lucky as we are."

"I know," I reply, holding out my hand to Malcolm. He takes it into his and squeezes it. "I still can't believe you're real sometimes."

"Well," Malcolm leans closer to me and whispers, "I could take you back to our bedroom and demonstrate to you just how real I am."

A genuine smile stretches my lips this time, and I almost give in to Malcolm's suggestion when our flirtation is interrupted.

"Might I have a word with the two of you?" Jered says in a low voice as he approaches the front of our dais.

"Do you have a count?" Malcolm asks eagerly.

I understand what he's asking Jered. The whole purpose for having this ball was to determine what percentage of the vote I have versus how much support Catherine has among the citizens of Cirrus.

"I'm afraid it looks dead even," Jered reports with a disappointed sigh. "At least for now. We'll see what happens tomorrow after people talk to those who didn't join us this evening."

"Fifty percent of the vote isn't exactly encouraging," I say, feeling as though I failed half the citizens of Cirrus in some way during my reign thus far.

"Don't get discouraged," Jered tells me. "I'm sure the others will come around to support you."

"Or Catherine will make so many promises for favors that she'll gain the support of the other fifty percent," I say, realizing that my vision of having an honest election might not be possible.

"If you would let me," Malcolm says, "I could ensure your win in this election, Anna."

"No," I say resolutely. "Either the people want the changes I'm proposing, or they don't, Malcolm. There's no other way to handle things. If you use your money to bribe people to vote for me, you'll have to pay those same people over and over again every time I want to make an improvement. That isn't going to work in the long run. We need to convince people that helping the down-worlders is the best thing to do for all of us, but I'm running out of ideas as to how to make them care."

"We'll figure something out," Malcolm says confidently. "We always do."

"We still have a week to win over enough voters to ensure Anna retains the throne," Jered reminds us. "That's when the election is set for. If cither of you have any suggestions on how to ensure a win, I would be happy to carry them out."

"I think I should go talk to Catherine," I tell them. "The only reason this is even happening is because of her. If I can convince her to back out of the election, we won't have to worry about this anymore."

"You can try," Malcolm says, sounding unconvinced about my plan, "but I really wish you wouldn't. I don't think she's right in the head anymore, Anna. I fear the torture Levi put her through broke her in more ways than one."

"I need to try, Malcolm."

"Then I'm going with you, because you're not going anywhere near that woman without me," Malcolm says, his expression daring me to say no to him.

"No," I dare. "She won't listen to a word I say if you're standing right beside me. She probably hates you just as much as or more than she hates me."

"I'll go with Anna," Jered volunteers. "I won't let anything happen to her."

"I don't just mean physically either, Jered," Malcolm stresses. "If that woman says anything to upset Anna, you bring her straight home. Is that understood?"

"Absolutely," Jered replies with an acknowledging nod of his head. "You have my word."

Malcolm relaxes slightly and slumps back in his throne, looking miserable about the whole situation.

"I still don't like it," he grumbles to me.

I don't say anything. We've made a compromise, and that's all that matters.

At the close of the evening, Malcolm and I say our thanks and goodbyes to our guests. Afterwards, we make our way to Lucas' suite of rooms to check on him and Linn's children. It's so late, we don't expect to find them awake, which we don't. Nevertheless, I wanted to check on the kids to make sure they were all right.

It appears that the children decided to make the sleepover a true slumber party. Mats have been arranged in a circle on the floor of Lucas' playroom. When I search for Lucas, I find him sleeping beside Bai. I feel the sting of tears when I see that they fell asleep holding each other's hand.

"We have to keep them together," I whisper to Malcolm, wiping at the tears trailing down my cheeks. "We just have to, Malcolm."

Malcolm nods his head in full agreement.

"I need to go see Linn tomorrow and settle this once and for all," I tell him. "I know you think we should wait until Linn is ready to talk to us, but we've been waiting for that to happen for months now. I would like to go to her tomorrow and beg her to let Bai be a part of Lucas' life. Are you all right with me doing that?"

"Yes," Malcolm says as he drags his eyes away from Lucas and Bai's joined hands to look at me. "I don't think we can wait."

I return my gaze to Lucas and Bai. "Then I'll convince her that they deserve to be together. Even if she can't forgive me for what I did to Daniel, I'll find a way to make sure Gabe and JoJo get their happily-ever-after."

The next morning, I get up early to prepare myself for the two visits I have planned that day. I know neither of them will be pleasant, but each is meant to solve a unique problem. If I can convince Catherine to back down, we won't have to worry about campaigning so that I can keep my place as

Empress of Cirrus. The conversation with Linn is simply one that's been a long time coming. I hope she and I can repair the friendship we had before Daniel's death, but I know that might not be possible. If she can at least stand to be around me for Lucas and Bai's sake, I'll take that as a small victory.

"Are you sure you don't want me to come with you to see Linn?" Malcolm asks me as I'm brushing out my hair.

"Yes, I'm sure. If you're with me, she may not feel like she can speak her mind freely. I want her to say everything she needs to, no matter how much it might hurt my feelings."

Malcolm walks up behind me and places his warm hands on my shoulders to bring me some much-needed comfort.

"But I don't like seeing you hurt," he tells me, staring at my reflection in the mirror. I meet his gaze and try to smile reassuringly.

"And that's another reason you don't need to be there," I explain.

Malcolm sighs in resignation, knowing he won't be able to change my mind. He leans down to kiss me on top of my head.

"I think I'll spend the time you're away with the kids," he informs me. "I want to see if I can figure out a way to use Bai's artistic talents to make talismans for the War Angels like JoJo made for the Watchers. If we can ensure their safety against the remaining princes, I would feel a lot better."

"I'm sure you'll figure something out," I say, standing from my chair. "JoJo and Gabe may have been sent back to get a second chance at a life together, but I'm sure God also intended for us to use their gifts to our advantage."

Malcolm wraps his arms around me. "Are you absolutely sure you don't want me to go with you today?"

I nod. "Yes. I'm sure. I'll be fine. Jered won't let me stay longer than I should."

Malcolm lowers his head, touching his forehead to mine as he sighs deeply and closes his eyes.

"If I could take your place today, I would do it in a heartbeat," he tells me fervently. "If there's one thing I know for certain, neither of them will welcome you with open arms. They're both bound to say things that will hurt you, and just the thought of that tears me apart inside."

"You can't protect me from all the bad in the world, Malcolm," I gently remind him.

"I know that," he replies, pulling his head back and looking into my eyes. "It doesn't change the fact that I still want to."

"Anna?" I hear Jered call out from the sitting room. "I'm here when you're ready!"

Malcolm drops his arms from around me, and we walk out of the bedroom hand- in-hand.

"Remember your promise to me," Malcolm reminds Jered as soon as we enter the room.

"I'll watch over her," Jered vows once again. "I love her, too, you know."

Malcolm nods, indicating he understands that fact all too well. All of my Watcher guardians feel protective of me. They waited a thousand years for me to be born and to fulfill my destiny. I've succeeded in part of my life's purpose, but I know uniting the down-world with the could cities and realizing the full potential of a world filled with the progeny of angel and humankind is also what I was sent to Earth to do.

"Who do you want to visit first?" Jered asks me.

"Catherine," I say without hesitation, because that visit will be the less emotional of the two.

"She's staying here in Cirrus," Jered informs us. "I'm sure she decided to take up residence in the city to make it easier to win over votes."

"You mean bribe people for their votes," I correct. "Where is she staying?"

"Lady Sophia offered her home for Catherine's use," Jered informs me.

"Lady Sophia?" I ask, remembering her attendance at the ball the night before. "Did she come to the palace to spy on us?"

"That would be my guess," Jered confirms.

"Wait," I say, remembering something else that happened at the ball, "is that why Ethan was glued to her hip all night long? Was he making sure she didn't cause any trouble?"

"I'm sure that was part of his reasoning," Jered replies. "I think he also wanted to find out as much as he could about Catherine's plans."

"Have you seen Ethan this morning?"

Jered looks over at Malcolm, and I can tell by his expression that he doesn't want to answer my question. His obvious reluctance tells me more than words, and confirms what I already suspected.

"Will we be seeing Ethan at Lady Sophia's this morning?" I ask, assuming Ethan's fact-finding mission probably included an overnight stay.

"I assume that's where he is," Jered says hesitantly.

"Let's go." I walk over to Jered and grip his arm. "If Ethan is still there, he might be keeping Lady Sophia occupied this morning. I would much rather speak with Catherine in private and not have to worry about her host interrupting our discussion."

"Good luck," Malcolm says just before Jered phases us to Lady Sophia's home.

After Jered knocks on the front door, it's promptly answered by a very skittish- looking maid.

"Empress Anna," the maid says, curtseying deeply. "We were not warned that you would be visiting us today."

"I'm sorry for my unannounced arrival," I tell her. "I'm here to see Catherine Amador. I was told she's staying here."

"Yes, Your Majesty. Is she expecting you?"

"No, she isn't. Is she available to accept visitors?"

"Yes, Your Majesty. She's having her breakfast in the sunroom. I can take you to her, if you want."

"Yes, please. I would like to speak with her as soon as possible."

The maid opens the door wider, allowing us entry into Lady Sophia's home.

"Is Lady Sophia here?" Jered asks.

"Yes but she's entertaining a guest at the moment," the maid answers, looking uncomfortable divulging this piece of information to us.

"That's fine," I say, giving the maid a reassuring smile. I feel a sense of relief that I won't have to deal with Lady Sophia personally. "We don't need to bother her. I only need to speak with Catherine for a moment."

"Yes, Your Majesty. Please, follow me."

Lady Sophia's home is one of the largest in Cirrus. Her late husband was best friends with Auggie's father when both men were still alive. Being close to the royal family definitely had its benefits.

We follow the maid to the far end of the east wing of the home, where the sunroom is located. The morning sunlight filters in through the glass walls and ceiling, giving the area a soft, almost ethereal, glow. We find Catherine sitting at a small, round white table, nibbling on a scone, with a cup of tea set beside her plate. She's watching the morning news, which is currently reporting on the ball at the palace the night before. When Catherine notices us enter the room, she lifts her hand and waves it through the holographic projection over the table to make it disappear.

"Well," Catherine says, setting the scone on her plate before sitting up straighter in her white wicker chair, "I have to say, this is an unexpected social call. To what do I owe the displeasure of your company this early in the morning, Anna?"

"Now, now, Catherine," Jered says as we come to stand in front of her table. "I expected better manners from you."

"And I expected Anna to have more sense than to come here," Catherine counters heatedly. "Let me guess, you're here to persuade me to back out of the election. How boringly predictable of you, my dear."

"It would be the best thing you could do for the people of Cirrus, Catherine," I say, hoping to reach her sensible side. "You have to know that."

"What I know is that a traitorous creature like you shouldn't be sitting on the Cirrun throne. My son is probably rolling over in his grave, wherever that might be, at the thought of you ruling Cirrus with your lover by your side. Tell me, Anna, how much did you have to spend to make Malcolm emperor? How long have you and he been conspiring against my family, to take control of Cirrus? Did Malcolm help you kill my poor, sweet Augustus?"

"We didn't kill Auggie," I tell her, doing my best to keep my temper in check. "You have to know how much I loved your son. He was my best friend. I loved him like a brother."

"You took advantage of his love for you and married him so you could have a legal right to the throne," Catherine accuses scathingly. "After all the years I spent grooming you to rule Cirrus, I never suspected you were devious enough to kill my only son so you could rule it the way you wanted to."

"If Auggie had lived, we would have governed it just like Malcolm and I have so far. It's almost like you didn't even know your own son, or the things he wanted for his citizens."

"How did you do it?" Catherine asks harshly. "How did you transform Augustus into that monster? At first, I thought someone was masquerading as my son, perhaps with some new technology I didn't know about, but when the torture began," I see Catherine visibly start to shake at the memory, "he brought up things from his childhood that only my Augustus could know. What did you do to make my sweet boy lose his mind so completely?"

"I didn't do anything to him," I tell her, realizing what I have to do if I have any hope of reaching Catherine's sensible side. I have to tell her the truth. "A demon inhabited Auggie's body. His name is Levi, and he's the one who killed your son."

Catherine lets out a derisive snort. "I suppose I'm supposed to believe that, just like we're supposed to believe your War Angel guard is composed of actual angels sent straight from Heaven."

"Why would you doubt that to be true?" I ask, not having realized before now that some people didn't trust my word about the origin of the War Angels.

"Some people believe you just made that story up to make your new guards appear more formidable than they actually are," Catherine informs me. "I have to say, it's a masterful plan. I mean, seriously, who would want to go up against an army of angels? Your deceitfulness is quite exceptional, Anna. I have to admit, you had me fooled into believing you were innocent and pure of heart. I never could have imagined what a bitch you truly are."

"Anna," Jered says, coming to stand in front of me to block Catherine from my view, "this conversation is pointless. She isn't in the right state of mind to listen to reason. We should leave now so I can keep my promise to Malcolm."

I look over Jered's shoulder to view Catherine's scowling face. I know he's right. Nothing I say to Catherine will change her mind about fighting me for the throne, but I can't leave without saying one more thing to her.

"I loved Auggie," I tell her, "and I'm so sorry that you had to lose him the way you did. You're not the only one who mourns his loss from this world. At least now you know that it wasn't your son who tortured you. I hope that brings you a small sense of peace. Auggie was too sweet a soul to have ever hurt you like that. I only rescued you from Levi because I knew how much Auggie loved you. I want you to understand that I did it for him, not you. One day, I hope you will believe the truth about me. I don't think you and I can ever be friends, but I don't want to be your enemy, either, Catherine."

"The very moment I'm declared the winner of the election," Catherine says, rising from her seat. "My first act as empress will be to cast you and your makeshift family out of Cirrus! I want to see you rot with the other down-worlders and never be allowed to step foot in my cloud city again!"

"You won't win," I say with equal conviction. "I'm meant to lead Cirrus into the future. I want you to know that, despite the disgraceful way you're treating me, I won't cast you out afterwards, Catherine. You will be welcome to live in Cirrus because it's your home, and that's what Auggie would have wanted."

"Get out!" Catherine screams, a look of true madness on her face. "And don't ever come back here, or I will strangle you with my own two hands!"

Without asking for my permission, Jered gently places his hand on my arm and phases me home, but not to the one I share with Malcolm. He phases me to my papa's house.

When I look at Jered questioningly, he replies, "I thought you might need a moment to compose yourself before we go see Linn."

We're standing on the veranda outside my old bedchamber. It's always been a place of sanctuary for me, and Jered seems to know this.

"It can be hard to have someone hate you so…vigorously," he says to me sympathetically. "Catherine was never the most compassionate person, but I hope you realize the things she said to you just now were out of anger. I'm not even sure she meant half of it, especially that last part."

"Well, if she didn't mean what she said, she's a better actress than I ever thought she could be."

"She's grieving," Jered explains, "and she's being masterfully manipulated by Helena and Levi. Misery loves company, and those two are using her grief to their best advantage."

"I know. It still doesn't make it any easier to hear, though."

"No, it doesn't," Jered agrees.

"I'm surprised you brought me here instead of taking me directly to Malcolm."

Jered smiles crookedly. "He would have insisted that you not go to Linn's today if I had. I didn't want to be responsible for an argument between the two of you."

"Very wise," I compliment, knowing Jered is right.

"Well, I can't say I expected to find the two of you standing here," I hear my papa say as he walks onto the veranda from the direction of my old chambers.

"How did you know we were even here?" I ask him as he walks up and kisses me on the cheek.

"Malcolm put in a new security system to let me know if anyone phases onto the property," my papa tells me. "I love seeing you, but can I ask why you're here?"

"I just talked with Catherine about bowing out of the election," I say.

"Ahh," my papa replies with a knowing nod. "I assume she still thinks you killed Auggie."

"Yes."

"She isn't thinking straight, Anna," my papa reassures me. "Once she's able to see past what she's lost over the past few months, I'm sure she'll realize how wrong she has been."

"I hope so," I reply, wanting to drop the subject of Catherine for a while. "Jered, would you mind giving us a moment alone?"

"Of course," Jered says graciously. "How long do you need?"

"Just a few minutes."

Jered bows his head and phases away.

"What's wrong, cherub?" my papa asks, sensing whatever I want to talk about must be important.

"Why didn't you tell me that you have a romantic interest in Olivia?"

"Ahh," my papa says with a small smile of understanding. "I probably should have before last night. To tell you the truth, I had no intentions of asking her to dance when I went to the ball, but then I realized that I'm not getting any younger, just older. I wanted to know if she was at all interested in me as more than just your father and a friend."

"From the way the two of you danced together," I say, "it looked like she was very interested in you as more than just a friend."

"Well, we'll see," my father replies, smiling shyly. I even think I notice a slight blush to his cheeks, something I don't recall ever seeing happen before when he spoke about someone of the opposite sex. "Matters of the heart should never be rushed. Considering everything Olivia has had to cope with this past year, I want to give her plenty of time to decide if I'm someone she's interested in starting a relationship with."

"Olivia has always struck me as a woman who knows exactly what she wants. If last night was any indication, I think you'll get what you're hoping for, Papa."

"I hope so."

There's a moment of silence before I say, "I'm going to talk with Linn when Jered comes back to get me."

"Are you nervous?"

I nod. "Yes."

"Linn is a good woman," my father reminds me. "She's had a long time to think about things. I'm sure she realizes what happened with Daniel hurt you just as much as it hurt her."

"But it didn't change the course of my life as much as it did hers."

"No, but it's a guilt you will always have to live with. Her sorrow will ease over time, but the depth of your guilt will never go away."

I know my father is right. I'll never be able to forgive myself for killing Daniel. It's a guilt I'll have to live with until the day I die.

"What should I say to her?" I ask, seeking his guidance in a matter that is too close to my heart for me to think clearly about it.

"I can't tell you that, but I do know that you need to give her time to say what's on her mind. Allow her the opportunity to relieve her heart of the sorrow she's been carrying around since Daniel's death. Some of what she has to say to you may be hard to hear, but you owe her the opportunity to say what she wants to and just listen."

"Did Malcolm share his suspicions with you about Bai being JoJo?"

"Yes, he told me about that a few months ago."

I take a deep breath, knowing I need to go see Linn before I lose my nerve. As if he can read my mind, Jered phases back into his spot on the veranda.

"Ready to go?" Jered asks me.

"Yes," I say, before I can second-guess my decision. "I'm ready."

CHAPTER FIFTEEN

Jered phases us to right outside the door to Linn's bedroom.

"Desmond should still be here," Jered tells me before raising his hand to knock on the door. "He told us that he would be staying the night to make sure there weren't any complications after the birth."

"I still can't believe she kept the pregnancy a secret from all of us," I say.

"I'm just thankful you and Malcolm arrived here yesterday when you did."

Desmond opens the door and greets us with a warm smile.

"Good morning, lass…Jered. Slade came over earlier and told us you would be visiting."

"Is now a good time?" I ask, half hoping it is and half hoping it isn't.

"She's been waiting for you," Desmond tells me, giving me a small, encouraging smile that also holds a warning. Desmond steps out of the room to stand beside the door. "Jered and I will stay out here while the two of you talk."

I take a deep breath and walk into the room. I'm absently aware that Desmond closes the door behind me. I find Linn sitting on the padded bench built into the bay window in the room. She's wearing a simple white robe and has a blue wool blanket covering her from the waist down. Her long black hair is braided into a side ponytail that lies over her shoulder.

When our eyes meet, I expect to see some form of emotion in Linn's expression, but she's keeping her thoughts carefully hidden from me behind a chilly reserve.

"Malcolm told me you had a baby girl," I say, not knowing how else to start our conversation. "Have you named her yet?"

"Sya," Linn answers.

An uncomfortable silence settles between us as we stare at one another. Not knowing what else to do, I walk over to the window and sit opposite Linn on the padded bench.

"I don't know what to say to you," I confess. "I could beg for your forgiveness and tell you how sorry I am for what I did to Daniel, but you already know all of that. There's nothing I can say or do to change what I did to him. I do want you to know that there isn't anything in this world that I wouldn't do for you and your children. I would die for all of you if it ever came to that."

"I know that, Anna," Linn says. "I want to apologize for the way I treated you yesterday. You were only trying to help me, and I reacted very poorly to your kindness. It made me realize that, in order for me to get over the anger I feel towards you, I need to unburden my heart of its resentment where you're concerned."

Linn looks down at my protruding belly, and smiles.

"Daniel would have been so happy to see you starting a family of your own," she tells me as her smiles turns wistful. "It's the little moments in life that are the most precious. I wish he could be here to see what a strong woman you've become. He dedicated his life to making sure you would be born and given the opportunity to fulfill your fate. I feel as though he was cheated out of that moment, or, I guess I feel like I was cheated out of being able to share in his joy over your successes. Since the day we met, he and I shared every sad and happy moment of our lives together. I know how much you meant to him, Anna, and I think he would be ashamed of me for treating you the way I have these past few months."

"You're human, Linn. I understood you needed time to grieve."

"I needed time to stop hating you," Linn tells me honestly.

I hesitate before asking my next question, because I'm not sure I'm ready to hear her answer. "And have you stopped hating me?"

"I don't think I'm a good enough person to ever completely forgive you for what happened," Linn admits as tears shimmer in her eyes, "but I don't hate you anymore."

"Can we ever be friends again?" I ask, having a hard time holding back my own tears because I fear I already know Linn's answer.

Linn's tears spill freely down her cheeks as she shakes her head. "No."

I wipe away my own tears because I understand there's no hope that Linn and I can go back to the way things were between us. Daniel's death will be a permanent chasm separating us from one another.

193

"Every time I see you," Linn begins to explain through a sob, "all I see is the woman who killed my husband. You are a constant reminder of what I've lost, and I will never find a way to separate the memory of his loss from you. I truly wish I could, Anna. I know you are a good person, but all I see is death when I look at you."

Linn's words tear my heart apart, but I understand her feelings. If our roles were reversed, and she had killed Malcolm, I would see her the same exact way.

"I understand," I say, knowing now that there won't be any way for me to change Linn's feelings towards me, "but is there any way you will allow Bai to be a part of my family's life?"

Linn tilts her head as she looks at me questioningly. "Why do you ask?"

I go on to explain who Bai truly is and her connection to Lucas.

"My little Bai is the reincarnation of JoJo?" Linn says in surprise. "Daniel never mentioned that to me."

"He didn't know. None of us did until recently."

Linn looks thoughtful as she absorbs this news. "Daniel told me about the vessels and what happened to Gabe when they went to that alternate reality. He would have been so proud and happy to know that JoJo chose him to be her father in her second life."

"I'm sure he would have," I agree. I know for a fact that Malcolm was overcome with emotions when he learned who Lucas was, and that Gabe chose him to be his father. It was a blessing and a privilege that Malcolm never expected to receive. To be chosen by one of your best friends to play such a pivotal role in their lives was a gift very few people ever received.

"Daniel would want Bai and Lucas to be together," Linn tells me with certainty. "She is free to visit Lucas whenever she wants. I don't want my feelings towards you to keep them apart."

"Thank you," I tell her before standing up. "I'll leave you now to recover from the delivery. I want you to know that if you or the kids ever need anything, all you have to do is tell us."

"I appreciate that, Anna."

I turn to walk towards the door. Once I'm on the other side of it, I find Jered pacing back and forth in the hallway.

"Where's Desmond?" I ask him, not seeing my other friend anywhere around.

"He went to check on the baby," Jered says, walking up to me. "How did things go?"

"She'll let Bai come to the palace to see Lucas whenever she wants," I say.

"Is that all she said?"

I shake my head and swallow hard to prevent myself from crying.

"There's no hope for the two of us," I tell him, not having to say more than that. "Can you take me home now, Jered?"

Jered touches my arm and phases me just outside the door leading to Lucas' chambers.

"Thank you for acting as my escort today," I tell him.

"I think by now you know I would do anything you asked of me."

"I do know that."

Jered looks at the closed door. "I have a feeling you'll find something in there that will cheer you up. Why don't you go see what Malcolm and the kids are doing?"

"We need to figure out how I'm going to win this election," I say, wanting nothing more than to go play with Malcolm and the children, but I don't want to waste time better spent in the pursuit of keeping my sovereignty.

"We can talk about that later this afternoon," Jered says. "Right now I think you need a good dose of happiness to take way the pain of this morning."

"I can't really think of a good enough argument against that suggestion," I admit.

"Then don't even try," Jered walks over to the door and opens it for me to walk through. "Just go."

The sound of laughter welcomes me as soon as I step into Lucas' playroom. I find Malcolm sitting in the middle of the floor behind Bai and beside Lucas as they watch her draw on Cade's left bicep with a tattooing pen. Vala and Luna are playing fetch with Linn's sons, which is where the laughter is coming from. When Vala sees me, she immediately shouts out my name and comes running towards me.

"How did your visits go?" she asks as she sits down in front of me. I see Malcolm stand and walk over to us.

"Catherine didn't back down," I tell her, knowing Malcolm will hear my answer, "and Linn said Bai can come here anytime she wants. One failure and one success, I suppose."

"Catherine was a long shot," Malcolm tells me. "We both knew that."

I nod. "Yes, we did. I'm just glad Linn is willing to let Bai come here to see Lucas." I look over at the two of them sitting together on the floor. "They need each other."

"Did Linn say anything else?" Malcolm asks.

"She said a lot of things. I'll tell you about them later."

Malcolm looks slightly worried about what I'm not saying, but doesn't push the issue.

"I see you have Bai drawing a tattoo on Cade's arm," I note, watching Bai as she carefully finishes her artwork on Cade.

"I thought it was worth a try," Malcolm says. "Since she's a painter, I thought tattoos might work as talismans."

"It's a good idea," I say hesitantly, "but how are we going to try them out to make sure they work?"

"Well, considering Cade's…uh…connection…with Helena, I thought he would be the best person to test the tattoo's effectiveness."

"And how exactly is he supposed to do that? Pick a fight with Helena's husband?" I ask jokingly. When Malcolm just looks at me without cracking a smile, I become angry.

"That is out of the question," I tell him. "I won't allow him to do it."

"You could order him not to," Malcolm relents, "but is that the best course of action for everyone?"

"How did you test the first talisman JoJo made? There has to be a better way than just throwing him into a situation he might not come back from alive."

"I tested the first talisman the same exact way," Malcolm tells me. "We had to know if they would work, and forcing a prince to use his power on me was the best way to do it."

"I have the same power," I remind my husband. "I can test it."

Malcolm's brow furrows at my suggestions. "I hate to bring this up, but Daniel had the talisman JoJo made us in his blood, remember? It did nothing to protect him from your power. Besides, in order for us to truly test the tattoo's usefulness, I think the person needs to actually feel like their life is in danger. You're their friend. They wouldn't truly feel threatened by you."

Malcolm's right, of course. Begrudgingly I say, "I still don't like this plan."

"Neither do I, but it's the best way to test it. We need to know if this will work so Bai can tattoo the others."

"She's just a little girl, Malcolm. She isn't going to be able to tattoo all two thousand War Angels in a day."

"No, she won't, but given enough time she can get to them all. The tattoos don't have to be large. She can do simple ones. Plus, with the tattoo pen it doesn't take her very long at all. She's been working on Cade's for about twenty minutes, and she's almost done."

"Did he pick his own design?"

Malcolm holds out his hand for me to take. "Yes. He did. Come see it."

Malcolm, Vala, and I walk over to look at Bai's artwork on Cade's arm.

It's a take on the yin and yang symbol. One tear-drop-shaped side is black with white lines drawn within, giving it the look of a feather. The other side is red but drawn in such a way to look like a dragon. The symbolism isn't lost on me. I assume the dragon represents Helena and the feather Cade. Yin and yang, indeed.

"What's to prevent someone from just ripping Cade's arm off and negating the effects of the tattoo?" I ask Malcolm in a whisper, not wanting to disturb Bai's concentration.

"Well, that's one of the restrictions she's trying to place on it," Malcolm whispers back. "Only someone who truly cares about Cade's welfare can see the tattoo. That way his enemies won't even know it's there."

"All done!" Bai announces as she pulls the tattoo pen away from Cade's skin and looks up at us with a bright smile.

"It's beautiful, Bai," I tell her. "You did such a good job."

"Thanks, Anna," Bai says, looking bashful after my praise. She hands Malcolm the tattoo pen.

"Can we go play now?" Lucas almost whines. "I want Bai to help me with the robot I've been working on."

"Go ahead," Malcolm tells Lucas. "But don't get too involved in it. Lunch will be served in a few minutes. Even crazy geniuses need to eat."

Lucas giggles. "Ok, Dad. I promise we won't forget to eat."

Lucas grabs one of Bai's hands, and the two of them set off to his small workshop connected to the playroom.

"So," I say as Cade stands up and pulls his black shirtsleeve down over his new tattoo, "when do you intend to go pick a fight with Levi?"

"As soon as possible," Cade tells me.

"Are you in that big a hurry to die?" I ask, not seeing the need for him to rush into what could be a certain death sentence for him.

"The sooner the princes know that they can't hurt us, the better," Cade insists. "I think one of the only reasons they haven't attacked us yet is because they know you would kill them if they did."

"And how exactly do you intend to start this fight with Levi?" I have to ask.

"I haven't quite figured that part out yet," Cade admits, "but I'm sure I'll be able to find a way at the party in Nimbo."

"What party?"

"Emperor Solarin and his new empress are having a wedding reception at their palace tonight," Malcolm tells me. "Cade and a few of the other War Angels intend to crash it."

"Seems like fair play to me," Cade says with a shrug of his shoulders. "They came to your party uninvited. I don't see any reason not to go to theirs the same way."

"Just promise me that you'll all be careful," I practically beg. "You might be protected, but the others won't be. Odds are that the other princes will be there, too."

"We'll be careful," Cade promises. "You won't be losing any of us tonight."

"Cade," Malcolm says, "would you mind watching over the children for a while? I need to discuss something with Anna in private."

"You two go on," Cade says with a smile. "I've got them until I need to leave."

Malcolm takes my arm and places his free hand on Vala's head. He phases us to the living room in our private chambers. We sit on the couch together, and Vala rests her head in my lap. While I'm stroking her soft fur, Malcolm says, "Now, tell us what happened today."

I go on to recount my two visits in greater detail to both of them. I can't prevent myself from crying over the loss of my friendship with Linn, even though, deep down in my heart, I knew the connection between us might be irreparable.

"I'm just glad she's letting Bai spend time with Lucas," I tell them both, trying to look on the bright side of things. "I'm not sure what I would have done if she had refused to allow them to remain friends."

"I didn't have any doubts she would," Malcolm tells me. "It's their destiny to be together."

"Malcolm, do you really think it's wise to allow Cade and the others to go to Nimbo? I realize we need to test the effectiveness of the tattoo, but I feel as though we're letting them walk into a hungry lion's den. You know what Levi is capable of doing. Even if he doesn't kill Cade, he could torture him just for fun."

"It's a risk we have to take, Anna. We have to know if the talisman works, for the sake of the other War Angels. You need to trust in their judgment. They'll be able to handle any situation they might face while they're there."

"And what if they cause an international incident that starts a war with Nimbo?"

"They won't. They'll be discreet."

I raise a dubious eyebrow at my husband. "Have you met our War Angels? Discretion doesn't seem to be one of their talents."

"True, but I don't think they'll start a war, Anna."

"I guess we'll see," I say, sitting back on the couch and wishing I could be at the party to watch over my angels.

Ever since they came to Earth and pledged their fealty to me, I've felt like they're my responsibility. Malcolm has reminded me time and time again that they're grown men who can take care of themselves, but I don't feel the same way he does. I feel like they're still learning what's right and what's wrong as they try to figure out their roles on Earth. Some of them have quickly adjusted to their new lives, while others, like Xander, are still struggling to find their way.

I send up a silent prayer to God to guide my angels tonight and make sure they all return home safely.

CHAPTER SIXTEEN
(From Helena's Point of View)

Humans and their incessant need to celebrate every little life event with a party. I don't understand it, but perhaps that's because I've never had a reason to celebrate anything in my life. It wasn't as if Lucifer threw parties with balloons and cake for me on my birthdays, although maybe that was because he simply thought of me as a place instead of a sentient lifeform.

I can clearly remember the first time I appeared to him in human form. He didn't react very well, but that's probably because I tried to look like an eight-year-old Anna. I thought if I looked like her, he wouldn't feel the need to go see her every year on her birthday. I can still remember the look of disgust on his face as I twirled around in my frilly red dress in front of him. He snatched me up, nearly shattering my illusion of a body, and ordered me to never assume Anna's shape again. I never did. I decided to mimic another form, one that I had a lot of respect for from Lucifer's memory.

Her name was Ravan Draeke…or was it Lillith? Whatever. They were one and the same. I mimicked her facial features at first, but over time, I refined them to suit me better. Though, her penchant for wearing red is something I've kept over the years.

Lucifer met her when he went to that alternate reality with Jess. What a mind- job that little adventure did on the pathetic old fool. I wasn't sure if Lucifer would ever recover. In actuality, he never did…not completely. Then when that bitch Amalie tried to take him away from me, I thought I was going to lose him forever. Though, as it turned out, that tragic romance gave me more of an advantage over him than I ever could have hoped for.

The grief Lucifer suffered through by losing his soul-mate and child in the same night was like being given a lifetime of missed birthday presents all at once. Lucifer became weak and pliable to my will as I drained him of power. If I were able to feel guilt, I suppose I might have felt that particular emotion from using him the way I did. Luckily for me, my moral compass isn't that sensitive. If I learned one thing from Lucifer, it was that loving others weakens you. He was weak with Jess. He was weak with Amalie, and his love for Anna almost destroyed him. Sure, he made it back to Heaven, but just barely. If God wasn't such a sucker for those who ask for His forgiveness, Lucifer would have been able to stay with me forever so I could feed off his sorrow for all eternity. Things worked out for me in the end, though. Taking five of the seals from Anna gave me enough power to become corporeal, and finally break through the veil separating me from Earth. I'm still not as strong as I want to be, but I have a plan to solve that little problem.

"Are you ready?" Levi asks me as he strolls into my bedroom, tugging on a sleeve of his white tuxedo jacket.

I stare hard at Levi's reflection in the full-length mirror I'm standing before.

"What have I told you about coming in here?" I ask him, doing nothing to contain my annoyance at his annoying habit of disobeying my orders.

"And what have I told you about us needing to at least appear to be happily married? If you don't play along, Helena, people will become suspicious."

"I'm fine with playing my part when we're in front of the humans," I say scathingly, turning away from the mirror to face him, "but when we're in private, there's no need for us to be pleasant to one another."

"Don't you find this body at least a little bit desirable?" Levi asks, smiling charmingly with Zuri Solarin's full lips. Levi looks me up and down appreciatively. "We could have fun together in ways we never could in Hell. Human bodies are very sensitive when you know how and where to touch your lover."

"Are you honestly trying to lure me into your bed?" I ask, not knowing whether I should laugh in Levi's face or punch it.

"I'm just offering my services to you if you ever want to try sex," Levi says with a shrug. "You took on a human form to experience everything it has to offer, didn't you? Humans enjoy sex immensely; just ask your sister."

"I don't think Anna would willingly share tales of her sexual exploits with Malcolm with anyone, much less me."

"So you *are* curious about it," Levi says triumphantly. "I thought you might be."

"Not curious enough to let you paw at my body with your grubby little hands. I worked too hard to become real. I won't degrade myself by lying with a filthy little mongrel as repellent as you, Levi."

Levi shrugs, as if my belittling of him has no effect on his ego. "Your loss."

I turn back around to look at the dress I've chosen to wear to the wedding reception. Since Nimbo chose Egyptian fashion, the dress I'm wearing reflects their heritage. Gold overlays emulating the rays of the sun cover the body of the red-tinged, see-through material from shoulders to ankle. Strategically-placed strips of pleated maroon chiffon cover my breasts and fall elegantly along my sides. The skirt is composed of one strip of chiffon hanging from my waist to the floor, and a large swath of the material in the back covers me from the hips down. The fabric is so thin it practically floats behind me as I walk. I chose to have my hair styled in a loose, low-hanging, inverted ponytail.

"You should wear your crown," Levi advises as he considers my appearance with a critical eye. "It might make you look more intimidating. It certainly works for Anna."

"Are you telling me I don't scare you enough as I am?" I ask, intensely interested in Levi's answer.

"I know who you are," Levi answers. "The humans don't. To them you just look like a beautiful woman who caught their emperor's affections. Wait just a moment."

Levi phases away but returns a couple of minutes later with my crown in his hands. It's a bit smaller than Anna's, with the diamonds arranged in a floral design within the gold.

"May I?" he asks as he walks up to me, holding up the crown.

I turn to face him so he can set the crown on my head and secure it into place.

"There," Levi says approvingly, "much better."

I turn around to look at my reflection, and have to agree with his assessment.

"Many of our guests have already arrived," he informs me. "Are you ready to meet more of your subjects, my empress?"

"The whole world will be kneeling down to me before long," I vow to my reflection.

"Yes, yes," Levi says, like he's bored, "but tonight you'll have to settle for the citizens of Nimbo accepting you as their leader. Tomorrow you can conquer the world, if that's what you most desire."

Slowly, I turn around to face Levi again and say, "This universe will soon be my domain. Make no mistake about that, Levi."

Levi holds up his hands in surrender. "Have at it. I'd rather have you in control than that Goody-Two-Shoes, Anna. Can you imagine how boring the world will be if she gets her way?"

"I can't let that happen," I admit, but keep the rest to myself.

Most of my power still comes from the energy generated by the hate and anger that flows through the universe. The Earth is ripe with negative energy, and it's the most important of all the planets with sentient life. I can't allow Anna to have dominion here. If she leads the humans to a place of peace and tranquility, I'll starve, more or less. Even the seals I carry need the negative energy humans love to produce in order to work properly. I can't prevent a smile as a brilliant idea forms in my mind. What I need…what the world needs…is a good war.

"Are you ready now?" Levi asks impatiently.

"Yes," I say with a true smile. "I think I am."

Levi takes my hand into his and phases us down to the palace's ballroom.

The space is filled with gold pillars and white marble. Levi has phased us directly to our golden thrones. As soon as the people at the reception notice our arrival, they all begin to clap and bow in our direction.

Levi holds up a hand, motioning the crowd to silence with the small gesture.

"Ladies and lords of Nimbo," he says, "I know most of you haven't had a chance to meet my lovely new wife, Empress Helena Solarin, but I'm sure you'll all fall in love with her as instantly as I did. Thank you for coming to celebrate this happy time in our lives. Drink, eat, and dance to your hearts' content!"

Everyone claps, and I plaster a well-practiced smile on my face. Humans feel comfort when they see you smile. Although, very few take the time to notice whether the smile is genuinely felt by the wearer. How these simple-minded creatures became God's favorite is beyond my understanding. Lucifer and I had been of one mind on that subject, at least until Jess came into his life. Her influence on him ended up changing everything.

At first, I thought it was just the fact that she was Michael's vessel that made Lucifer want to be with her. However, that excuse grew thin over time. Every year after they returned from alternate Earth, he would spend one entire day and an hour on her birthday with her. Oddly enough, she seemed to enjoy being with him; most of the time anyway. I was glad when Jess finally died. I would have danced on her grave if I had been allowed to. The spell she wove over Lucifer finally broke after her death, and he started to act more like his old self. We had so much fun during the years between Jess' death and the first time he met Amalie. I should have found a way to kill that bitch before she got knocked up with Anna. Because of them, I lost my only true companion in this world.

I spend a good half hour greeting our guests with Levi by my side, and learning the names of the lords and ladies who influence Nimbo society the most. Not that it really mattered. All of them would be groveling at my feet before too long.

About an hour into our reception, the large gold double doors at the entrance to the room are unexpectedly opened. I sit up a little straighter on my throne when I see some of Anna's War Angels walk in, causing quite a disturbance among our guests with their arrival. After my first conversation with Cade, I did my research on Anna's angels. I knew all of their names now so I never had to ask again.

Cade, dressed in a dark blue suit, leads his brother angels as they walk into the room in a strategic V-formation. Counting Cade, there are six of them in all.

"Did you invite them here?" Levi asks me angrily. It's obvious he assumes that I did. He suspects Cade and I have a connection, but I have neither confirmed nor denied his assumption.

"No," I answer. "I did not."

Levi stands from his throne as the rather impressive looking group of angels walk up to us.

"Please excuse our unannounced arrival," Cade says to me, completely ignoring Levi's presence. "Our empress asked that we attend your reception in her place. She apologizes for not being able to come in person, but her pregnancy tends to put limitations on her ability to attend social functions. She did, however, ask me to give you her best wishes on your marriage."

"Please thank the Empress of Cirrus for her well-wishes, and you are all welcome in our home," I say, slightly confused by Cade's presence here. I seriously doubt Anna sent me any sort of well-wishes. Perhaps she sent Cade here in an effort to confuse me. I see she'll have to learn I'm not that easily confounded. "I hope you and your friends enjoy yourselves while you're in Nimbo."

Cade smiles. "I'm sure we will, Your Majesty."

Cade bows at the waist, but the others don't. They remain ramrod-straight, and look as if they all want to kill me. I smile at them because I know Anna hasn't given them permission to touch me yet. My big sister doesn't want to cause an international incident on the brink of her election. That would be a certain way for her to lose her crown to Catherine. Perhaps I should start the fight and force her angels to attack me. If there is one thing that is a certainty, I can't allow Anna to remain in power of Cirrus. It would cause too many complications.

"So," the War Angel I know as Xander says, "how's the wine here in Nimbo? I heard it was some of the best produced on Earth."

"Feel free to drink your fill," I encourage, sensing that this particular War Angel isn't like the others. He might actually be useful.

"We won't be staying that long," the one named Zane, Xander's true brother, informs me. I see him give Xander a disapproving sideways glare.

"Please don't feel as though you have to leave any time soon," I tell them. "You are all welcome to stay here in Nimbo for as long as you want."

"Not really our kind of city," Atticus says, looking around at his surroundings as if he expects something to materialize out of thin air and attack him.

"Oh, I don't know," Gideon says, smiling at a group of lovely young ladies to the left of him. "It might not be so bad."

"We'll stay for a little while," Roan tells me, "but we'll need to return to our empress soon."

"As I said, stay for as long as you want," I say, looking at Cade.

Cade nods to me as he turns and fades into the crowd with the other War Angels. I lose sight of Cade for a while. Even though I can't see him, I can feel his eyes on me during the evening. Levi and I continue our pretense of being love-besotted newlyweds as we dance and give each other small touches and kisses during the evening. I know I'll have to take a long shower when I return to my chambers. I may even have to make a quick trip to Hell to burn off any remaining traces of him from my skin.

When I notice Cade escort an exceptionally beautiful brunette onto the dance floor, I feel something unpleasant flutter within the depths of my soul. I watch as he twirls her around effortlessly, causing her to giggle in delight as he manhandles her. When they pass by my throne, Cade glances up at me with a pleased smile on his face.

"You should watch your expressions," Levi warns me in a low voice so no one else can hear. "Your jealousy is showing."

I snap my head to the side to look at Levi. "I'm not jealous."

"That might be what your mouth is saying, but your face is telling another story. You're supposed to be in love with me, remember? *I'm* your forever devoted husband, not him."

"I need some fresh air," I say, standing from my throne. "Don't follow me. I really don't want to be around you right now."

Without waiting for Levi's response, I step over to the far side of the room and pass through the glass doors that lead out onto a large veranda. Thankfully, the space is empty, and I'm allowed to steal a moment to myself.

"Are you all right?"

Cade's voice and presence take me by surprise. I whirl around to discover he's standing directly behind me.

"What are you doing out here?" I ask harshly. "Shouldn't you be finishing your dance with that pretty little thing that was just in your arms?"

"I saw you come out here," Cade replies, taking a step closer to me. "I wanted to make sure there wasn't anything wrong with you."

"Of course I'm fine," I say irritably. I place my hands on Cade's chest and push him a couple of steps back from me. "Haven't you ever heard of personal space? I don't need you looming over me like some overprotective watchdog. Why don't you go back to your dance partner? I'm sure she's not very happy that you left her on the dance floor all alone."

"Is that what you want?" Cade asks. "Do you want me to go back to her, or would you rather have me stay here with you?"

I hesitate before finally saying, "Do whatever you want. I really don't care."

Cade smiles. "Why are you trying to lie to me, Helena? Don't you know I can distinguish between a lie and the truth?"

"How? Is that one of your angelic superpowers?"

"All War Angels can do it," he explains. "I thought you knew that."

"Obviously, I don't know everything."

"Obviously, or you wouldn't be trying to push me away when you know you've already lost the battle."

"I haven't lost anything," I inform him heatedly. "I'm my own person. I decide what happens in my life, not some predestined love match mumbo jumbo!"

Cade takes a step closer. "Prove it," he challenges. "Prove to yourself that you can ignore what's between us. If you can do that, I'll leave you alone. I won't speak to you if we're in the same room. I won't even look at you. I'll stay away forever if that's what you really want me to do."

"And how am I supposed to prove that I want you to leave me alone?"

"Kiss me," Cade says, stepping so close now that I can feel his warm breath on my face. "If the kiss makes you feel nothing, then I'll go away. I won't ever seek you out again. You have my word."

"I may be infected," I inform him.

Cade's eyes squint in confusion, but his lips smile in amusement at my statement.

"And why would you be infected with something?"

"Levi's been playing the role of the dutiful husband all evening long. I'm not sure I'll ever be able to get the stench of him off my skin."

Cade lifts his hands and rests them gently against the sides of my neck, using his thumbs to tilt my head up towards his.

"Do you trust me?" he asks in a whisper, watching me closely for my reaction to his question.

"No," I say without a doubt. "You're dangerous to me."

"Only because what you feel for me scares you," he murmurs as he lowers his head down to mine. "You need to learn to trust people, Helena. You can trust me."

Against my better judgment, I do place a small bit of faith in Cade. I close my eyes, finding myself breathless with anticipation for the first touch of his lips against mine.

Unfortunately, it never happens.

"Get the hell off my wife!" I hear Levi roar as Cade is ripped away from me.

When I open my eyes, I see Cade sprawled out on the marble floor of the veranda between Levi and me. Cade quickly gets to his feet and turns to face a fuming Levi.

"I'll kiss who I want," Cade taunts him with a lazy grin. "She wanted it, too. I wasn't taking advantage of her. Or are you just jealous that Helena was about to willingly kiss me, when you know how much she detests you even touching her?"

Levi charges at Cade, but Cade easily sidesteps Levi's clumsy attack.

Cade considers Levi and seems to find him lacking as he shakes his head disappointedly. "I expected you to be more of a challenge, or has living on Earth all these years made you lazy, Levi? I seem to remember you being a better fighter than this during the war."

I see Levi conjure his lightning whip in his left hand. He flicks it against the marble between him and Cade, causing a crackle of electricity to fill the air.

"What?" Cade says, looking at the whip. "You've stooped so low you would use that thing on an unarmed man? What's wrong with you, Levi?

Can't you win in an honest fight anymore? There was a time when even you had a small amount of honor during combat."

Levi disintegrates his lightning whip. "Is that what you want, Cade? To fight me in hand to hand combat?" Levi's hands become covered in blue flames. "You'd fare better against my whip."

"Do your worst," Cade taunts, like a complete fool.

"Both of you need to stop this!" I order, trying to bring reason back into the situation, the irony of which isn't lost on me. "You're acting like a couple of school boys fighting over a girl. It's beneath you both."

"Stay out of this, Helena," Levi says to me tersely. "I'm tired of following all your damn rules. If you want to stop me, kill me…if you can."

Cade rushes Levi, taking him by surprise but not completely. Levi has enough time to react, and wraps his hands around Cade's neck. I feel a wave of his rage as he lets loose his ability to kill angels.

I let out a strangled cry of dismay. The sound is strange to my ears, but what's even stranger is the fact that Cade doesn't disintegrate before my eyes.

"What the hell!" Levi storms, letting loose his power on Cade once again, but receiving the same result. Finally, Levi simply pushes Cade away from him. "How?"

Cade smiles as he rubs his neck with one hand. "I guess we War Angels are just harder to kill than you thought."

"That's not it," Levi says with certainty. "You've got something. I've seen this before."

Cade shrugs his shoulders. "Sorry, I can't tell you our secret. But thank you."

"What the hell are you thanking me for?" Levi demands.

"I needed to know if you could kill me. Now I know you can't. Thank you for being so predictable."

"You used me to start a fight with him?" I ask, not sure if I'm impressed that Cade pulled one over on me, or if I'm insulted.

"I'm sorry," Cade tells me sincerely. "I do want to kiss you, but I would rather do it under better circumstances."

"Leave," I tell him, "and take your friends with you. If you ever come here again, I'll find a way to kill you myself!"

"Helena…" Cade says beseechingly as he takes a step closer.

"Get out!" My voice carries farther than I intended, and draws the attention of those inside the ballroom.

Cade stares at me for a moment, looking conflicted about what he just did. Finally, he does what I told him to do. I watch as he walks back into the ballroom. He's quickly surrounded by the other War Angels, and they all phase back to Cirrus as one.

I turn away from the sea of questioning faces within the room, and look out over the veranda. I raise a hand to cover my chest as my heart begins to constrict, causing a sharp pain I don't quite understand. All I do know is that I feel like someone I should have been able to trust has betrayed me. I feel like Cade used me to get what he wanted, just like Lucifer used me. At least Lucifer never lied about what he wanted from me. I always knew where I stood with him.

As another jolt of pain courses through my body, I realize what it is I'm feeling. I just didn't know I had the capacity to feel it. For the first time in my entire existence, I know what sorrow feels like.

CHAPTER SEVENTEEN

(Back to Anna's Point of View)

"Anna, come sit with me," Malcolm begs. "You shouldn't be pacing the floor in your condition."

"I can't help it," I say, continuing to tread the same path around the couch in our sitting room, for about the hundredth time. "I'm worried about them."

Malcolm phases to stand directly in front of me. Without asking for permission, he scoops me up easily into his arms to cradle me against him.

"And you're making me worry about you," Malcolm chastises gently.

He walks us over to the couch and sits down, keeping me firmly on his lap. I rest my head against his shoulder and close my eyes, finding peace as he holds me in his embrace.

"I'm not really worried about Cade being killed by Levi tonight," I say. "My heart tells me that the tattoo will work."

"Then what is it, my love?" Malcolm asks, resting his cheek against the top of my head. "What's worrying you so much? Maybe I can help."

"I think I'm more troubled about his connection to Helena," I confess. "You and I both know nothing good can come from it."

"You never know," Malcolm says. "Maybe love will change her."

I shake my head. "I don't think so. As you've so often reminded me, she's pure evil."

"She was," Malcolm concedes, not sounding so sure about his earlier statement.

I lift my head and look at Malcolm. "What do you mean by that?"

"I've been thinking about her since our last conversation. She has a body now," he starts to explain. "She has to eat, sleep, and shower like the rest of us."

"But she's not human."

"No," Malcolm agrees. "She's not human, but that doesn't mean her body doesn't react and feel like a human one. I'm not human, but I have the same feelings and needs as you do. Helena might actually be able to feel love, sadness, and pain now."

"If that's true, I almost feel sorry for her. I can't imagine having to sort through all those emotions for the first time, but she's the one who wanted to be real. She only has herself to blame for what she's going through."

"True, but it also opens up a host of possibilities for her. Maybe she can learn to be more than she was created to be."

"I never thought I would hear you talk about her like this," I have to admit. "It's almost like you hope she finds a way to become a better person."

"You know I was lost for a long time," Malcolm reminds me. "I guess I do feel a little sorry for someone who was never shown how to love. The two of you were both created from Lucifer's soul, but he never loved her like he did you. During your life in Heaven and on Earth, Lucifer showed you how much he cared. Helena didn't get that part of him. All she ever received was his hate and anger. Can you imagine growing up like that?"

"She wasn't a child *in* Hell, Malcolm. She *was* Hell."

"But she was still a sentient being, Anna. She understood what was going on around her. She was alive. She just didn't have a form until she made one for herself."

"Now you're making me feel bad for wanting to kill her," I grumble.

Malcolm chuckles. "Oh, no…I agree she has to go. We would only be killing the body she made for herself and sending her back to where she belongs. We can't have her running around in the Origin unchecked, causing havoc and mayhem."

"Which brings up a good point: How do we kill the body she has?"

"I've been thinking about that too," Malcolm says. "You might be able to do it with your sword."

"Do you think I'm the only one who can kill her?"

"You're the descendant of two archangels. As far as I know, you're the most powerful person in the universe because of that fact. I don't think there's much you couldn't destroy if you really wanted to."

"That makes me sound rather ominous," I say jokingly, but Malcolm doesn't laugh. "I don't want people to see me as a destroyer of worlds."

Malcolm lifts his hand and rests it on my belly.

"You're also the bringer of life," he reminds me. "Don't forget that."

"I don't think the babies would let me forget," I say. "Would you mind giving me a back rub? It's killing me tonight."

Malcolm stands easily from the couch, with me in his arms, and walks into our bedroom. After he lays me on my side, he lies down behind me and opens the closure at the back of my dress. He uses the heel of his hand to massage from the base of my spine all the way up to my shoulders. His touch has always brought me comfort, from the very first moment we met.

"That feels so good," I tell him, closing my eyes and letting his touch heal my aches. "I think I'll keep you."

Malcolm chuckles as he inches closer to me, and pulls my gown down over my left shoulder to plant small kisses against my flesh.

"Being married to me does have its fringe benefits," he murmurs against my skin as he slides his hand down my side to rest gingerly on my hip.

"Yes, it does," I sigh, luxuriating in his attention.

Malcolm lavishes me with his love and comfort for a few more minutes. Then, I feel him pull the back of my dress together to close it.

"It's almost time for them to return," Malcolm informs me with a note of disappointment.

"Stupid angel punctuality," I complain because it's definitely putting a crimp in my private time with Malcolm.

"Come on," Malcolm urges, getting out of bed to walk around and help me up. "Let's see what happened in Nimbo."

As soon as we walk back into the sitting room, Cade and his entourage phase into the room. I do a quick head-count, and sigh in relief to see that everyone made it back safe and sound.

"It worked," Cade tells us, since he knows exactly what we want to know first. "Levi tried to kill me twice, but was unsuccessful."

"Can I get the next tattoo?" Gideon asks excitedly, like a child asking for a new toy. "I've always wanted one."

"Always," Xander says condescendingly. "You've only been on Earth a few months, Gideon."

"Just because my always isn't very long doesn't make it any less significant," Gideon defends.

"Do you even know what you want the tattoo to look like?" Xander questions.

"Well...no," Gideon admits. "But I'll figure it out."

"Well, I already know what I want," Xander replies cockily. "Maybe you should just wait and get yours after I get mine. You might like what I have planned."

"Did anything else happen at the party that we need to know about?" Malcolm asks.

"I did notice something strange," Roan says, looking worried about his observation, "or maybe it wasn't, but I thought I should make a note of it."

"What did you see?" I ask.

"None of the princes were present. In fact, the only other cloud city royal there was Lorcan Halloran."

"Really?" I ask, finding this fact strange. "I thought for sure they would all attend to show their support. Why would they come to my ball, but completely ignore Helena's wedding reception?"

"I'm not sure," Roan admits, "but I thought you should know."

"Thank you all for going, and reporting back to us," I tell them.

I look at Cade and see that he has a drawn expression on his face, like he's upset about something that happened at the party.

I quickly do my best impression of a yawn, but it actually turns into a real one.

"Oh, excuse me," I say to the group. "I guess I'm more tired than I realized. Cade, would you mind bringing me up a glass of warm milk?"

"Of course," Cade says, immediately phasing down to the kitchen to do as I ask.

"Have you had time to talk about what needs to be done in order to ensure that Anna wins the election?" Roan asks. "Is there anything that we can do to help?"

"We decided to wait until the morning to discuss things," Malcolm answers. "Jered is looking into a few options for us first. We'll all meet in the family room at nine o'clock tomorrow morning."

"Sounds good," Roan answers. "We should leave so Anna can get some rest. We'll see you both in the morning."

My angels phase back to their own homes.

Malcolm turns to me and says, "I assume you sent Cade on his errand so you can talk to him in private when he comes back."

"Am I that obvious?"

"Just a little," Malcolm says with a smile, "but I do know you very well. Probably better than most people, I would wager."

"You would definitely win that bet," I admit, just as Cade phases back into the room.

"Don't be too long," Malcolm says. "You actually do need to get some sleep."

Malcolm kisses me on the forehead and walks back into our bedroom, but leaves the door open. I turn to Cade and see that he's still wearing the same strained expression of worry on his face.

"Sit with me," I tell him, walking to the couch.

Cade sits down beside me and hands me my glass of warm milk.

"Thank you. Now, tell me what has you looking so upset. Did something happen between you and Helena?"

"I used her to make Levi mad," Cade confesses, refusing to meet my gaze. "I shouldn't have, but I knew his jealousy was the one thing that I could count on and exploit."

"Does she know you used her?"

"Yes."

"Was she upset?

"Yes."

"How upset?"

"Very."

"How do you know?"

"Because I can feel her pain." Cade looks up at me, like he's hurting just as much as she is. "Should I go to her, or do you think that would just make matters worse?"

"I can't really tell you what you need to do, Cade. All I can say is that you need to follow your heart where she's concerned, at least to an extent. You know, Malcolm and I were just talking about Helena. She's obviously feeling emotions now that she's never felt before. It's going to take some time for her to learn how to cope with them."

"So you think I should stay away from her for a little while."

"I'm not saying that. I'm saying that you need to decide what needs to be done. Only you know what she needs and when she needs it. If you think going to her now will help, then go. If you think it would only make matters worse, well, then, don't go."

Cade leans back on the couch and lets out a long, troubled sigh. "Right now, I think her feelings are a jumbled mess. I don't think seeing me will help her."

"Cade," I say, hating to broach the subject, but knowing I have to, "you know that we can't let Helena remain on Earth."

Slowly, Cade nods. "I know that, Anna."

"And you know we'll have to kill the body she's in so we can send her back to Hell."

"Yes," Cade says quietly.

"Are you going to let me kill her when the time comes for it to happen?"

Cade is silent. He stares at me for a moment before he admits, "I'm not sure."

This time, it's my turn to let out a deep sigh. "What are we going to do about that?"

Cade shakes his head, appearing conflicted between his duty as one of my War Angels and his newfound affections toward Helena. "I don't know, Anna. I know sending her back to Hell is the right thing to do, but something inside me is holding out hope that I can change her."

Considering the conversation Malcolm and I just had about this very subject, I know Cade's desire isn't outside the realm of possibility, but I also know Helena.

"You need to prepare yourself for the worst-case scenario here," I tell Cade. "I know Helena." I twirl a section of my white hair and lift it up. "She and I are connected, remember?"

"That's one reason I still have hope for her," Cade says, his expression reflecting that emotion. "She must have connected to you for a reason, Anna. Maybe she wanted to share herself with someone else, and you were the only one she could do that with at the time."

"You think she was reaching out to me?" I ask, not having considered this possibility before. As far as I knew, Helena did it so she could pull me to her whenever she wanted to. It was how she'd stopped me from phasing into Heaven to return the seals.

"I don't know if that was her initial intention," Cade shrugs. "I could just be fooling myself by thinking her motives weren't anything but selfish and destructive. I know she isn't a good person, but I have a hard time believing she's all bad."

"Why? Because she's your soul-mate?"

"Maybe," Cade acknowledges. "I guess I've always tried to see the best in people."

"She's not exactly a real person, though. You need to remember that, Cade."

"Why don't you think of her as a real person? What is she lacking to make her real to you?"

"Well, she's real, but she isn't like us."

"How?"

I have to admit I'm stumped for an answer to Cade's question.

"Maybe it's just easier for you to kill her if you don't think of her as real," Cade says, on the verge of becoming angry. "If she's not real, then it's not murder."

"Are we having a problem in here?"

Both Cade and I look over to the doorway of the bedroom. Malcolm
has his arms crossed over his chest and feet spread apart as he stares hard at
Cade, appearing quite menacing as he waits for an answer.

"No," Cade replies, standing from his seat. "There's no problem,
Malcolm. I was just leaving."

"Good," Malcolm proclaims.

Cade looks down at me. "I'm sorry for the tone I just used with you. I
hope you can forgive me."

"You asked a good question," I told him. "And I will think about what
you said."

Cade nods his head, unable to meet my eyes. "I'll see you both in the
morning."

After Cade phases, I feel conflicted about our conversation.

"He thinks he's in love with her," Malcolm says as he walks over to
me. "I wouldn't take anything he said to heart. He knows Helena needs to be
taken care of as soon as possible. He just doesn't want to face that fact."

"Can you blame him?" I ask, trying to place myself in Cade's
position. "If you were Cade and I was Helena, how would you feel? What
would you do?"

"You know what I would do," Malcolm says with certainty.

"Protect me."

Malcolm takes my hands and pulls me up off the couch and up against
him.

"Let's not dwell on impossible questions right now," he says. "All I
want to do is take you to bed and snuggle."

I smile. "Who would have thought you were the snuggling type?"

"Why? Don't I look like a snuggler to you?"

"To me, yes. To the rest of the world, no."

"Then I would have to say that I'm perfect, because that's exactly the way it should be."

"And I would have to agree with you, but they do say that love is blind."

"Others maybe, but never you, my love."

"Take me to bed, husband. I've had a rough day."

Malcolm takes me to our bedroom and helps me change into pajamas. I drink the warm milk Cade brought me, and fall asleep in my husband's arms almost as soon as I lie down. It is the perfect ending to a day that has been far from ideal.

At least, until I hear the first scream...

CHAPTER EIGHTEEN

That first scream is soon joined by a multitude of them, sounding like a chorus of terror.

Dressed in only the black silk pajama pants he wore to bed, Malcolm quickly phases out from underneath the covers to snatch up his wolf-head cane and pull out the sword hidden within. I try to phase to where my own sword is, but quickly discover that I can't. Obviously, the babies are still blocking my ability to phase where and when I want.

Malcolm phases to the tall chest of drawers in the room, and pushes against its side to pop open a hidden compartment to retrieve my sword.

"Anna! Malcolm!" I hear Ethan yell from the sitting room. Without knocking, Ethan rushes into the bedroom to find us.

"What's happening?" I ask Ethan as I stand up from the bed and take my sword from Malcolm.

"There are hellspawn everywhere in the city, attacking people," Ethan quickly informs us. "I've already instructed Cade to take the children and dogs down to Brutus and Kyna on the surface for now. He'll stay there to protect them just in case."

"Has anyone gone to Linn's to get her and the baby out?" I ask anxiously.

"Desmond is still at her house, as far as I know," Ethan says.

"Go over there and check to make sure he's phased her somewhere safe," Malcolm orders Ethan.

Ethan phases to Linn's home, and Malcolm and I swiftly make our way out of the bedroom. We rush onto the veranda to evaluate the situation from its high vantage point.

After our first fight against the hellspawn, I ended up having nightmares about them for weeks afterwards. They are horrific creatures, resembling severely deformed human corpses. Their rotting stench is almost as overwhelming as their unsightliness. As Malcolm and I survey their numbers, I know there have to be thousands of them in Cirrus, and that's only from what we're able to see roaming around on the streets below us.

"You need to get out of here," Malcolm says, grabbing my arm.

I quickly snatch it out of his grasp before he can act on his intent.

"I am not leaving!" I inform him tersely. "Not when the people of my city are being attacked by those things. We need to get everyone who can't self-teleport out of the city to the escape pods. There's no way we can kill all of these hellspawn before they murder the people here."

All of the escape pods are located on the underside of Cirrus. Malcolm and I used one to flee from the city after my wedding to Levi.

"Anna!" I hear my papa yell from direction of the sitting room.

I rush back inside, and find him standing there dressed in white pajama pants and a matching robe left hanging open at the front, holding his sword in his right hand.

"You need to teleport yourself down to the surface," I tell him, knowing how vulnerable his humanity makes him against the hellspawn. "I need you to go to Brutus' home to watch over Lucas and the others for me."

"I'll go if you come with me," my papa says stubbornly. "I'm not leaving unless you do too."

"Please, Papa," I beg. "I can't think straight if I know you're in danger. Go to Lucas and protect my son for me. I have no way of knowing what else Helena might have planned. If anything happened to him because of me..."

We all know only Helena can control the hellspawn. Until they're slain, her minions will continuously kill anyone who has the misfortune of crossing their path. Unfortunately, what I just said to my papa is painfully true. We have no way of knowing what else Helena has arranged next. Lucas is one of my vulnerabilities, and Helena isn't above exploiting that to make me do what she wants. Since she seems determined to find a way to make me lose my throne, I wouldn't put it past her to be employing the hellspawn as a diversion tactic to find some way to endanger his safety to get me to do what she wants.

"I'll go," my papa says reluctantly, "but you need to get out of the city as soon as possible. Is that understood?"

"Yes," I tell him. "I understand."

Papa looks up at Malcolm. "Keep her safe."

"Always," Malcolm promises.

My papa raises his right hand, bringing up the holographic controls of his personal teleporter, and transports himself to the down-world.

Roan appears in my sitting room, followed in short succession by the other War Angels in my personal guard.

"I've sent word to my brothers on the surface to come up here to help us with the hellspawn," Roan tells us. "The rest of the guard stationed here in Cirrus is making sure people can get to the escape pods and public teleporters. We've also started evacuating everyone living here in the palace."

I'm thankful that Roan has already set into motion what I had planned. It's a relief to know that I can count on my War Angels to keep their heads during nightmare scenarios like this.

"Then let's start cleaning this mess up," I tell the others.

Roan looks pointedly at my protruding belly. "Anna, we can handle these things. There's no need for you to put yourself in a dangerous situation. Don't you trust us to take care of it for you?"

"It's not a matter of trust," I tell him. "It's a matter of responsibility. The people of Cirrus count on me to protect them. I will not leave until I know those who can be saved have been, so stop questioning my decision and wasting our time. Let's get these things out of my city!"

"And that's why I like you so much," Gideon says with an approving smile. "You never back down from a fight."

"No, I don't," I confirm. "Now, where do we need to go to be most effective?"

"All of you should go down to the area where the escape pods are located," Roan says. "I'll handle stationing the rest of the War Angels in the most populated areas to help people get down there to you. Hopefully, you won't have to fight off many of the creatures. We should be able to kill them before they reach the lower levels."

"And if you're not able to?" I ask.

"If you see a horde of hellspawn making its way down that far, you'll know that we were overrun and couldn't contain them. I would advise you to leave the city at that point to protect the lives of your unborn children,

Anna," Roan stresses to me. "Whatever happens, the three of you *must* survive."

"If we see a horde heading our way," Malcolm says, "I'll get her out whether she wants to go or not."

Roan nods, knowing he can rely on Malcolm to do what needs to be done in order to keep the babies and me safe.

"Then let's go," Roan says, phasing to do his job while the rest of us go to perform ours.

Malcolm phases us down to the staging area where the escape pods are kept. It's complete pandemonium as terrified people rush past us to get to the awaiting pods. I see a young girl around Lucas' age trip and fall behind a woman I presume to be her mother. The mother isn't immediately aware of her daughter's plight. The crying girl makes several attempts to stand up, but the crush of frightened people behind her keeps pushing her back down. Finally, the mother notices her daughter isn't following her anymore, but the advancing crowd holds her back, keeping her just out of reach of her daughter.

I make my way to the girl, but even I have a hard time staying upright in the maddening crowd.

When I first began to absorb the seals from the princes, my temper became something I had to learn how to control. Sometimes I was successful and sometimes I wasn't. I feel my temper start to get the best of me in this situation, but I try to keep calm and sympathize with my frightened citizens.

All of a sudden, I'm pushed so hard I almost lose my balance. If Malcolm hadn't remained close enough to catch me, I would have ended up face-down on the concrete floor. The incident causes a switch to flip inside me, and my patience abruptly evaporates.

I fly straight up into the air above the crowd, which certainly catches everyone's attention.

Since the moment I saved Alto from total destruction by using the power the seals gave me, everyone knew I was something more than human. I'm sure the change in my physical appearance didn't help matters either. Malcolm liked the white hair, but, for me, it and my bright blue eyes are a constant reminder of my connection to Helena. Perhaps that was one reason some in Cirrus didn't want me to remain in power. They feared what they couldn't understand. It's a theme that has been prevalent throughout all of human history. If you're unable to understand something, fear takes hold of your heart, and you either find a way to control what scares you or you destroy it. Since Helena took five of the seals away from me, I'm sure I don't possess the same type of powers as I did when I saved Alto, but the people looking at me right now, in a mixture of awe and trepidation, aren't aware of that fact.

"Stop acting like frightened animals!" I chastise them. "I know you're scared, but you need to calm yourselves down. Don't let fear make you forget who you are."

I fly over to the girl I saw fall and who is still sitting on the floor. As I hover above the child, the people around her move away. With the scattering of the crowd, the little girl's mother is finally able to lift her up into her arms.

"Thank you, Empress Anna," the tearful mother tells me, hugging her daughter tightly to her chest.

I look back at the sea of people looking to me for direction and tell them, "There are plenty of escape pods for everyone. Get to them quickly, but remember that we're all in this together. If you see someone having trouble, stop to help them. Don't let your own panic make you forget your humanity." No one in the crowd moves as they all continue to stare up at me. "Go," I urge them.

In a more orderly fashion, the citizens of Cirrus begin to fill the escape pods to capacity before deploying them down to the surface. I continue floating above them to monitor the crowd's behavior and to act as a reminder that I'm keeping my eyes on them.

Malcolm and my other War Angels guard the four entrances to the staging area while I maintain my position in the air. Honestly, I think Malcolm is perfectly fine with having me off the ground and out of immediate danger. Everything seems to be going smoothly.

At least, until I see her.

From my position in the air, I'm able to see above the crowd and through the upper glass portion of the wall separating the staging area from the larger outer chamber. The fifty or so stone steps leading from the city streets down to the outer chamber are directly in my line of sight. Malcolm and the others can't see what I can.

And what I see is Helena standing behind my new personal maid, Jenny. Helena stares directly as me, as if she wants to make absolutely sure I see her. She has one hand clasped around Jenny's throat. From the redness of the girl's face, I can tell Helena's touch is not light. Helena phases, and I can see where her trail leads. I can only assume she expects me to follow her.

"Malcolm!" I yell down, instantly gaining his attention and also Xander's, who is standing right beside him at one of the center entrances. "Follow me!"

Helena may have thought I would blindly pursue her alone, and once upon a time I probably would have. But not now. I have two lives growing inside me who don't need me to be reckless with myself or them.

"Come on, babies," I say, rubbing my belly with my free hand and hoping they can hear me. "We need to follow her and see what she's up to."

Without my having to do anything else, I'm phased by the babies to the spot Helena seems to want me to follow her to. It's in the center of the city by the twenty-foot- high bronze water fountain that has a dove with outstretched wings adorning the top of it. The once-clear water now flows thick and crimson with blood, and I see the bodies of at least twenty of my citizens floating in the large pool of water of the fountain. Men, women, and even children drift lifeless in its depths.

I'm still hovering in the air, so the hellspawn filling the large open area between the fountain and the surrounding buildings can't reach me. However, when Malcolm and Xander phase in below, they immediately have to defend themselves. I'm shaking so violently with rage at what I see that I physically feel something break inside me. It urges me to seek vengeance against the one who has caused so much misery to the innocent.

"I'm going to kill you!" I promise Helena, seeing no other way to quickly end the chaos she seems determined to orchestrate.

"Not before I kill this one," Helena sneers. Poor Jenny isn't even given the opportunity to voice the terror I see in her eyes as she realizes her life is about to come to an abrupt end.

Helena rips out the front of Jenny's throat and tosses the poor girl's lifeless shell into the water with all the other dead bodies.

My sword bursts into flames without me even having to ask it to as I fly straight towards Helena, my arm outstretched. As ruthlessly as Helena just killed Jenny, I stab her straight in the gut until the hilt of my sword is rammed up against her flesh. Helena places her hands on my shoulders to prevent herself from falling down, and grunts in pain as I twist the blade of my weapon inside her body.

"Well," she says, breathing hard, "that certainly stings, but I'm afraid it isn't enough to kill me, Sister."

I grab Helena's arm with my free hand and try to call upon my power to kill angels, but nothing happens. My hands don't burst into blue flames at all, making me wonder if the babies are somehow blocking my power. It's the only explanation that makes any sense.

Helena takes a step back from me, and then another as she completely slides her body off my blade. I watch as the cut I just made to her midsection seals up, revealing skin that looks unblemished by my mark. Her body shakes slightly, but it's as if she's merely shrugging off the effects of my attack instead of recovering from what should have been a mortal wound, if she had been mortal.

"Get these things out of my city, Helena!" I shout threateningly.

"Or what?" Helena taunts, unaffected by my demand. "I don't take orders from you, Anna, and you need to heed my next words, because they might just save your life."

Confused, I ask, "What are you talking about?"

"This may be hard for you to believe, but I'm not your enemy in this situation. I need you to stay alive, but there are others who want to make sure you and your babies die. I'm doing what I can to keep you safe, but you're making it increasingly difficult to work that small miracle, Sister."

"Who wants me dead?" I ask, obviously needing to know this information.

"That isn't important right now," Helena says. "Just know that if you win the election, you might as well slice open your own throat. They won't stop until one of them is able to catch you off-guard and kill you and the babies. You and your children may have a guardian angel, but I don't think even Will is strong enough to bring your babies back from what the others have planned for them."

"Are you talking about the other princes?"

Helena begins to cackle. "Goodness, no. I mean, don't get me wrong, they do want you dead, but they also want you to win your little election, Anna. They want the others to do their dirty work for them."

"Then who are you talking about?"

"It doesn't matter," Helena says, sounding irritated with me. "Just stop trying to win. It'll only cause you heartbreak in the end, and I'm not sure if I can stop them from killing you."

Seeing that I'm not going to get a clear answer from Helena, I ask, "If what you're saying is true, why are you trying to protect me?"

"Can't we just chalk that up to sisterly love?"

"No. I'm not even sure you can feel that emotion."

"Neither am I," Helena admits. "Let's just contribute it to me looking out for my own best interests then. I'm sure you can believe that."

"Yes, I can, but I still don't understand how my staying alive helps you."

Helena shrugs. "Just take it as your own little miracle. I don't have time to explain it to you. What you need to do now is get out of the city, and take your War Angel army with you. They'll never be able to rid Cirrus of my hellspawn because, for every one your angels kill, two more will automatically take its place. I have an endless supply of them in Hell, you know. This is not a battle you can win, Anna, so don't even try. Go to your precious down-world for a while and spend some quality time with your family."

"You're not making any sense, Helena."

"I know," she sighs wearily. "Just go, Anna."

Helena phases back to Hell.

I look out at the hellspawn that fill the surrounding area, but notice none of them have any interest in attacking me. Since they're all under Helena's command, I'm not exactly surprised by this development. If she doesn't want me dead, then her minions certainly wouldn't be the ones to do the job. The slack-jawed face of Jenny draws my attention back to the bodies of innocent people who are dead, either directly or indirectly by Helena's hand.

I feel powerless because I know what Helena just said to me was as close as she would ever get to a promise. For every hellspawn we kill, she'll send two more up to take its place. There's no way for us to obliterate their numbers. She has my city at her mercy, and there's nothing I can do to stop her.

As I walk through the horde of hellspawn, they clear an unobstructed path for me to walk down. When I'm standing beside the spot where Malcolm and Xander are furiously killing them, I say, "Let's go. There's nothing we can do here. For all of the ones you just killed, she'll be bringing up twice as many to take their place. We need to evacuate the city, and stay away until we can figure out how to get rid of them for good."

"We can't just leave Cirrus to the mercy of these things," Malcolm protests as he slices the head off the hellspawn standing in front of him.

"We have to…for now," I say. "Killing them is pointless."

Malcolm finally relents and grabs my arm to phase us back to the terminal where the escape pods are. There are only a handful of humans left in the area now, and I begin to wonder if any of us will ever step foot into my city again. Have I lost the world's most powerful cloud city to Helena?

For the moment, that's exactly how it seems.

CHAPTER NINETEEN

Disheartened is a mild word to describe how I feel as the last citizens of Cirrus enter the final escape pod. I watch its descent to the surface, and wish the ones inside the best of luck. They'll have to figure out how to live there on their own, at least for a little while.

"What can we do for them?" I ask Malcolm, feeling helpless.

Over a million people call Cirrus their home. I wasn't sure if there was any way I could help them all, or even provide them a place to live while we tried to figure out a solution to our problem. Some of them would be able to find sanctuary with friends in the other cloud cities, but most of them would have to make due in the down-world until we found a way to clear out the hellspawn. How we were going to work that small miracle was beyond me for the moment.

"The people here in Cirrus are among the brightest and most innovative in the world," Malcolm reminds me. "They'll figure things out on their own until we can help them, Anna."

"But they won't have access to their money," I say worriedly. "They're going down there with nothing but the clothes on their backs."

"That's more than some people have," Malcolm replies. "We'll come up with a plan to help as many as we can, but, right now, I would feel more comfortable if I could get you out of this city."

"I'm probably the safest person here," I tell him, wondering if that's a blessing or a curse. "The hellspawn won't attack me."

"For that, I am eternally grateful, but there's obviously someone out there who wants to kill you. That's what Helena said, right?"

I nod. "Yes."

"Then let's go. I feel too open here," Malcolm says, looking at the empty terminal.

Strangely enough, the hellspawn never came down this far. It was almost as if Helena gave us time to get as many people out as we could. I'm not sure what the final death toll will be, but I know thousands of Cirruns have probably been massacred by her minions. I feel sick to my stomach thinking about their deaths.

"Gideon," Malcolm says, gaining that man's attention. "Go to my New Orleans home and tell Overlord Giles that we'll be staying there with him until we can figure out a way to remove the hellspawn from our city."

Gideon bows slightly at the waist to us before phasing to complete his task.

"What do you want the rest of us to do?" Xander asks as the other members of my personal guard gather around us.

"I want you to stay close to Anna," Malcolm tells them all. "Right now, we need to go get Lucas from Brutus' home in New York. Follow us there first, and then we'll head to New Orleans."

Malcolm takes my hand and phases us into Brutus' living room.

The room is cozy and inviting in an old-world kind of way. The walls are painted a dark rose color that gives the room an intimate, welcoming feeling. The dark- stained wood, waffle-style ceiling, and accent furnishings bring out the warmth of the beiges and golds within the fabric of the seating. The ornate stone fireplace is the focal point of the room, and commands attention due to its artisanship and elegant curves.

It seems like everyone in the house is gathered here. Lucas is the first one to notice our arrival, and immediately runs to us. Malcolm picks him up easily with one arm while still maintaining his grip on his sword. As always, Vala and Luna aren't far behind our son.

"I was so scared something would happen to you and Mommy," Lucas says, hugging his father tightly around the neck as if he never intends to let Malcolm out of his sight again.

I place my hand on Lucas' back to give him a small bit of reassurance that we're all safe from the nightmare creatures that now have free rein to roam the streets of Cirrus.

"We were never in any danger," Malcolm tells Lucas to alleviate his worry. Malcolm's words aren't completely true, but Lucas doesn't need to know that. Right now, he needs to be reassured that nothing bad is going to happen to his parents.

"We were all very worried about you, Anna," Vala tells me. "Cade phased us down here before we were able to see what was going on."

I'm thankful for that small miracle. I didn't want any of the children to develop nightmares of the hellspawn like I did after I first saw them.

"Was everyone able to get out safely?" Cade asks worriedly.

"Those who were left alive," I tell him, wondering what he thinks of his precious Helena now.

How can you love someone who just purposely orchestrated the death of so many innocent people? Cade's never been witness to Helena's cruelty before tonight. Now, he knows the kind of savagery she's capable of committing. Is he still holding out hope that he can change her? Unfortunately, I have very little faith that she can alter her natural instinct towards destruction. She was born to be cruel and punish those who were sent to her realm to live out all of eternity in their worst nightmares. Can someone like that even fathom the concepts of peace and love?

I look around the room and see that Linn was also brought here. Her children surround her like a protective circle of innocence as she sits in a chair by the unlit fireplace. Our eyes meet briefly, and I know I need to leave as soon as possible. She shouldn't have to tolerate my presence any longer than necessary.

"How are you doing?" Kyna asks me as she walks up and gives me a small hug of comfort. "Do you need anything? We can have rooms prepared for you here, if you want to get some rest."

"We'll be staying at the house in New Orleans," I tell her, loud enough for Linn to hear me, too. I don't want her to have to worry that she'll be obliged to see me any more than she has to. "Thank you for offering, though."

"Brutus," Malcolm says as Brutus comes to stand beside his wife, "I need you to gather all of the other Overlords and bring them to my New Orleans home as soon as they can get away from their normal duties. We need to come up with a plan to help the Cirrun refugees as quickly as possible."

"Consider it already done," Brutus says.

"Give us at least a couple of hours, though," Malcolm suggests, looking at me with undisguised worry. "Anna could use some rest first."

"I can manage," I say, even though I hate to admit that I'm bone-tired.

"You need to rest," Malcolm says caringly, not being fooled by my words. "You're of no use to anyone if you can't think straight."

I nod, too tired to put up a believable fight over the issue.

"We'll see you in a couple of hours," Malcolm tells Brutus. Malcolm looks over at Atticus and says, "Phase Vala and Luna for me. I have my hands full at the moment." He touches my arm and phases Lucas and me.

Xander, Roan, Zane, Cade, and Atticus, with Vala and Luna in tow, follow us to the sitting room in our New Orleans home. It's been months since we were last here. Almost all of our time has been spent in Cirrus, setting up and trying to secure our reign there. I'd almost forgotten how much this house feels like home to me. So much happened within its walls to change my life for the better. I was born here, I married here, and I conceived here. It is a place filled with treasured moments, and it will always hold a special place in my heart because of them.

"Why did you decide we should stay here instead of the beach house?" I ask Malcolm.

"I figured we could let someone else stay there, since it's so close to New York," he tells me. "Don't you think that would be a better use of the space?"

"Yes, just make sure you secure the nursery," I tell him, feeling overly-protective of that part of the house. "I don't want my window broken by carelessness."

"I'll make sure to secure the room before anyone is allowed to live there," he promises.

"Malcolm and Anna," Giles greets us, walking into the room with Gideon and Alex, the War Angel stationed in New Orleans.

Alex is slightly shorter than Gideon, with a narrow, boyishly handsome face. His light brown hair is all one length, the tips of which just brush the tops of his shoulders. His face is clean-shaven today, but the few times I've seen him he usually has a little stubble across the lower half of his face. His penetrating hazel eyes are his most prominent feature.

Since coming to Earth, Alex has barely spoken two sentences to me, and those instances were only because I prompted him to with direct questions. For whatever reason, he tends to act rather reserved in my presence. I'm not sure why, and I haven't had the time to delve into that particular peculiarity of his. I wasn't offended by his behavior, just curious as to the reason behind it.

When we were replacing the corrupt overlords in the down-world, Malcolm and I appointed Giles as overlord responsible for livestock. It was an important post because it placed him in charge of the distribution of meat products in both the down-world and up-world. I was just thankful we could place someone we trusted in such an important position.

"I was surprised when Gideon arrived to say you would all be staying here," Giles says as he walks up to Malcolm and shakes his hand. "I just wish it could have been under better circumstances."

"Yes, we'll be having a meeting to discuss what needs to be done next in a couple of hours," Malcolm informs Giles. "I've asked Brutus to gather the other overlords and bring them here. We're all going to have to work together to handle the influx of people from Cirrus. They'll need a place to live for a while until we can figure out a way to get rid of the hellspawn up there."

"I'll have the cook prepare some food for the meeting," Giles says. "It'll be almost morning by then, so I'm sure the other overlords will be hungry when they get here."

"That actually sounds kind of wonderful," I say, realizing how hungry I am.

"I'll make sure to put a little extra on your plate, Empress," Giles promises with a conspiratorial smile and wink.

I place one hand on my belly. "We would heartily appreciate the extra food. Trust me, it won't go to waste."

I look over at the quietest of War Angels. "How are you doing, Alex? It's been a while since you last visited us in Cirrus."

"I'm doing quite well, Anna," Alex answers, with a small nod and a reserved smile. "Thank you for asking."

"Roan," Malcolm says, "I need you to handle securing this site. We don't know what Helena has planned next, and I would rather not have any more surprises for a while. There's no way for us to make any place completely safe from Helena, but we can at least try."

"We'll do everything we can to keep all of you safe," Roan promises.

"Come on, you two," Malcolm says to Lucas and me. "Let's get a little rest while we wait for the others to arrive."

Malcolm phases us all to our old bedroom.

"I'm not sure I can sleep," I tell Malcolm, even though we only slept for a few hours before all Hell literally broke loose in Cirrus. I lean my sword against the wall near my side of the bed. Out of the corner of my eye, I see Malcolm do the same with his own blade.

Malcolm tosses Lucas onto the bed, adding some much-needed laughter into our lives. When I sit down on the side of the bed, Lucas comes up behind me and wraps his arms around my shoulders.

"Everything will be all right, Mommy," he declares in a way that makes me want to believe him.

"How can you be so sure?" I ask wearily.

"Because I've seen it," he says, subtly reminding me that he has the power to see into the future.

I turn slightly, making Lucas let go of me so I can look at his face.

"What have you seen?" I ask him, hoping he knows how to regain control over Cirrus.

"I've seen us living in the palace with Liam and Liana, remember?"

I nod. "Yes, I remember you telling me that once. Have you seen anything recently? Perhaps something that will help us figure out how to get those creatures out of Cirrus?"

Lucas shakes his head, looking a little dismayed. "No. I'm sorry. I haven't seen anything helpful."

I reach out and caress the top of Lucas' head. "That's ok. I'm sure we'll figure something out. We always do, don't we?"

"Yep!" Lucas say, with the enthusiasm only a child can have.

I watch as he crawls up towards the pillows on the bed and lays his head down.

"Come on, you two," Lucas urges, holding out his arms towards Malcolm and me and wiggling his fingers to beckon us closer. "I don't know about you, but I need a family hug."

Despite the dire straits we find ourselves in, I can't help but smile. I scoot further onto the bed before attempting to lie down. After Malcolm lies on the other side of Lucas, we clasp our hands together and rest them on Lucas' chest. Lucas grabs our joined hands with his little ones, and sighs contentedly as he closes his eyes. I look away from Lucas' happy face to Malcolm. His expression is a mixture of love and concern for me. I try to smile reassuringly, but fail miserably at the endeavor.

"He hasn't been wrong yet," Malcolm whispers, reminding me of Lucas' track record in prophesying the future.

"Nope!" Lucas chirps with his eyes still closed. "I haven't been. We'll be able to go back home soon. I just know it."

Even though he's only six years old, I trust that Lucas' vision will come true. We'll eventually go back to Cirrus. I'm just not sure how long it will take to regain control of it.

Lucas' warmth and reassurance about the future allows me to relax enough to allow weariness to overcome me, and, before I even realize it, I'm fast asleep.

"Anna…"

I'm slowly coaxed from my dreamless sleep by the sensation of tender kisses being planted randomly across my cheek. When I open my eyes, I discover Malcolm leaning over me. His long dark hair frames his face, making him look like a true angel to my eyes. I reach a hand up and caress him, treasuring the warmth of his skin against mine. His eyes close, silently letting me know that he's finding joy in the gentleness of my touch. Sometimes, the quiet moments between us mean more to me than any other. They're the ones that keep our connection strong enough to withstand all the trials we've faced in our life together so far.

"I hope you know what you mean to me," I whisper. "I could tell you a million times that I love you and it still wouldn't seem like I say it enough."

Malcolm's lips stretch into a content smile. When he opens his eyes to look into mine, I feel my heart melt into a puddle of bliss at the love I see inside his soul for me. No one will ever love me the way he does, and I will never love another man the way I do him. To say that Malcolm holds my heart doesn't come close to describing his claim to me.

"How do you do that?" he asks me with a look of amazement.

Confused, I ask, "Do what exactly?"

"Make me feel worthy enough to have someone like you love me."

"It's simple. You're a man worth loving. You always have been. It's only now that you're realizing that for yourself."

Malcolm leans down and kisses me gently on the lips. It isn't a kiss meant to lead to a passionate encounter, even though I wouldn't have minded that. It's one given in a single, fleeting moment in time to share the love he has in his heart for me.

When he pulls away, we smile at one another and know that our kiss will forever be frozen in our memories.

"Are they here?" I ask, assuming he woke me for the meeting with the overlords.

"Yes. They're here. Do you feel up to going down and speaking with them?"

I give him my answer by trying to sit up. Malcolm helps me with that task, since my belly can make such a small movement awkward for me to do alone.

"Where is Lucas?" I ask, noticing he isn't in the bed anymore.

"I sent him down to the kitchen to get something to eat. I think he wanted to check on Vala and Luna anyway."

I notice Malcolm is dressed in a crisp-looking white shirt and black pants. I look down at myself and begin to worry about my disheveled appearance. Trying to preside over a meeting in my pajamas doesn't seem like something an empress should do.

"I need some clothes," I say, pointing out the obvious.

"Already thought about that," Malcolm assures me, walking over to the walk-in closet in the room. He soon reappears with one of my maternity dresses draped over an arm.

"You went back to Cirrus?" I practically yell.

Malcolm shrugs. "You needed things. I went and got them. It's not like those creatures can actually kill me anyway."

"Yes, but they can still hurt you," I admonish. "Did you at least take someone up there to watch your back?"

"Jered went with me, but, strangely enough, there weren't any hellspawn inside the palace."

I scowl at Malcolm so he knows how upset I am with him.

He just smiles back.

"I do love it when you get all feisty over my safety," he says, taking me into his arms as if I forgive him, which I do not. Not by a long shot.

I slap him hard on one arm, which makes him grunt in pain.

"I wasn't joking, Malcolm. If anyone is safe up there, it's me. I can go get my own belongings."

"I would rather you didn't have to look at those creatures," he says. "I remember the nightmares you had after our fight with them. You're too close to giving birth to begin having those night terrors again, Anna."

"What would upset me more is losing you." I wrap my arms around Malcolm's waist and rest my head against his chest.

"You won't lose me anytime soon, my love. I promise I won't die until after you do. I love you enough to make that sacrifice."

I lift my head and look up at him. "How can you make such a promise to me?"

"I plan to ask my father to do to me what he did for Mason. Mason was able to keep all of his angelic traits but physically age with Jess. Considering what we're fighting against, I think that's a better option than asking for true humanity. If I became human, I would become a liability to you. If I stay the way I am, and just age alongside you, I can be more useful in keeping our family safe."

"I do like that idea," I say. "Why did you just call it a sacrifice, though?"

"Because I would end up living here without you until I died a natural death. After you die, I'll ask to become human so that can happen. Maybe I'll pick a fight with a demon and end my torture quickly."

"You can't do that to our children," I tell him. "At least give them time to get over my loss before you die. It's not like I can't come back here to see you."

"True, but for you Earth would feel like it does when you go to Heaven now. You wouldn't feel like you should be here anymore."

"Well, that's too far in the future for me to even want to worry about right now. Let's just focus on what we need to do today."

Malcolm helps me get dressed, and I simply brush my hair out straight and braid it into a side ponytail. I sigh at my reflection, which Malcolm hears.

"What's wrong?" he asks, coming to stand behind me at my vanity.

"I hate this white hair," I complain. "Maybe I should start wearing a wig."

"Don't you dare," Malcolm says, aghast at my suggestion. "I like your hair just the way it is."

"It's not the color, really," I tell him. "It's the fact that I have it because of Helena. I feel like as long as I have it, she has a small bit of control over me."

"She can't control who you are or what you do, Anna."

"But she did use our connection to one another to pull me down to Hell."

"She hasn't done it since then, has she?"

"No. But that doesn't mean that she can't. Maybe she just hasn't had any reason to."

"Let's not worry about it. It's not a problem that we can solve yet, and, like you said earlier, we have enough to deal with today."

Malcolm holds out his hand for me to take and helps me stand from my chair.

My stomach grumbles its protest at not being fed yet. I hope Giles stays true to his promise to me about breakfast.

Malcolm phases us directly down to the dining room, where we find most everyone in the house sitting around the table eating breakfast. All five of my overlords are present and grouped at one end of the table, eating and talking amongst themselves. Of course, Brutus and Giles are present. Also among the group is Barlow Stokes, who we made Overlord of Manufacturing; David Dean, who is Overlord of Agriculture; and Sean Rhodes, Overlord of Raw Minerals.

After Malcolm and I assumed control over Cirrus, we fired two of the five overlords because of their cruelty to the down-worlders who worked for them. We only allowed David and Sean to keep their posts because Malcolm knew them to be good men who treated their workers fairly.

David was a tall, lean man with brown hair and kind brown eyes. This was only the third time that I had ever been in his presence, but he gave off an effortless warmth that filled you from head to toe whenever he looked at you. There wasn't any doubt in my mind that he was a man who could be trusted.

Sean Rhodes, on the other hand, did not hold my trust, even though Malcolm assured me that we could rely on him. Sean was the eldest of the overlords and slightly past his prime at the age of sixty-eight. His skin was the color of rich caramel, and he always kept his greying hair cut close to the scalp. Whenever he looked at me, I felt like I was being judged and found lacking in his estimation of my character. I wasn't comfortable around him, but I trusted Malcolm to know what was best concerning Sean's leadership skills.

The rest of the table is filled by all seven members of my War Angel guard, along with Jered, Desmond, and my papa.

"It's about time you showed up, lass," Desmond says when he sees us. "How are you feeling? Do I need to do a quick examination of the babies?"

"I'm fine, and I think the babies are fine, too," I say, feeling an ache in my belly that has nothing to do with the children growing inside my womb. Well, not directly anyway. "We're all just very hungry at the moment."

Giles stands up and walks over to a silver cart in the room where two plates sit, wrapped in foil.

Malcolm escorts me to the two chairs at the head of the table and pulls out my chair for me to sit in. Giles brings us our plates and uncovers them. I smile when I see that my plate does, indeed, have twice as much food as Malcolm's plate.

"You're going to spoil her, Giles," Malcolm half-heartedly complains.

"Well, I think she deserves to be spoiled a little, don't you?"

"More than a little," Malcolm agrees, taking his seat beside me.

I'm so hungry, I don't give anyone a chance to say anything else to me before I grab my fork and dig in.

"Wow," Desmond says in amazement, "she must have inherited that from Jess."

"Jess *was* quite a vigorous eater," Jered agrees.

I look up at the two men as I chew a mouthful of eggs. I swallow before I say, "If the two of you were responsible for growing two babies inside your bodies, I have no doubt that you would be eating just as heartily."

"Unquestionably," Jered agrees with a smile before taking a sip from his coffee cup. "I think we were just all having fond memories of Jess and her total lack of table manners."

Malcolm chuckles. "I have to admit it was amusing to watch her eat sometimes."

"Was she always a messy eater?" I have to ask.

"No. Just when she was hungry like you are now."

"Well, she probably just didn't want to waste time," I say, as an excuse for my ancestor. "I can totally sympathize with her plight, especially if she was pregnant."

"She did seem to eat more…uh… energetically when she was with child," Jered agrees. "I thought she was going to eat Mason out of house and home when she was pregnant with Luke."

"Was there any particular reason why?" I ask out of curiosity.

"We're still not entirely sure," Desmond answers, sounding baffled. "Luke was conceived while we were on alternate Earth, and Jess' pregnancy was rather difficult for her. Lucifer seemed to suggest it was because of where he was conceived, but he never did explain why it mattered."

"Well," Jered says, "we do sort of know why it mattered."

"What do you mean?" I ask.

Jered looks thoughtful as he remembers Jess' son. "Luke was somehow connected to alternate Earth by being conceived there."

"Connected?"

"He would…" Jered stops to collect his thoughts on the matter. "He would sometimes have dreams about it. It was almost like he could see what was happening there in real time. Did you know he and Caylin's daughter, Kate, were the ones who married to join the two families together?"

"Yes," I say, still finding this information about my family's past immensely interesting. "I've seen their names on the family tree my mother painted."

Jered nods his head. "Strangely enough, some of the descendants ended up inheriting his ability to see what was happening on alternate Earth through their dreams. Have you ever experienced dreams about it?"

"I don't think so," I say hesitantly. "Even if I had, I'm not sure I would know it."

"True," Jered concedes. "And not every descendant was born with the capability."

The story about my ancestors fascinates me, but I find any information concerning my family's past interesting. I begin to wonder if I will ever have dreams about the alternate Earth Malcolm went to with Jess. In fact, if I remember correctly, Jered also went there with them. Neither man seemed to like to talk about the experience too much. From what I could gather, it wasn't a pleasant period in their lives. It was where they lost Gabe. Considering Lucas is Gabe reincarnated, I can only imagine how hard his death was on all of them. I don't even want to imagine my life without Lucas in it.

After we eat, Giles and his servants clear the table so we can discuss what to do about the refugees from Cirrus.

"Well," Sean Rhodes says, "I know they're scattered all over New York State, but we're going to have to move them. We simply don't have enough resources there to keep them all housed and fed."

"Would some of the down-worlders be willing to let them stay in their homes?" I ask, coming up with a plan that might help us all in the long run. "Perhaps we should look at this catastrophe as a blessing in disguise."

"What do you mean?" Malcolm asks, looking confused by my suggestion.

"Well, for months now we've been trying to think of a way for the people of Cirrus to get to know the down-worlders. This might be the perfect opportunity to do just that."

"I have to say," Barlow chimes in, "that's actually a brilliant idea. There's no better way for the Cirruns to understand the conditions down here than by living in them. Maybe if they have to live outside their cushy lifestyles for a little while, they'll see what needs to be done and start supporting the changes you want to make."

"Well, that's all well and good," Sean says, not sounding too enthusiastic about my suggestion, "but I don't see the people down here offering what little they have to a bunch of puffed-up cloud city folk. Most down-worlders resent the people who live in Cirrus. They're not going to just open their doors and invite them to stay in their homes."

"You don't know that," I say defensively. "Deep down, I believe people will do the right thing, and, in this moment, the right thing to do is give aid to those who have been run out of their homes in the middle of the night by creatures sent straight from Hell!"

My outburst causes immediate silence, and I belatedly realize I shouldn't have yelled at Sean. He was simply speaking the truth. There was no way to make the down-worlders help the people who had lorded over them for years, and I wouldn't force them to do it. They would have to make the decision of whether or not they wanted to help their fellow man on their own.

"I'm sorry," I tell Sean. "I didn't mean to raise my voice to you. Please accept my apology."

"There's no need for you to apologize," Sean says with a small shake of his head, looking at me with newfound respect. "I'm glad to see you passionate about something. It shows how different you are from Catherine."

"Where is Catherine, by the way?" I ask. Surely, one of them knows what happened to Auggie's mother.

"She's safe," Ethan informs me. "After I made sure Desmond was taking care of Linn, I went to Lady Sophia's home and got her and Catherine out."

"Where are they now?" I ask.

Ethan fidgets in his chair and looks down at the table's surface before saying, "They're in Nimbo."

"Doesn't Catherine know that Helena is the one who caused this problem?"

"No," Ethan tells me, looking me in the eyes. "No one does."

"What do you mean no one does? Someone had to have seen her in Cirrus. Wasn't there any video surveillance running when she killed Jenny?"

"Everything was down," Ethan replies. "Only the emergency energy supplies were running at the time, and video surveillance isn't considered necessary during a power failure. Only we saw what she is capable of."

I look at Cade, who is remaining suspiciously quiet. He's staring down at his plate, either unwilling or unable to meet my gaze. Since he now understands the horror she is capable of unleashing into the world, I wonder if he still thinks Helena is worth saving. What little pity I had for Helena immediately evaporated when I saw her rip out Jenny's throat like she was simply stepping on a bug in her path. Her total disregard for human life seemed to indicate to me that she is beyond redemption.

"And no one is going to believe us if we begin to slander my accusers," I say, realizing how well Helena had thought everything out.

"Well," Brutus says, "I think we need to concentrate on one thing at a time. Let's figure out how we're going to move people and get them settled."

We decide to send out a broadcast to all the escape pods and tell people to stay where they are for now. Since each pod had a homing beacon, we could easily track each one and pick people up in transporters to move them to safety. There were always transport ships coming and going from the various ports in the down-world. We would simply have to interrupt their shipping schedules so that they could help us transport people throughout the down-world. David Dean volunteers to coordinate with the more affluent down-worlders to see if they can house some of the Cirruns. Barlow even offers to take a couple thousand refugees to live with his people near the mountains. The more we talk about what we can do, the less dire the situation seems to be. The solution isn't as impossible as I first believed, and I have hope we can indeed use this as an opportunity to unite the people of Cirrus with the down-worlders.

Once our meeting is over and a plan is agreed upon, I know I need to do one more thing that day. I pull Malcolm aside and out of earshot of the others.

"What's going on?" Malcolm asks me, looking worried.

"Nothing is wrong," I tell him in a low voice. "I just need to take a little trip somewhere. I pray the babies will phase me there."

"Where do you need to go?"

"Heaven. I need to talk to Lucifer about Helena. Maybe he can lend me some insight into what will help us defeat her."

"I think that's a good idea, actually," Malcolm says. He leans down and gives me a less-than-chaste kiss. I wonder if he's purposely trying to make my world spin even more out of control than it already is. When he draws his lips away from mine, he whispers, "Come back to me."

"Will that kiss continue when I do?"

Malcolm smiles. "Among other things, if you want."

"If I want," I say with a roll of my eyes. "Silly man. You shouldn't even feel the need to wonder."

I rub my hands over my stomach and mentally prepare myself for my visit to Heaven. Malcolm was right earlier when he mentioned the difference between being in Heaven and being on Earth. The living didn't belong in Heaven, and the dead didn't belong on Earth. Every time I visited Heaven, I felt like something was pushing me to return to my own realm of existence. It stood to reason that the same could be said for the dearly departed when they came back here. I suppose that was one reason I rarely saw my ancestors. However, Lilly did say she would come down when the babies were born, to see the next generation.

"Ok Liana and Liam, Mommy needs to go see her dad in Heaven. Would you mind taking me to him?"

Without needing to say another word, the children phase me to Heaven for a reunion with Lucifer that is long overdue.

Awakening

CHAPTER TWENTY

Once upon a time, the first of all angels was conceived by God to fill the lonely void His existence had become. This angel was created to be second only to God in strength of mind and form. His love for his father was unparalled by any and all who were made after him. He was so stubborn and headstrong that only he could ever fathom defying God's orders and raging a celestial war against Him. This angel's name was Lucifer, and I am honored to call him my father. I'm proud because, in the end, he chose the right path and humbled himself before God to ask for His forgiveness. He didn't lose who he was in that moment. He found it.

For some reason, I expected the babies to phase me to Lilly's piece of Heaven, which looks like the Colorado home Malcolm built for her back on Earth. Instead, I'm standing in front of an exact replica of the home Lucifer and my mother shared while they were married. I've been to it a few times, but, of course, after years of neglect it had fallen into ruin.

Rays of warm sunlight stream down through the canopy of trees surrounding their small, heavenly home. The house itself is quaint in a storybook sort of way. From its steeply-pitched cedar-shingled roof to its rustic stone walls and lead-paned windows, the home exudes the very definition of old-world charm. Vines with small pink roses grow along the corners of the dwelling, reaching up to the balconies on the sides and front of the house. The flowers appear to be spectators wishing to take part in the happiness residing within the interior of the walls, if only for a little while.

Suddenly, the front door opens, and I see my mother and father standing in the entryway, smiling at me. The warmth of their love for one another fills my heart, giving me hope that all will be well in my reality, given enough time. Before I can take a step forward, my mother phases and has her arms wrapped around me.

"Oh, Anna," she says, her voiced filled with the love only a mother can have for her child, "it's so good to see you." My mother pulls back from me, her hands still on my forearms as she looks down at my protruding belly. "And to see the evidence of my unborn grandchildren. I told Lucifer that you would be having them any day now, but he insisted that it was months away."

"Well," Lucifer says, walking out of the house to stand in front of me, "my sense of time has been off by a lot since I returned. I haven't quite gotten used to being back on Heaven time yet."

Lucifer leans in and gives me a peck on the cheek.

"You look ravishing, Anna," Lucifer tells me with a proud smile. "I guess that big oaf is treating you well enough."

"I thought you would have given up on making condescending remarks about Malcolm by now," I say in exasperation.

"What can I say? Old habits die hard. I think I can tease my daughter about the man she's chosen to make a life with on Earth. Isn't that what most fathers do?"

"Not quite as vocally as you."

Lucifer shrugs. "I can't make any excuses for myself. I am who I am, and some things will never change about me. I will, however, concede that I know he treats you well. If he didn't, I feel sure I would know about it and find a way to come back and knock some sense into him."

I can't help but let out a small laugh. "That won't be necessary. If anything, Malcolm gives overprotectiveness a whole new meaning."

"He does realize you're more powerful than he is, doesn't he?"

"Of course he does, but he's still my husband."

"Besides, this is Malcolm we're talking about," my mother adds. "He was always protective of us girls. You remember the lengths he went to in order to try to keep you and me apart, Lucifer."

"Yes," Lucifer says ominously. "I remember his attempts quite well."

"Why don't we change the subject before you lose that halo you earned back?" I suggest to Lucifer, not wanting to upset him. "I actually came up here to get some advice from you."

"How can I help you?" Lucifer asks, looking concerned about the fact that I felt the need to come all the way to Heaven to seek his counsel.

"Helena has become a problem," I begin. I go on to tell my parents exactly what's been happening on Earth the past few days.

Lucifer looks troubled by the recount of Helena's antics.

"If I hadn't wallowed in self-pity and grief for so long," he says, "she never would have become powerful enough to steal the seals from you or connect to you the way she has. I'm sorry for making you go through this, Anna. It was never my intention to leave you a mess to clean up on my behalf."

"I don't blame you," I tell him. "And you shouldn't blame yourself. What's done is done. I just need to know if there is a way that I can trap her back in Hell or not."

"If you can kill the body she made herself," Lucifer says, "that should be enough to force the part of her soul which resides in the body back to Hell, but…"

From the look of worry on my father's face, I know I won't like what he has to say next.

"But, what?" I prod.

"But, if she retains the energy she derived from the seals, there's really nothing to prevent her from making a new body in Hell and traveling back through the veil again. The only way to ensure that she stays in Hell is to take the seals away from her; if not all, at least some."

"Can I do that?" I ask.

Lucifer shrugs. "I'm really not sure. The only way to know is for you to try."

"Ok, let's say I can take at least some of the seals from her; how do I destroy the body she's in? I stabbed her with my sword, but it didn't do anything. Her body instantly healed from the wound."

"Really?" Lucifer asks, sounding alarmed but also intrigued by this bit of new information. "I thought your sword would be enough. Did you use your power on her? The one you use to kill archangels."

"I tried, but …" I hate to say what happened. I haven't even told Malcolm this part yet. "I think the babies prevented me from using it on her. They've been controlling my phasing, too."

I decide not to tell them that the children keep phasing me to Helena. What I just told them is more than I wanted them to know as it is.

"Well, that's troubling," my mother says, looking worried.

"It's possible it wouldn't have worked anyway," Lucifer states. "She isn't an angel. I'm not quite sure what you would categorize her as, to be honest. She doesn't exactly fit into any class of known creature."

"That's basically what Malcolm said."

"Well, he and I don't agree often, but on this point we do. What's troubling me now is this unknown factor that's trying to kill you. She didn't say anything more to you about it?"

"No," I say with a shake of my head. "She just said that if I win the election, this person or persons will try to kill me and the babies."

"I can tell you one thing: I wouldn't trust anything Helena says. She's keeping you alive for her own reasons, and I'm sure they are selfish ones. Don't ever make the mistake of thinking she cares about you, Anna. She isn't capable of loving the way you think of love."

"She has a soul-mate," I reveal to my parents, just now remembering that I forgot to mention that important fact earlier.

"Oh, my goodness," my mom says, looking aghast by the prospect. "Who's the unlucky person?"

"Cade. You might have known him as Dumah up here."

"Are you telling me her soul-mate is the War Angel you made to protect you during the war?" Lucifer asks.

"Apparently."

"Talk about ironic."

"That poor man," my mom says, looking distressed by this news.

I feel that tug on my soul telling me that it's time for me to leave Heaven. I've stayed longer than I intended to, but I had hoped one of my parents would be able to come up with a plan to take care of my Helena problem. Since it seems like neither of them can suggest something I haven't already thought of, I decide it's time to leave.

"I'll let the two of you get back to whatever it is you were doing," I say, not wanting to pry into their privacy. "Thanks for trying to help. If you happen to think of something else, please let me know."

"Of course we will," Lucifer says, leaning over to kiss me on the cheek before I go. "You take care of yourself and those babies. I have to admit, it gives me an almost guilty pleasure envisioning Malcolm changing dirty diapers."

I laugh. "I'm afraid we both will, but I'm looking forward to meeting my little girl and boy."

"Lucifer," my mom says, "would you mind giving me a moment alone with Anna? I would like to ask her about that little concern I've been having."

Lucifer nods his head understandingly. "Of course. I'll wait for you inside. Be careful, Anna, and keep safe."

"I will," I promise.

Lucifer walks back into the house, and my mother takes my arm to escort me a short distance up the cobblestone walkway to an iron bench underneath a trellis of blooming wisteria.

After we sit down, she turns to me and asks, "Tell me, how is Alex doing on Earth? Is he adapting well?"

"Honestly, I don't know. He decided he wanted to be stationed in the down-world not long after we assumed control of Cirrus. He hasn't really said that much to me since the War Angels arrived."

"I see," my mom says, looking troubled by this news.

"Why are you asking about him?" I inquire, wondering why she seems so concerned about this War Angel in particular.

My mother smiles wanly. "He and I spent a great deal of time together after I arrived in Heaven. He was floundering here, and God thought we might be able to help one another."

"Floundering?" I ask. "How so?"

"When he was created by his Guardian in the Guf, something went wrong during the process. He ended up having a hard time verbally articulating his thoughts to other people. It was extremely frustrating for him, and he tended to keep his distance from the other angels because of it. After I came here, God asked me if I would act as a nurturing force in Alex's life. I think He knew that we both needed what the other could provide."

"And what was that exactly?"

"He needed someone who wouldn't push him to talk, and I needed someone I could take care of. Since I couldn't be with you, he was the next best thing."

I know I shouldn't, but I feel offended that my mother lavished Alex with her love while I got nothing from her while I was growing up. It's a ridiculous form of jealously, but I can't help it. I'm having a human moment. I feel as though I was cheated out of experiencing my mother's affection while Alex was showered with it.

"I was wondering," she says, "if you could look out for him for me."

"He's a grown man," I say defensively. "Why do I need to do that?"

My mother looks a little taken aback by my tone with her, but I can't help it. I want to be the bigger person in this scenario, but my heart just won't let me.

"He doesn't make friends easily," my mother goes on to explain. "I was hoping you would be one to him."

"If he wants to be my friend, he can ask me himself," I say, pushing my hands against the bench to help me stand to my feet. "I need to go. I have things that need to be done back home."

"Anna," my mother says in alarm, "have I said something that's upset you? I didn't think you would mind helping Alex out, especially after you learned how much he means to me."

"Help him?" I ask, almost angrily. "Why do you think I would help someone who got to experience things with you that I never will? It's obvious you're more concerned about his feelings than you are mine, but I guess I shouldn't be surprised by that."

"That's not true, Anna," my mother says, on the verge of tears. "I do love Alex, but I never used him to replace you in my life. You have had a place in my heart since the moment you were conceived. I began loving you while you were still inside my womb, just like I know you love the babies growing inside your own right now. Alex is a dear friend to me, but you're my baby. You always will be, even when you're old and gray. Please, don't be mad at him because he chose to show me kindness when I needed it the most. I was so lonely here without you and your father. I remained that way for a very long time, but Alex helped me through the worst periods by being a true friend to me. We helped each other cope with our own frailties and came out a little bit stronger because of it. So please, don't punish him because you think I love him more than I do you. There's no one in Heaven or Earth that I love more than you, Anna. No one."

The threads of jealously that were strangling my heart are slowly drawn back into their dark crevice after my mother's words.

"I'm sorry," I say, feeling embarrassed by my small tantrum. "I shouldn't have become so jealous."

"You're human," my mother reminds me. "And we humans are delicate creatures when it comes to our love for one another. I should have thought of your feelings before asking you to look after Alex for me."

"I'll watch over him for you," I promise her, hoping it makes up for my foolish outburst. "Though that might be easier said than done. He hasn't wanted to be around me much since the War Angels came to Earth. He's purposely kept his distance from me."

"It could be that he doesn't want to upset you like I just did," my mom suggests. "If you had learned about our relationship from him, how do you think you would have reacted?"

"Probably the way I just did," I admit, feeling ashamed of myself.

"Then that's most likely why he has kept away. He didn't want to run the risk of upsetting you, especially while you're pregnant. That's just the kind of person he is, always looking out for others."

"Well, now I feel like a complete heel," I confess, feeling doubly ashamed. "I'll reach out to him. I don't want him to feel as though he has to hide from me."

"Thank you," my mom says, leaning in and giving me a hug. "I love you, Anna. I always have and I always will. Please remember that."

"I love you, too, Mom," I say, hugging her back.

"Now, go home and solve your Helena problem. I know you'll find a way to deal with her, and try to keep faith that you'll make the right decisions."

"I'll try," I say, hugging my mom one more time before I go.

After I pull away from her, I place my hands on my belly and say, "Okay, babies. It's time to go home."

I always feel a mixture of relief and regret when I phase out of Heaven. I'm glad to be going, but, then again, I hate leaving behind my loved ones. In time, I'll be able to share more moments with my mother and father, but I'm not in any hurry. I have a lot of life to live and a host of memories to make with Malcolm and our children. Heaven will always be waiting for me.

The babies phase me back to the bedroom I share with Malcolm in our New Orleans home. Unfortunately, my husband is nowhere to be seen, so I make my way out of the room. As I'm walking down the hallway, towards the staircase leading to the first floor, I notice Malcolm's study door is ajar. Taking the chance that he might be in there, I walk over to the door and push it completely open.

Instead of finding my husband, I find the other soul I need to talk to today. I surmise that Devine intervention may be playing a role in this fortuitous happenstance.

Alex is sitting on the couch with a book in his hands. I seem to startle him with my unannounced entry. His head jerks up so fast I fear he may have injured it in some way.

"I'm sorry," I tell him. "I didn't mean to interrupt you. I thought Malcolm might be in here."

"No, he's downstairs in the living room with the others," Alex says in a quiet voice.

Remembering the promise I just made to my mother, I walk further into the room and ask, "What are you reading that has you so captivated?"

Alex closes the book in his hands and holds it up for me to see the cover.

"*The Campaigns of Alexander the Great*," I read aloud. "Got something against a good romance novel?"

Alex smiles. "Not at all; I love any story that makes me feel something, but Alexander's ability to lead men has always intrigued me. You have that same quality."

"Thank you," I reply. "At the moment I feel like I'm treading water and just trying not to drown."

Alex smiles shyly. "If there's one thing I'm absolutely sure of, it's that you will come out victorious in this war with Helena. There may be losses. There may even have to be sacrifices, but you won't allow her to win."

"How can you say that with so much conviction? You barely know me."

Alex sets his book on the coffee table in front of him before meeting my gaze again.

"Malcolm told us you went to see Lucifer and Amalie in Heaven," he replies. "I assume she asked you about me."

I nod. "Yes, she did. My mother wanted to know how you were getting along here."

"I thought so," Alex says with a look of acceptance. "She's always worried over me too much. I can confidently say you will win because I see a lot of your mother in you. You're both stubborn to a fault and will always fight for what you believe in. I don't believe your destiny is to fail in this life, Anna. You were born to accomplish great deeds, and I don't see Helena in the same light. She wants things she was never supposed to have. She thinks she wants to be real, but I'm not sure she thought through all the consequences of having a corporeal body. I certainly doubt she thought she would meet her soul-mate in a man who couldn't be more her opposite if he tried."

"You almost sound sorry for her."

"Not sorry, really, but I can sympathize with her plight."

"Do you think she deserves our mercy?"

"No. She is evil and must be stopped no matter how you choose to do it. I think we've all seen just how cruel and ruthless she can be. Helena doesn't cherish life like we do, but I think that's because she's never lost someone she truly loves."

"I'm not even sure she can love."

"I suppose the debate could go either way on that subject, but whether she can or not isn't relevant. She's incapable of treasuring humanity; that much seems clear. She just sees them as future disciples in a universe she believes belongs to her. You will have to make her see the error in her thinking, Anna. You're the only one she views as an equal to her."

"I'll stop her," I promise. "Somehow."

Without much else to say, I ask, "Would you like to come down with me and join the others? I'm sure they would love to have you with us."

Alex shakes his head. "No, thank you. I would rather stay and finish my book, if that's all right."

I nod. "Of course, but I want you to know that I consider you a part of my family, just like I do all the others. You are always welcome in whatever home we might be staying in."

"Thank you."

I turn to leave, pulling the door shut, but leave it slightly ajar, just as I found it, when I re-enter the hallway.

After I make my way downstairs, I find my family gathered in the living room. Before I can go to Malcolm and Lucas, who are playing a game of checkers, Cade approaches me.

"Can I have a private word with you?" he asks urgently.

"Of course."

Cade motions that I should precede him into the foyer, away from the others.

"What's wrong, Cade?"

"I heard what Helena said about someone trying to kill you. I would like your permission to go to her to see if I can learn anything else."

"Do you realize how dangerous that could be for you? We don't even know if she was telling me the truth. It could just be a scare tactic, for all we know."

"I think it's worth investigating at least. I might learn something, or I might not. We won't know unless I try."

"Are you really going to her because you want to see if she will confide in you, or are you going to her in hopes of understanding how she can be so cruel? It can't be easy for you to rationalize your feelings towards her and know the atrocities she's capable of committing."

"No. It's not easy," Cade admits. "I don't know if she can change who she is. I may be hoping for the impossible, but maybe all she needs is someone to show her she doesn't have to be the person Lucifer created her to be."

"What if she likes being the way she is? What if, instead of you changing her, she changes you?"

"That won't happen," Cade says confidently. "I could never be like her."

"Have you thought about the fact that she might be saying the same exact thing? That she will never be like you?"

"I don't understand how anyone would want to care for no one but themselves. It makes for a lonely, unfulfilling life."

"Yes," I agree, "it does for us, but perhaps not for her." I study Cade for a moment before I say, "Go to her. See what you can learn, but don't stay there long. Don't make me come look for you."

"I won't stay long," Cade pledges. "It probably won't take much time to find out if she plans to answer my questions truthfully or if she's just stringing me along."

"Watch your back, and return to us in one piece."

Cade nods his head and phases.

From his phase trail, I see that he's gone to Nimbo. I wish him the best of luck in his fact-finding mission. He's going to need it.

CHAPTER TWENTY-ONE

(Helena's Point of View: After Cade's departure from the party in Nimbo the night before)

I thought when I took on a physical form my life would be made easier, but ever since I became flesh and bone, everything has felt like a jumbled mess. I *feel* too much. I find it hard to concentrate sometimes because my body is in a constant confused state of raging chemical reactions and sensitive nerve endings trying to make me connect to the world around me. I go to Hell sometimes just to clear my mind and find a little peace. That might be exactly what I need to do right now to get rid of this overwhelming sadness I feel. I don't like it. I don't like feeling vulnerable. It's a sign of weakness that I can't afford to show.

"Well, I guess I don't have to worry about lover boy after all," Levi sneers smugly. "Like most men, he was just using you to get what he wanted, and I guess he didn't particularly want you as much as you thought."

"Leave," I order through clenched teeth, striving to keep my composure when all I want to do is kill Levi. "Get out of my sight, or, so help me, I will strangle that body you call home and toss it over this railing without a second thought!"

"Tsk, tsk. Cade really does bring out the beast in you," Levi gloats. "If I didn't know any better, I would say you have feelings for him."

I whirl around and grab Levi by the throat, lifting him a few feet in the air.

"Don't say I didn't warn you!" I state in a low, menacing growl to avoid drawing the attention of the partygoers in the ballroom.

"Wait," Levi strangles out, desperately clutching at my hand with both of his. "You need me."

I laugh derisively. "I can live without you, but you're right. For the moment, I do need you in order to retain my position here in Nimbo, at least until I can get that stupid law changed about the succession of only male heirs. Anna circumvented the law in Cirrus. I'm sure I can do it here in Nimbo, too. So, count your lucky stars, Levi. I will allow you to live until your presence in my life is no longer required."

I loosen my grip to allow Levi to drop to the floor. He lands on his feet, but the redness around the front of his throat won't go away anytime soon. I hope it acts as a reminder that he's only alive because of my benevolence.

"Get away from me," I order in disgust, "before I change my mind."

Levi's scowl is almost amusing as he turns to walk back into our wedding party. When he opens the glass door to the room, someone else darkens its opening. I begin to wonder if I'll ever get any peace this night.

"What do you want, Hale?" I ask the leader of a rebellion angel faction that has been trying to interfere with my plans for Anna since I arrived.

The man steps through the door and comes to stand with me on the veranda. Hale chose a rather nice-looking human form: tall, light brown skin, a handsome face, and short brown hair.

"I want what you promised us," Hale says, his hazel eyes daring to accuse me of not keeping my end of our bargain.

"What more do you want?" I ask, becoming irritated with his demands. "I've humiliated Anna in front of the whole world. Once this election goes through, she'll lose her throne and be shamed even further. That's what I promised you in exchange for your patience in this matter. Isn't that enough to pacify you until the babies are born?"

"The only reason we are being so patient," Hale says, placing a special emphasis on the last word, "is because we don't want one of the other princes thinking they can take Lucifer's place and control us. At least with you we know where we stand."

"And as soon as the babies are born, I'll have everything I need to remain more powerful than the princes. We've already had this conversation once, Hale. I'm not sure what else it is that you want me to do."

"I want you to make her feel pain," Hale says vehemently, his face contorted by barely-controlled rage. "I want her to suffer so much loss in her life that it hurts Lucifer as much as he hurt us."

"I know you feel like he abandoned you…"

"He did abandon us! He's the one who led us all into a war against God! Now, he's back in Heaven, living in paradise with his little wifey, while we remain stuck here on this god-forsaken planet. How is that fair? How is that justice for what he did to our lives?"

"Lucifer never forced you to follow him," I remind Hale. "You chose to do that all on your own. So, don't blame him for your failings. Look in a mirror and blame the person who stares back at you."

"We still want retribution," Hale says ominously, "and there are many of us who don't think you're doing enough to make Anna suffer. We're losing patience, Helena. You may be able to kill some of us, but certainly not all of us at once. We number in the thousands. One of us *can* get to Anna before she's able to react. We can slice her throat wide open and stab those babies dead while they're still inside her womb. Her little Guardian Angel Will might be able to save her life, but there won't be enough left of the babies for him to piece back together to save theirs. You know we can do it if we all band together, and there's nothing like mutual hatred to ensure victory."

"So you're asking me to do more to make her suffer sufficiently to satisfy your craving for revenge?" I ask, knowing Hale's threat isn't an empty one. I've been keeping him and his followers at bay for a while now, but their impatience for blood seems to be reaching a fever pitch.

"Yes," Hale answers, making the word sound like a snake's hiss.

"Fine. Tell your people to go to Cirrus tonight. I need a few hours to put things together, but I think they'll enjoy the show once it begins."

"Is there any particular location in Cirrus that you want us to be?"

"Tell them to make sure they don't stand on the streets. I would advise them to choose a high vantage point to stay safe."

"Care to share what you have planned?"

"And ruin the surprise for you? Never."

I phase to Hell because I'm weary of having to talk to a lowly rebellion angel with a superiority complex. As soon as I'm home, I instantly feel at peace. It makes me wonder why I torture myself on Earth, and then I remember my plan.

Hale and the others aren't the only ones Lucifer deserted. He left me here to fend for myself, too. Though, strangely enough, I don't blame Anna for what happened. Lucifer had been weakened by that bitch, Amalie, long before Anna was born. What happened to Lucifer was more Amalie's fault than my sister's. Oh, how I wish I had the ability to phase into Heaven and disrupt their happy little afterlife together. Unfortunately, I'm not that powerful… at least not yet.

I phase into my favorite part of Hell, where the leviathans are kept. They may be grotesque to some, but they are one of my favorite creations; so large and bloodthirsty. Yet their true majesty has only been realized on that alternate Earth Lucifer visited. When he came back and shared his memories of that place with me, I felt envious of that Earth's version of Hell. I probably would have wept with joy to see my favorite creations roam free in the living world.

I wish I had enough power to break open a big enough tear in the veil between Heaven and Earth to transport them all into the land of the living, but even I can't do that yet.

I phase to another section of Hell which contains what is essentially an experiment gone terribly wrong. The hellspawn are certainly nightmare-inducing, just like I wanted them to be, but they are also quite dimwitted. I'm not sure what went wrong when I made them, but even mindless drones can have their uses. One advantage that they have is their hive-mind. If I give an instruction to one, all the hellspawn hear it. The stench in this part of Hell is overpowering, to say the least. It was tolerable enough before I had a functioning body, but now the smell makes me want to vomit.

"Listen up!" I tell them as I stand on a rocky cliff above more than a million hellspawn, trapped together in their small corner of Hell. "I have a job for some of you to do, but there is one rule you *must* obey. None of you, and I mean not even one of you, is to touch my sister, Anna. Eat, maim, murder all the humans and angels you want, but she is off-limits. Is that understood?"

The hellspawn grunt in response, because that's about all they can manage with their limited intellect.

"For every one of you that dies on the surface, two of you are instructed to take their place. You have free rein of the streets and most of the buildings in Cirrus, but you are not allowed to go into the palace or underground passageways. I don't want every citizen within the city annihilated, just scared witless. Grunt if you understand what I'm saying."

From the chorus of guttural responses, I take it they comprehend my instructions.

"Prepare yourselves," I tell them. "We'll be leaving shortly."

I phase up to my private sanctuary, and sit on the bench Lucifer himself loved to rest on to watch his own memories play out. I need a solitary moment to compose myself. It's never a good idea to rush into things without a clear head.

My thoughts end up centering on Cade. Perhaps I should kill him and be done with the whole 'soul-mates meet and fall in love' scenario. It's a ridiculous notion anyway. How can you fall in love with someone you don't even know? Ludicrous.

Yet…

I can't deny that there is some sort of kismet attraction between the two of us. Although, after tonight, I doubt I will have to deal with his puppy-love mentality anymore. He'll see how little I care about human life when I unleash my hellspawn on Cirrus. After that, he'll probably bolt like a scalded dog. Still, I hate to admit it, even to myself, but a part of me wants to see where this will all lead with Cade. If what I do tonight doesn't run him off, I may play with him some more just to see what happens. If nothing else, I could use him for sex. Levi was uncharacteristically astute about my curiosity concerning that particular pastime between humans. I do want to know what it feels like, and Cade seems physically fit enough to get the job done. Why shouldn't I do it with someone I at least consider attractive? I'm definitely not going to allow Levi into my bed.

I shiver with revulsion just at the thought of such a thing.

I have no doubt Cade would make a suitable lover. I'll just have to wait and see how his feelings change for me after tonight's events.

I sit for a little while longer, soaking up the comfort of my home. I know time is passing, but it doesn't really matter. I have plenty of it.

After I begin to feel like my old self again, I stand up from the bench and go back to the hellspawn. I lead them to a large fissure in the veil between Hell and Earth. I've been able to seal up many of the smaller cracks my ascension to the Earthly veil caused, but the larger ones like this will take more power than I possess to close. With a little manipulation, I'm able to force the crack to change positions and connect it directly to Cirrus.

I walk out onto a paved area in the center of town, where a gigantic bronze fountain is erected, splashing cool, clear water into the pool at its base.

"Go," I tell the hellspawn behind me. "Enjoy yourselves."

I phase to the ballroom in Anna's palace and walk out onto the balcony to bear witness to the chaos my hellspawn are about to unleash in the quiet streets of Cirrus. I almost feel sorry for the citizens of Anna's cloud city. They're about to face their worst nightmare come to life. Some of them will be able to keep their heads clear of fear, and escape, but some of them won't be as lucky. Really, if you think about it, I'm doing Anna a tremendous favor. I'm weeding out the weakest links in her city and making sure they don't pollute the gene pool any longer. The theory of survival of the fittest is about to be proven.

The first scream I hear sends a slight ripple of pleasure throughout my body. I wonder how many souls I'll reap tonight. The more I have in Hell, the stronger I become. Fear is a lovely thing to perpetuate, especially since the power of the seals increases exponentially when there's more of it floating around the universe. Every scream I hear is more power within my grasp. No matter what happens tonight, I'll grow stronger. Now that I think about it, I should have done this a long time ago.

As my hellspawn cover the streets below, I look around at the neighboring buildings and see a few rebellion angels taking in the show from their rooftop perches and balconies.

I watch the proceedings for a while before I'm rudely interrupted.

"Empress Solarin?"

I turn to find a pretty young thing wearing a black and white maid's uniform, standing a few feet behind me.

"Yes?" I say to her.

"I'm sorry, Your Majesty," the girl says with a curtsey, "but you need to leave. We're under attack and evacuating the city."

"How unfortunate," I say. "I guess you should be running along then. I'll be fine."

"I can't just allow you to stay here unprotected, Your Majesty. I was told to clear this area before I could leave. You need to come with me or use your personal transporter to escape."

I had one of the teleporters installed into my hand when I first came to Earth. Since my phasing was restricted to places that I had physically been to, it limited my ability to move around efficiently. With the teleporter, I am able to go almost anywhere I want.

"Let me help you," I say to the girl. "Where exactly do you need to go to get away from all of this?"

"We were told to go to the escape pods, Your Majesty."

I hold out my right hand and bring up my personal teleporter. I activate a 3-D map of Cirrus, and locate the area where the escape pods are stored. Every cloud city has a similar area built into their underbellies. I touch the spot on the map that I want to teleport to before I hold out my free hand to the girl.

"Come with me…" I leave the end hanging, for her to fill in her name.

"Jenny," the girl tells me. "I'm Empress Anna's personal maid."

I smile. "Well, that's just perfect, Jenny. I think you'll do just fine."

"Fine for what, Your Majesty?" Jenny asks as she accepts my hand.

"Fine for what I want to show Anna."

I place Jenny's hand in the crook of my arm before I press the button that activates my teleporter.

We find ourselves standing on the steps that lead down from the city streets to the area where the escape pods are housed. When I look straight ahead, I see my sister floating in the air above the crowd. I wonder if she realizes how magnificent she looks when she flies. It's almost as if she has an unseen wind blowing around her, making her white hair float slightly away from her body. Depending on your predisposition, you would either see her as an angel of mercy or one of certain doom.

I quickly twist Jenny's arm behind her back, forcing her to stand in front of me. Just before she lets out a startled cry for help, I wrap my other hand around the front of the girl's throat and squeeze, but not hard enough to kill. I stare straight ahead while the frightened masses of Cirrus pass us by without even giving us a first glance, much less a second one. They're more preoccupied with saving their own skins than worrying about little Miss Jenny and me.

I only have to wait a little while before Anna notices my presence. I phase back to where the crack in the veil between Hell and Earth is, to wait for my sister to follow. When she does, I can tell that she's more than mildly upset with me. True, I have made a shambles of her beautiful home, but, somewhere deep down inside, she had to expect it of me eventually.

Out of the corner of my eye, I notice Hale standing on a balcony of a house nearby. I can feel his intense stare without having to look him in the eye. He's watching and waiting to see what I'll do next. I know he wants to make Anna suffer, and what better way to do that than kill someone she cares at least a little bit about?

"I'm going to kill you!" Anna promises me.

Her anger just makes her even more striking to my eyes. It shows that she and I aren't that dissimilar from one another. We simply have different ways of expressing who we are.

"Not before I kill this one," I taunt her, hoping what I do next will satisfy Hale's need for bloodlust for at least a little while.

I hadn't planned to kill Anna's maid when I lured my sister here. In fact, I had intended to make a bargain with Anna. If she willingly abdicated her crown, I would gather up my toys from her city and take them back home. However, with Hale watching me, I can't afford to appear weak, and I know after I killed Jenny, Anna isn't going to be in any mood to enter into negotiations with me.

I grip the front of Jenny's throat and yank. It's a merciful death, probably one of the few I've ever performed myself. I toss the girl's corpse into the fountain's pool of blood so she can find peace among the dead bodies of her fellow citizens.

When I turn back to look at Anna, she's already upon me, stabbing her flaming sword directly into my gut. The pain is excruciating, but there's no way I would ever let her know that.

"Well," I say to her, doing my best not to grimace, "that certainly stings, but I'm afraid it isn't enough to kill me, Sister."

I force myself to drag my body off her sword, even though it hurts just as badly coming out as it did going in. Once the blade is removed, I feel my body begin to heal itself, and the pain quickly ebbs away.

"Get these things out of my city, Helena!" Anna shouts.

"Or what?" I ask her, seeing her demand as an empty one. "I don't take orders from you, Anna, and you need to heed my next words because they might just save your life."

"What are you talking about?"

Her confusion is almost cute.

"This may be hard for you to believe, but I'm not your enemy in this situation. I need you to stay alive, but there are others who want to make sure you and your babies die. I'm doing what I can to keep you safe, but you're making it increasingly difficult to work that small miracle, Sister."

The rest of our conversation is just me trying to convince her that she needs to lose the election in order to protect the babies gestating within her womb. Her children are the key to everything, and I won't have their lives placed in jeopardy. I don't know why Anna can't see that. She frustrates me beyond all reason sometimes.

Finally, I just tell her to go somewhere secure while I use an escape route I know she won't dare follow.

Once I'm back inside Hell, I collapse onto the bench to let my body fully recover from Anna's spiteful, and, quite frankly, childish act of vengeance. How can she not see that everything I'm doing is for her own good? She can become so blinded by her own emotions sometimes. I wish she could learn how to master her humanity.

I end up spending hours in my domain, soaking up its tranquility. It might seem odd to some to think of Hell as a place of sanctuary. For me, it's a direct extension of my soul that will always be a part of me, no matter what physical form I might take.

I allow myself the luxury of spending a few hours resting inside my home before returning to Nimbo.

By the time I go back, it's already morning in my cloud city. After I change clothes, I realize I'm ravenous. I seek out the dining room, where I know breakfast will be served, but, once I'm there, I wish I hadn't returned at all. Sitting at my table is Levi and the one-time Empress of Cirrus, Catherine Amador.

"Good morning!" Levi says cheerily as I walk in. He sits at one end of the table, with Catherine by his side. I decide to sit at the opposite end of the long table, doing my best to avoid having to converse with either one of them. I soon realize it's a hopeless cause.

"I hope you don't mind me staying here for a while, Helena," Catherine says to me, as if we're old friends. Little does she know that I only think of her as a pawn in my game of wills against Anna. "Zuri said I was welcome here for as long as I needed."

I smile tightlipped at Catherine. "By all means, you should stay as long as you like, Catherine. Our home is yours."

Catherine sighs heavily. "Well, I'm not sure how long that will be. It may take some time to figure out how to vanquish those hellish creatures that invaded Cirrus. I just hope this catastrophe has taught my citizens a valuable lesson. Anna will only lead them into further ruin. I'm sure it's all her fault those things invaded my city."

"I suppose winning the election will be a lot easier for you to do now," I say, motioning to a servant to bring me my food.

"Whenever we're able to have it," Catherine says worriedly. "Now that everyone is scattered in the down-world, I don't know when that will be."

"Anna is resourceful. I'm sure she'll have the situation handled shortly."

"Yes, well, since she's no doubt the cause for the whole state of affairs in the first place, she should be the one who has to clean this mess up," Catherine says haughtily.

The words 'over-privileged diva' come to my mind when I look at Catherine. She's lived the posh life for far too long and forgotten what it means to be humble, if that word was ever in her vocabulary to begin with. That was one of the main differences between Catherine and Anna. Even though Anna grew up with everything a girl could ask for, she still maintained her humbleness, and knew that being empress was an honor, not a right. It made Anna an idealistic fool who believed good would always conqueror evil, but I can't fault her for that. It's the way she was raised to think. Andre Greco coddled her too much as a child and protected her from all that was evil in the world. She didn't have to struggle for anything, yet even someone as sheltered as Anna understood that an empress shouldn't just be a figurehead. She had the power to change the world, and that's what she was at least attempting to do. In any other circumstance, I would probably applaud her aplomb, but I couldn't afford to do that now. Not when I was so close to making the world into what I wanted it to be.

I don't say much during the rest of the meal, even when either Catherine or Levi attempts to drag me into their banal conversation. I just don't have the patience to deal with their petting of each other's egos. I make up an excuse about having a headache after I eat, and retire to my private chambers for some peace and quiet.

As soon as I walk into the room, I feel his presence. I close my eyes and curse softly when I realize my moment of peace has been yanked completely out of my grasp.

Cade stands in my chambers, by the large window overlooking the city I now rule. He either senses or hears me enter and turns around to face me. The look of unmitigated disappointment on his face causes my heart to twist involuntarily inside my chest. I turn my back to him as I close the door behind me, in order to give myself a moment to compose my emotions.

When I turn around to face him, he's wearing the exact same expression. I allow my fury to rise to the surface and remember what he did to me the night before.

"Don't even look at me like that," I say tersely, refusing to forgive him so easily. "You have no right to, considering how you used me to get what you wanted last night."

"What I did didn't end thousands of innocent lives, Helena," Cade says disappointedly. "Is that why you did it? To get back at me?"

I stare at Cade for a moment before I bust out in laughter.

"Wow," I say, taking a breath, "I knew I had an ego, but that, my dear, takes the cake, as the humans say. Do you honestly believe that I would do all of that just to spite you for humiliating me? Please, stop thinking you mean that much to me, Cade. Arrogance doesn't become you."

"Then why did you do it?" Cade pleads, wanting to understand my motives. "Was it truly to protect Anna from these people you say want to kill her?"

"All you need to know is that Anna is safe for now. I've handled things."

"Who is trying to hurt Anna?"

I narrow my eyes at Cade, finally understanding why he's really here.

"Is that the only reason you came to see me? Are you hoping to use our connection to one another to persuade me to answer that question?"

"I don't know why you won't tell us," Cade says, not denying that he's only here to get information Anna needs from me. "If your motive last night was to protect her and the babies, you should tell me who is trying to harm Anna so we can protect her even more. How are we supposed to fight against an unseen force?"

"I don't need you and the other War Angels slaying a group of people I will need later on," I reply irritably. "Just leave things as they are, Cade, and everything will work out the way it's supposed to."

"What's your motivation to protect Anna?" Cade asks directly. "She doesn't believe it's out of the goodness of your heart."

"And what do you believe? Do you think there actually is goodness in my heart?"

"I hope that there is," Cade admits, looking doubtful, "but, considering what you did last night, I'm not sure hoping is enough."

"I'm a selfish bitch. I make no excuses for that, Cade. I do whatever I feel is necessary. Don't stand there and think that you will ever be able to change who or what I am, because you won't. That, my dear, is a fact of life."

"Don't you want to become better than you are?"

"Yes, but on my terms. Who are you to judge when I become better than I am now? What does that even mean to you? Does your definition of better have me helping the elderly, or fawning over puppies and babies? If it is, then you don't know me at all."

"What do you think will make you better?"

"Power," I answer succinctly. "That will give me what I desire most."

"And what is that? What is your end-game in all of this?"

I shake my head. "I'm not that easily played, Cade. Your natural charm won't persuade me to tell you all of my secrets. I'm not some witless female who would do anything for the man she loves just because he asked her to."

Cade's face registers shock as he continues to look at me. I wait for him to speak, but he doesn't.

"What's wrong with you?" I ask crossly. "Why are you looking at me like that?"

"*I'm not some witless female who would do anything for the man she loves just because he asked her to,*" he says, repeating my exact words back to me. "Do you love me, Helena?"

I hesitate, but then quickly recover to say, "It's just an expression. Humans say them all the time without truly meaning the words."

"But you're not human," he points out. "You always say what you mean and never waste words. Do you feel love for me, Helena?"

I shrug my shoulders and look away from him. "I don't know what I feel for you. Even if it is, don't be fool enough to believe love will conqueror all in this situation. It won't. I'm not made that way. Love is a weapon that can be used against you if you allow it. Don't be that reckless, Cade. Stay sensible, and maybe you'll figure out how to let me go. That's the only way you'll survive this with your sanity intact."

"I don't know if I *can* let you go," Cade confesses. "I'm not even sure I want to."

"And here I thought what I did last night would finally break the hold I have over you. What will it take for you to realize that I will never be the person you need in your life?"

"I'm not sure. All I know is that I still have hope that you can change. I don't know if I'm the one who will be able to do that for you, but maybe I can help you in my small way."

"And that's your problem, Cade," I scoff. "You believe I need help. I don't need your help. I don't want your help. I'm extremely content with the person I am today. Why would I want to change? Do you think my feelings for you will suddenly make me into the person you want me to be? Stop deluding yourself. It will save us both a lot of time."

"Then what do you see happening between the two of us? What kind of future can we have with one another?"

"We have no future, at least not in the way you imagine it." I phase over to Cade so that I'm standing directly in front of him. "The one thing I can offer you," I say as I begin to glide my right hand up his muscular arm, "is my body. What do you say? Would you like to take me to bed, Cade? Do you still find me desirable enough to do that?"

"Yes," Cade whispers reluctantly, "I still find you desirable."

"Have you taken a woman into your bed yet?"

"No."

I look into Cade's blue eyes and see that he's being truthful.

"Why not?" I ask, finding this strange.

"I was waiting for the right person to come along."

"And am I the right one?"

Cade remains silent, but sometimes actions speak louder than words.

Cade wraps his arms around me and pulls me to him roughly. When he lowers his lips to mine, I feel as though the air in my lungs is being snatched away by his demanding kiss. I was disappointed that our kiss was interrupted the night before, but now I'm glad that it was. The kiss last night was destined to be soft and romantic. However, this kiss, our first of what I hope to be many, is filled with raw passion and need. I wrap my arms around Cade's neck, enjoying the play of our tongues and yearning for more than just this innocent dalliance.

I pull my arms back away from his neck and grip the front of his shirt with both hands. In one quick jerk, I tear the piece of cloth down the middle to expose his flesh to me. Cade groans against my mouth as my hands touch his chest for the first time. As I glide the tips of my fingers from his shoulders to his abs, I can feel his physical need for me reach new heights. When I grab the waistband of his pants, I nimbly pull open the closure in the front, and slide one hand in to take hold of the hard proof of his desire for me.

Cade breaks our kiss and stumbles backwards a few steps, forcing me to let go of him.

"Don't run away," I tell him, in a voice that's at once a plea and an order. "You want this as much as I do. I think that's painfully obvious, considering what I just had in my hand. Or are you trying to play hard to get?"

Breathing heavily, Cade quickly closes the front of his pants.

"I'm not playing with you, Helena," Cade says, taking in a deep breath. "This isn't a game to me. It's my life, and, if we're going to go any further, I need to know this isn't just your way of gaining control over me."

"Are you that easily controlled?" I ask. "Does my playing with that thing in your pants give me power over you? I seriously doubt it. Otherwise, you wouldn't be so far away from me right now. You would be hauling me to my bed and finishing what you started."

"I made a mistake coming here," Cade says, sounding disappointed in himself as he runs a shaky hand through his hair, looking distraught. "I should have known you wouldn't tell me what I need to know."

"Yes," I agree, "you should have known me a little better than that. I won't be manipulated by you."

"I won't be manipulated by you, either," he tells me.

"Then I guess we're at an impasse for the moment."

"I guess we are."

Cade stands there in his ripped-open shirt, and just stares at me for what seems like a long time.

"You should probably go now," I tell him, seeing no point in him staying if he isn't going to take me to bed. "And tell Anna to watch her back. I can only do so much. I hope last night was enough to satisfy the people who want to kill her."

"If you would just tell us who they are, we could take care of them."

"Like I told you, I need them. What I don't want is you and your brothers hunting them down and exterminating them. Just go, Cade. Neither of us is going to get what we each want from the other."

"I won't give up on you."

The desperation in Cade's eyes almost makes me feel sorry for him. Almost.

"Good-bye, Cade."

Cade gives me one more hopeful look of longing before he phases back to Anna.

I hate to admit it, but I instantly miss his presence. The room feels empty without him in it.

"Damn him," I curse, even though it does nothing to make me feel better.

CHAPTER TWENTY-TWO

(Back to Anna's Point of View)

Malcolm and I decide to allow our overlords to handle the relocation of the Cirrun refugees. We trust them to do what's right, and feel our presence might be a hindrance to all the work they need to do. Instead, we decide to go to our beach house to lock up the few items we don't want our future guests to inadvertently break during their stay in our home.

Since Malcolm has a house in every major city in Cirrun-controlled down-world territory, he offered them all to the overlords to use as housing for our displaced citizens. However, the beach house was the only property we were concerned about. We never stayed in the other homes, besides the one in New Orleans, so they didn't contain many personal belongings. Malcolm said most of them hadn't been used in years by him and Lucas.

My husband held the respect of many of the people in the down-world. They had gifted him the homes to show their admiration. We had talked about donating the houses to the less fortunate since we spent most of our time in Cirrus, but lack of time had delayed that plan. I was grateful for that now since we had another way to put the space to good use.

As I stand on the front porch, watching Lucas play fetch on the beach with Vala and Luna, I being to wonder how people in the down-world survive the summers here. Even in the shade of the porch, I feel as though my skin is about to melt off.

"Lucas!" I call out. "Five more minutes, then you and the dogs need to come inside. It's too hot out here!"

"Ok, Mommy," Lucas says with a wave of his arm at me.

"I don't know how he can stand this heat," I complain to Ethan, who has stayed glued to my side since we arrived at the beach house Malcolm and the other Watchers built for me. "I'm having a hard time breathing, it's so hot."

"Go inside, Anna," Ethan urges. "I'll bring Lucas in when his time is up."

"I would argue, but I'm just too hot to make the effort. Are you sure you don't mind?"

"Why would I mind watching him? Cade does it all the time."

The mention of Cade makes me feel anxious over his welfare. My emotions must be written on my face.

"Cade will be fine," Ethan assures me. "He won't be swayed by her womanly wiles."

I have to giggle at Ethan's euphemism. "Until you meet your soul-mate, I think the connection is almost impossible to explain."

"I'm sure it's strong," Ethan concedes, "but so is the bond we War Angels feel for one another. It's a sense of brotherhood that won't allow Cade to betray us."

"I didn't think he would," I'm quick to say. "I know how loyal Cade is to us all. Otherwise, I wouldn't have allowed him to remain Lucas' protector after he met Helena."

"Then don't worry about him, Anna. He's a big boy. He can take care of himself."

"Strangely enough, I'm not worried about his physical well-being. I'm more concerned about keeping his heart intact."

"You make it sound like finding your soul-mate is the best and worst thing that can happen to a person," Ethan says jokingly.

"It all depends on who your soul-mate is, I guess," I say. "I wish Cade's was anyone but Helena."

"I do, too," Ethan replies, "but maybe there's a purpose in such madness."

"So poetic," I tease, fanning my face with my hand in a vain attempt to cool myself.

"Go inside before you faint," Ethan begs.

"Ok. Don't let Lucas stay more than a couple of more minutes, though."

"I won't."

I walk into the coolness of the house and sigh in relief. Thankfully, Malcolm was able to install a temperature-control system in the home to keep it at a constant seventy degrees during the summer and toasty warm in the winter. I walk up the stairs leading to the second floor to find my husband. When I reach the nursery, Malcolm is holding a small white disk, the last of ten disks that already surround the window with my family tree painted on it. When he first built this house for me, he had it moved from the home Lucifer and my mom shared while they were married. It was a reminder of my roots and of all the generations who preceded me.

"Does it work?" I ask Malcolm as I step into the room.

"We're about to find out," he says, pushing a small button on the underside of the last disk in his hand before positioning it on the wall beside the window. "No one but me can turn off the force-field these disks produce. The security code is imprinted with my DNA."

"Good," I say in relief. "Now I won't worry about whoever uses this house breaking my family heirloom."

"I'll tell Brutus to look for a couple with a baby," Malcolm tells me as he stands in front of the window. "They can use this room now that the window is protected."

"Are you sure the force-field is up?" I ask dubiously, since I don't actually see any signs of it being on.

Before I can react, Malcolm rears back one fist and punches it towards the window with all his might.

Involuntarily, I let out a loud gasp in dismay and feel my heart jump into my throat.

Malcolm's hand is stopped a few inches away from the window by an unseen force, and I breathe out a sigh of relief.

"It works," Malcolm declares, lowering his fist.

"I'm glad you were so confident that it would," I laugh nervously. "You nearly gave me a heart attack!"

Malcolm turns away from the window and walks over to me.

"I'm sorry I scared you," he apologizes. "I didn't mean to, but you wanted to know if the force-field was up."

"Couldn't you have just tried to place your hand on it slowly instead of a shattering blow directly at it?"

Malcolm shrugs. "Yeah, I could have," he concedes. "But I don't do small. You should know that about me by now."

"Yes, I do," I admit, immensely liking that fact about my husband. "And we all know I like big things."

Malcolm takes me into his arms and smiles down at me. "Are you flirting with me, Empress? Or are you daring me to ravish you here on the spot?"

"Flirting, yes," I say as I look up at him. "Ravish, no, considering our son is so close, and we have a house full of War Angels who might mistake my cries of pleasure for pain. I don't think I could ever live down that shame."

"Shame?" Malcolm asks, aghast. "There's absolutely no shame in finding pleasure with your husband. But you're right; we might cause your bodyguards to panic unnecessarily. You can get quite loud while I indulge your every desire."

"Well, what woman wouldn't get loud with you making love to her?" I ask, drawing an even bigger, well-deserved smile from my husband.

"If you keep this up, I may have to phase you somewhere more private to ravish you until both our needs are quenched."

"I wouldn't complain," I reply, but then remember that I should add, "as long as it's a temperature-controlled place. Honestly, I don't know how the people down here can live in this heat during the summer months."

"If you had been raised in the down-world, your body would be used to the extremes in temperatures here."

"I guess living the pampered life in Cirrus spoiled me."

"Nothing wrong with being a little spoiled. You still turned out to be one of the best people I know. You truly care what happens to others. That's a rare quality nowadays."

"Why can't anything ever be easy?" I ask as I wrap my arms around Malcolm's waist and rest my head against his chest.

"I don't know," Malcolm tells me, rubbing my back with his hands comfortingly. "If I could make things easier for you, I would, my love."

"I know."

We stand there quietly, each of us lost in our own thoughts until we hear the clash of swords.

"What the…" Malcolm jerks his head up just before the room is filled with angels fighting.

Malcolm quickly phases me back to our New Orleans home.

"Shouldn't we go help them?" I ask urgently, my heart pounding so hard I can barely breathe.

"No, Ethan and the others can handle them."

"Dad! Mommy!"

Lucas comes running in from the foyer with Vala and Luna by his sides. As soon as he reaches me, he wraps his arms around me as tightly as he can.

"Oh, sweetie," I say, holding Lucas close. "Are you hurt?"

"I got them out as soon as I saw the others phase in," Cade tells us.

"I didn't realize you were back," I say, wondering why Cade's shirt is ripped open but not having the time to delve into such a superfluous matter.

"I came back a few seconds before they struck."

"They, who?" I ask, looking between Malcolm and Cade.

"Rebellion scum," Malcolm tells me, sounding disgusted by the fact.

"I don't understand," I say. "Why are they attacking us?"

"They have to be the ones trying to kill you," Cade concludes.

"Helena didn't confirm that fact, I gather?"

"No. She wouldn't tell me, but it makes perfect sense now. She said it was a group that she would need later on. That was one reason she wouldn't tell me who they were. She was afraid we would try to hunt down and slay all the rebellion angels."

"But why do they want to kill me? I don't understand."

"I think I do," Malcolm says, looking thoughtful. "Lucifer is gone. He was their leader and he just up and left them here. I think if I were them, I would be mad at him, too. What better way to get their revenge on him than to hurt you?"

It made sense, even if I didn't like to hear it.

"Well, we won the war in Heaven against them," Cade says. "I guess we'll just have to beat them here on Earth, too. In fact, I'm going back to help the others. I can't let my brothers have all the fun."

Cade phases back to the beach house.

I keep Lucas close, wondering how in the world I'm going keep him and the babies safe.

If the rebellion angels want to kill me, there is a very good chance that they will find a way to do it. If nothing else, their vast numbers will give them a slight advantage. How am I supposed to protect my children from an army of angels?

"Malcolm…" I say, preparing to ask him what we should do next, when the solution is suddenly decided for me.

I find myself standing inside a room that looks decidedly unwelcoming. It's beautifully decorated, in a gothic sort of way; perhaps a room a teenager who lived in Nacreous might have. There are no windows in the walls, which makes it feel slightly claustrophobic. There is a large canopy bed made out of black wood situated directly in front of me. Its four thick posts look like miniature church steeples. The gold velvet coverlet and pillows look comfortable enough. There are two cribs situated against the walls directly across from the sides of the bed. They are also made of black wood, with decorative silver appliques across the tops of the back and front pieces.

"Mommy," Lucas asks me, tightening his arms around my hips, "where are we?"

"You're in my home, little angel."

I look to my right and see Helena standing there, with a surprised but pleased smile on her face. Her expression does nothing to ease my worry. I try to phase us away, but of course, I can't.

"I have to admit," she tells to me with a slight tilt of her head, "I didn't expect for it to be this easy to have you come here on your own."

"I didn't choose to come to you," I inform her. "The babies phased us here."

"Ahh," Helena says, nodding her head, "that makes perfect sense. They know they're safe here."

"How in the world are we safe being with you?"

"Well, they probably know I have no desire to kill you or them, Anna," she says, holding out her hands as if to prove she isn't hiding a weapon of any sort. "I want you all to live, and your little cherubs seem to understand that fact."

"What is this room?" I ask, looking around at the black and silver wallpaper and sparse furnishings. "It's almost like you expected us to come here."

"Oh, I wouldn't say expected, but I knew if things became dire I would need to bring you here to stay with me."

"And where exactly are we?" I ask her, but already fear I know the answer to my own question. I seriously doubt we're in Nimbo.

"My domain," Helena says with a grin. "Welcome back to Hell, Anna."

CHAPTER TWENTY-THREE

(From Malcolm's Point of View)

"Malcolm…" I hear Anna say to me, but during the split-second it takes me to look over at her, she and Lucas unexpectedly disappear from my sight.

I stare at her phase trail as my heart sinks to the bottom of my stomach, weighted down by so much dread I feel as though it's about to suffocate me. Blood surges through my veins as worry threatens to consume me, but I know I don't have the luxury of acting weak. My family needs me. Of all the places the babies could have phased their mother to, why did they choose to take her to Hell? And not only have they taken their mother there, yet again, but they've also taken Lucas this time.

I immediately reach out a hand to follow the trail, but I instantly discover that I can't phase through it.

Helena has shut the door to Hell and is wisely denying me access. She's done this once before, but back then it was my willingness to venture into her domain that made her reopen its gates. Obviously, that trick isn't going to work a second time.

Lucifer took me there to get Anna back after she killed Daniel. The only reason I went was because I knew Helena couldn't pass up the opportunity to feed off my guilt. At the time, she was blocking Lucifer from entering her realm, but when she felt my presence trying to phase down with him, she allowed us entry.

I've never experienced such excruciating mental anguish as I did while I was in Helena's clutches. It felt like my mind was being dissected by a million shards of ice, probing for all my weaknesses and darkest regrets. Anna saved me from going insane back then by abandoning her vengeful torture of Levi and phasing me home.

I need to go there now, but, if I do, will I lose myself to Hell again and get lost in the memories of my own sins? Will it gorge on me like I'm a buffet of guilt? How am I supposed to protect my family if I can't even protect myself down there? Maybe the babies will return Anna and Lucas soon, and I won't have to figure out a way to get her back.

"Malcolm," I hear a comforting voice from my past say to me, "we'll help you."

I turn to look behind me, and see Jess and Mason standing there. If they've come all the way from Heaven to help me, my hope that the babies would return my family to me swiftly isn't going to be realized.

"How are the two of you here?" I ask them, wondering if my mind is playing tricks on me and conjuring them up during a time I need their support the most.

Jess walks up and gives me a hug, proving she's real.

"I told God that if there ever came a day I was needed back here, He had better let me come," she tells me, before pulling away. "We weren't just going to sit up there in Heaven and let you face going to Hell on your own. We suspected you wouldn't ask anyone to go down there with you either. In fact, I was pretty sure you would make the boneheaded mistake of refusing help when you actually need it. You're just too stubborn for your own good sometimes."

"I won't be responsible for someone else losing their soul or their mind to Helena."

"We know," Mason tells me. "That's why we're here. We're not in any danger of having either of those things happen to us. If you get into trouble, we can help you."

"Danger of having what happening?" a new voice questions.

I look to my right to see Jered enter the room.

"What's going on here?" he asks, looking at Jess and Mason like he's seeing ghosts. "And am I hallucinating, or are Jess and Mason really standing in front of you, Malcolm?"

Jess answers in her own way by going to Jered and giving him a hug, too.

"We're real," she declares. "And we're here to help."

"I don't understand," Jered says, looking as confused as he sounds. "What's happened?"

I quickly explain the situation to Jered.

"Then let's go get our girl and Lucas," Jered says without hesitation.

"Jered," Jess says, a great deal of hesitancy in her voice about his suggestion. "Do you think that's the best place for you to go? Helena's bound to try to torture you with your own guilt as much as she will Malcolm."

Jered's expression changes to one of fierce determination. "Malcolm and I have grown a lot since you left this world, Jess. I'm not the same broken man I was back then. True, I still have my demons, but I've worked through a lot of them. She won't break me. I won't allow it. Besides, I've been down there recently. I didn't suffer through any ill effects."

"Excuse me, but I would like to volunteer my services as well."

Alex steps inside the room from the foyer. "I don't have a lot of guilt that she can feed on. Maybe that will be a useful quality down there."

"Are you sure, Alex?" I ask. "This may be a one-way trip if you aren't confident you can handle yourself."

"I'm sure," Alex says resolutely. "I want to go."

"There's at least one more person we'll need to take with us," Jess says to me, sounding reluctant to tell me who else should be added to our rescue party. "Slade."

"No," I say vehemently. "I will *not* take that traitor with us!"

"We need him, Malcolm," Mason tells me, in that voice he would sometimes use, indicating that arguing with him is futile. "You saw for yourself that Helena won't let us just phase down there. We need him to locate a crack in the veil for us to travel through. Only a creature of Hell, or someone who died and was sent there, can see the fissures. He knows where one is for us to travel through."

"He betrayed us," I say, as argument enough for not taking Slade.

"And he paid the price for that betrayal," Jess reminds me. "Give him an opportunity to redeem himself in your eyes, Malcolm. Everyone deserves a second chance. Even Lucifer was given one."

"Why not have Lucifer come down here and act as our guide?" I suggest. "He designed the place. Surely he would be the preferred escort."

"I didn't tell him what was going on," Jess informs me, looking uncomfortable about her admission. "I'm afraid of what might happen if he does go there again. Since he returned to Heaven, he's been reexamining his life here on Earth. For the first time, he fully realizes all of the pain and suffering he caused. If Helena thought he was a feast of sorrow and guilt after Amalie's death, she would have a party with all the trappings if she got her claws into his guilt now. He's worked too hard to find his happily-ever-after. I won't do anything to jeopardize that."

"So he has no idea Anna is in danger?" I ask.

"No. He doesn't know, and I pray he doesn't find out until after we have her back. Lilly and Brand are the only ones we told that we were coming here to help you. No one else needed to know."

"Malcolm?" I hear Ethan say. "What's going on?"

I look up and see him and the other members of Anna's personal War Angel guard now standing in the room. They're all covered with blood, and I know the battle at the beach house against the rebellion angels must be over.

I tell the new arrivals what's happened. I look pointedly at Cade because I hope he realizes how much danger Anna and Lucas are in. It's the first time I'm thankful that he's soul-mates with Helena because I know I can use it to my advantage.

"I need you to come with us in case you're able to sense where Helena is down there," I tell Cade as I continue to stare at him. "I'm sure she's with Anna. I seriously doubt she'll let her out of her sight."

"We're all going," Ethan informs me. "You don't know what you'll face when you get there. Helena will make you deal with more than just bad memories, Malcolm. There are probably a countless number of monstrosities in that place just waiting to attack you."

Ethan is almost certainly right. There are probably creatures in Hell that the handful of us can't fight off by ourselves, but I don't want them to risk their lives and souls for a mission I should be completing on my own. I already have too many people going with me as it is.

"If I ask you to stay here," I say addressing all of Anna's guard, "will any of you obey my request?"

"We have a great deal of respect for you," Ethan answers cautiously, "but I only obey God and Anna's commands. Since God isn't here telling us not to go, we'll be going with you whether you want us to or not."

I didn't have the authority to force them to stay. I nod my head in acceptance of their help.

I turn to Jered and say, "I need you to go find Slade so he can show us a way into Hell."

"It's probably not a bad idea to also have him go inside with us. Hell is like an ever- changing labyrinth," Jered informs me. "I'm sure spending a thousand years there taught him a thing or two. Maybe there's a pattern to its inner workings that we don't know about."

"Maybe," I concede, still not keen on the idea of having Slade join us. I'm not even sure his presence will help. He's already returned to Hell in a failed attempt to locate Helena. In fact, this expedition may be a fool's chase, but I have to try. I have to do something.

"I'll find him and bring him back here," Jered says just before phasing.

After Jered is gone, I look over at Ethan and the others. "I suggest you all go get cleaned up. Let's meet back here in fifteen minutes. I need to do some things to prepare first."

Before anyone can say another word, I phase up to my bedroom.

I want to hit something. I want to tear the room apart, but I know that won't solve my problem. And who exactly am I supposed to be mad at? The twins? Perhaps they thought they were safer with Helena than they were with me. They haven't even been born yet, and I feel like I've already failed them as a father.

"Malcolm…"

I look to my right and see my own father standing there.

"Can You bring them back?" I ask Him, belatedly realizing I've asked the wrong question. Of course He has the ability. The real question is, "Will You bring them back to me?"

"They are following a path I cannot disturb," God tells me.

I turn to face him fully and ask, "Then why are You here?"

"I wanted to help prepare you for your journey with a warning."

"That doesn't sound very encouraging," I admit, feeling my heart sink even further inside my chest. "A warning about what?"

"I know you realize Helena will make it difficult for you while you're in her domain, and there are certain things in your past that she will try to use to her advantage."

"I'm fully aware of that," I say. "I'm prepared to face whatever she intends to do."

"Those going with you will also be judged by her. You will need to remain strong for them when they lose faith in themselves. Can you do that my son?"

"I will," I say confidently. "I won't let them fall victim to her will. You have my word."

"That includes Slade, Malcolm."

Involuntarily, I bristle. "He betrayed us, Father. You know how hard it is for me to forgive people after they've broken my trust."

"I thought out of anyone you would be able to sympathize with what he went through, Malcolm," my father says.

"He was weak," I say in disgust. "I lived with my hellhound bite for a thousand years. How long did he suffer with it? A few days? I have no pity or respect for someone that spineless."

"Not everyone can be as strong as you, my son. If you think about it, Slade ended up suffering for just as long as you did. He was tortured by both Lucifer and Helena after his death. All I ask is that you give him a chance to prove that he isn't the same person he once was. He's asked for a fresh start, and I believe you should give it to him."

"I can't promise anything," I reply reluctantly, "but I will try."

"That's all I can ask of you."

I fall silent for a moment because I want to ask a question, even though I know I won't get a direct answer.

"Things will work out the way they should," God tells me, already knowing what my unasked query is. "Be vigilant in your quest, Malcolm. And remember…success can come in many different forms."

God phases away, leaving me surprised he said even that much.

I strip off my shirt and toss it onto the bed. I have a feeling Helena will use my hot nature against me in Hell. The less I wear there, the better. I make my way into the bathroom and open the top drawer of the vanity. I grab a black hairband from its interior and pull my hair back into a ponytail. As I turn to walk away, I catch a glimpse of myself in the mirror above the sink, and see a man whose face is filled with grim determination.

I am determined.

I'm determined to get my family back, and not even Hell itself will stop me.

Author's Note

Thanks so much for reading *Awakening*! The second book in the series will be titled *Reckoning*. I plan to have it available by spring of 2016. As always, you can follow my progress on the book every Sunday at either my Facebook page or my website.

Sincerely,

S.J. West

FB Book Page:

https://www.facebook.com/ReadTheWatchersTrilogy/timeline/

FB Author Page: https://www.facebook.com/sandra.west.585112

Website: www.sjwest.com

Email: sandrawest481@gmail.com

Newsletter Sign-up:

https://confirmsubscription.com/h/i/51B24C1DB7A7908B

Instagram: sandrawest481

Twitter: @SJWest2013

Made in the USA
Monee, IL
16 August 2022

11684029R00177